MURDER BY
COMMITTEE

MURDER BY COMMITTEE

Henry Marks

iUniverse, Inc.
Bloomington

Murder by Committee

iUniverse books may be ordered through booksellers or by contacting:

iUniverse
1663 Liberty Drive
Bloomington, IN 47403
www.iuniverse.com
1-800-Authors (1-800-288-4677)

ISBN: 978-1-4620-4397-2 (sc)
ISBN: 978-1-4620-4398-9 (ebk)

Printed in the United States of America

iUniverse rev. date: 08/05/2011

Acknowledgements

For a first time author, the support of family and friends makes the idea of writing a novel a real possibility. Sharon, Catherine, Celeste, and Dell thank you for your support and help. You not only made it possible, you made it better. Thanks also to the editors at iUniverse.

The cover art was created by Anna Moya-Delgado who took an idea and created a image.

PROLOGUE

Today was the day when I would start developing my plan. I had spent a great deal of time thinking about the remainder of my life. I had considered a variety of options; and hundreds of scenarios had run through my mind. My goal was to exact my revenge on Peter Stanford. I wanted to ruin his reputation. I wanted to leave him as nearly penniless as he had left me. I wanted him off the planet and I was prepared to do whatever was needed.

Chapter 1

The alarm went off. I thought I had selected a soft classical music station, but what came out of the radio was hard rock. Actually, I'd call it sulfuric acid rock. I slammed my hand down on the button to turn the alarm off and wondered if I should reread the instructions for setting the alarm.

I opened my eyes, raised my head from the pillow and looked out the window. It was a light gray overcast day with a soft rain falling and a very gentle breeze blowing from the West, but it was Oregon and it was late October—what else could one expect. My mood was warmer than the weather. I stretched and listened to the creaks and pops from the various parts of my body. I wondered when I had become so old that I creaked. In any case, it was time to get up and face the day. I pushed myself up to the edge of the bed, with the accompanying pops and cracks. Perhaps this was the music of old age.

I went into the bathroom and glanced at the mirror. Jesus, I thought. The creature staring back at me looked to be a survivor of some sort of disaster. My hair had been gray from my early 30s, but now there was less of it and it fanned out around my head reminding me a lot of that famous picture of Einstein. My skin had a sallow tone which underscored my large nose, or as I preferred to call it, my

Roman proboscis. I still stood just under 6 feet (that always sounded better than 5' 11") and was still a good twenty pounds overweight even though I had been eating better since I met Sheila. Enough of this self examination.

I emptied my bladder, brushed my teeth, and started the water for my shower. I liked it hot and, in this apartment, it took a while to get the water reasonably hot. I showered, shampooed, toweled off and put on my underwear and socks. I was my day off so I didn't wear my 'uniform' of white shirt and tie. I put on a purple sweatshirt that everyone in Portland liked to call a hoodie. A pair of somewhat wrinkled brown cord pants and well-worn Nike's completed my ensemble. A dozen strokes with a brush reduced my Einstein look to something more resembling a medieval monk.

I needed to get started. Today was the day. I had to develop a plan. I knew what I wanted as the result. Now all I needed was the method.

Perhaps I should start at the beginning. My name is Karol, Karol Rogers. I am, or perhaps I should say was, a bio-scientist. I was a partner in a company called SynthGen. SynthGen whose goal was to develop an anti-viral agent to attack the HIV virus. The initial tests showed we had a truly powerful anti-viral agent. The HIV virus mutates rapidly which makes it hard for any biological agent to successfully attack it. Our anti-viral agent attacked the protein shell, regardless of the degree of mutation. With the shell even partially destroyed, the body's own immune system took care of the rest. Two years of animal tests were positive, with relatively few significant side effects. Unfortunately, initial human tests were much less positive. In the first trial, the initial injection produced severe reactions in over half of the volunteers. The reactions included projectile vomiting and cramps. These reactions were strong enough to cause these volunteers to refuse further treatment. Further injections in the remaining volunteers produced these same extreme side effects. In two cases, volunteers had to be hospitalized and later developed additional symptoms which ultimately lead to death.

A slight variation in the genetic code of the anti-virus produced an equally powerful anti-viral agent, but with very substantially reduced side effects. Less than ten percent of the volunteers exhibited either cramps or vomiting. The severity was such that only two percent of the volunteers refused further treatment. Follow-up at one month, and three and six months demonstrated a very substantial reduction in the levels of the HIV virus in over sixty percent of the subjects. We had an effective treatment for HIV! SynthGen was going to be worth millions!

Peter, my partner, was responsible for marketing, advertising and all those other mundane tasks which have no relationship to the scientific creation of an anti-viral agent, but which are required to get it produced and into the hands of physicians where it could do some good. Peter was a slender, 6-foot 1 inch tall, platinum blond, icy blue-eyed, graduate of one of the better Northeastern Schools. He dressed with sartorial perfection and seemed to know almost everyone who it was important to know. Peter was also extremely good at what he did. He was a major reason that we got our National Institutes of Health (NIH) grant in the first place. While I could supply the hard science, I had a hard time putting much of the grant into the appropriate (politically correct) terminology that the Feds demand. Without Peter's skills, I would probably still be teaching undergraduates and doing research on a shoestring in my spare time.

Both Peter and his personal assistant knew how to ingratiate themselves with Federal officials. I had watched them *work* a room. As a couple who had little knowledge of how the biochemistry worked, they seemed to have no trouble charming officials who approved or reviewed federally funded projects. I'd often wish I'd had those skills, but when I enter a room full of strangers I immediately seek out corners or alcoves. Its not that I am afraid, its just that I don't really know what to say. Peter's personal assistant was a master at flirting with men and she had no difficulty changing the minds of some of the most stubborn males.

For more than ten months, I was unaware that Peter had published the results of the first human study. Even though his scientific knowledge was limited, it wasn't that hard. I had written up all the results for our NIH grant. However, the results that Peter published focused on the fact that two volunteers died. The implication was that they died as a result of the treatment, although I didn't get that information until well after the study was published. I felt my time was much better used figuring out what was wrong with the first anti-viral agent and correcting it to eliminate the unwanted side effects.

Naturally, his report produced a great deal of public comment, complaints, outrage, and calls for congressional hearings. As one might suspect, an investigation followed. Any human experiments resulting in the death of a subject are always followed by an investigation, but usually the investigation was a matter of filling out a ream of forms. These forms were designed to show that all appropriate warnings were provided to human subjects and that they were made aware of the fact that they were participating in an activity that had the potential of causing harm. Since we were working with a population who were very likely to die if my procedure did not work, there should have been no great outcry at the deaths of two individuals.

This time, however, forms would not be enough. This time the investigation would be done in person and under oath. A panel was formed to ask the questions demanded by the press. Being a Federal program, it would normally have been chaired by someone from NIH or the Food and Drug Administration. The demands from the press and the pressure of the upcoming election caused the standard committee to be replaced by a committee composed of individuals from the sciences and Members of Congress.

It took well over a year after the report had been published for a committee to be formed and start taking testimony. The final panel was composed of three individuals who had once been well known scientists, but who were now administrative drones who merely reviewed the work of others and did no research themselves. There were four members of Congress and at least a dozen Congressional aides. There was some maneuvering to be on this panel since it would invariably lead to substantial amounts of public exposure as the deaths had received a great deal of press coverage. I remember feeling very pleased at the time that Peter was handling everything since I don't really feel comfortable answering a bunch of questions from these non-scientific, political types.

While I was carrying out the preliminary tasks associated with the development of the newer version of the anti-viral agent and making sure that all of the written protocols would be carefully followed, Peter was testifying to the investigators. I was later told that his testimony indicated that the information provided to the subjects did not adequately detail the possible risks associated with their participation in the study and that the informed consent forms from the two dead subjects were mysteriously missing.

Informed consent is one of the basic tenets of human research. Subjects must be clearly informed of any risks associated with their participation in the study. They must be made aware of the fact that some risks were unknown by the very nature of an experimental trial. All subjects were required to sign a statement that they had been informed of these risks. Somehow, the paperwork from the two subjects who had died could not be found. Peter assured the investigating panel that he was sure that I would have informed all subjects of the risks; however, he was never directly involved with the subjects. Consequently, he could not absolutely confirm that these subjects had given informed consent.

I still remember bits and pieces of my appearance before the panel. I was so focused on the current study that I was having trouble paying attention to the inane questions I was being asked.

"Dr. Rogers would you please describe the specific setting in which you obtained informed consent," I was asked by the committee chairman. If I had been casting a movie, I would have chosen him as epitomizing almost everyone's idea of the overweight, pompous, arrogant Senator from one of the Southern States. His greasy, fat neck seemed to flow over his shirt collar and his face was the same color found on packages of ground turkey. His little beady eyes in his fat face had been caricaturized in hundreds of cartoons on editorial pages and his thinning white hair must have been two feet long to allow a comb-over such as he wore. Even his name would have been perfect for my fictional movie: Randolph Beauregard III.

"Mr. Chairman, as I remember, for each group, we gathered all of the participants in the main conference room. Everyone was seated around the large table with the printed briefing materials in front of them. My lab assistant, Terri, was responsible for reviewing all of the material orally and then answering any questions the subjects had. She then obtained a signed consent for from each subject indicating that they understood the risks of the study and had all of their questions satisfactorily answered. She filed these signed statements in the protocol file cabinet."

"Dr Rogers, did you witness any of these subjects providing informed consent?"

"Well, not directly. But I had complete confidence in Terri. She had worked for me before on an experimental project and had done an excellent job." Luckily I had been smart enough to avoid mentioning that the research I was referring to had been done while Terri was an undergraduate senior.

"And, who was this Terri?"

"As I mentioned before, she was my lab assistant. She was responsible for the initial paperwork, orienting the subjects, and recording the experimental data. Terri was a fourth year graduate student who was working on her dissertation proposal."

"And, where is Terri now?"

"Well, I had to let her go."

"And why was that?"

"I found out that she . . . . ah . . . . did not follow the established protocol for recording data."

"What does that mean . . . she failed to follow established protocol for recording data? Do you mean she falsified data?"

"Ah. She sometimes failed to record data immediately upon collecting it, relying on her memory to fill in the data forms at a later time."

"And this was the person entrusted with assuring informed consent for all subjects?"

"Yes, she was."

"Why then are the signed consents missing for some of the subjects?"

"I don't know. I just assumed that Terri had done her job. Mr. Chairman, I may have erred in not supervising my assistant closely enough, but I am sure that all of the subjects had given informed consent.

When we first observed side effects, we immediately sought additional medical support and provided the best services available. All of our subjects were at high risk for death and this was addressed both in the screening process and in the informed consent procedure."

"Why then are their no records of informed consent for these two individuals who died?"

"As I said, I don't know."

"We also found several other pieces of documentation missing. I have provided you with a list of the missing materials."

I was handed a packet of photocopies of paperwork from my studies. I glanced through them and found specific items circled in red. There were blank signature lines, missing data, and obvious erasures. How had I never encountered these items before? The checklist of individuals who had given informed consent had every name checked off, but there were two individual consent forms missing.

I checked the screening forms for the two individuals who had died. They were the only ones missing. There was nothing to substantiate any screening had occurred. How could I have not seen this? Could this all be Terri's fault?

"Mr. Chairman, could I have some time to review this material?"

"Is this not the material you used to produce your report for NIH? Why aren't you familiar with it?"

"I . . . . I worked with summary material. I saw very little of the original, raw data. I was unaware of these lapses in documentation."

"Yet, you told us that you fired Terri, your assistant, because she falsified your data. How could you know that if you didn't see any of the raw data?"

I tried to remember what it was that caused me to tell Terri she had to leave the project. Then I remembered, it was something Peter had told me. Peter had said he had noticed her entering data on a day when no data was being collected. He had described her as surreptitiously entering the lab when no one else was around. He said he thought it looked funny.

I had called her into my office and asked her directly about her data entries. She hemmed and hawed, but eventually confessed to very occasionally entering data well after 'collecting it.' I asked her how often this delayed data recording had occurred. She assured me that it had only occurred two or three times and the vast majority of the time the data was recorded accurately and in a timely fashion. There was no way I could keep Terri on as an assistant after she had confirmed that the accuracy and/or omission of data could not be confirmed.

I tried to figure out some way she could resign so her Curriculum Vitae would not show a termination for cause. She continued to claim that only an inconsequential amount of data was entered late and that she remembered almost all of it perfectly. I told her that there was no way that we could keep her on the project, especially since Peter had direct evidence that she falsified data. I tried to let her know that I would accept a resignation rather than actually firing her, but apparently that wasn't enough.

I remember her rushing out of the office sobbing, saying, "It was unfair. Mr. Stanford knew I was entering the data a little late. I'd told him. He'd said not to worry. He said it would be okay."

"Mr. Chairman, the material you have shown me definitely indicates that I was remiss in my supervision of my subordinates, but I don't think that there is any indication of any kind of systematic errors in data collection."

"Dr. Rogers, I noticed that you carefully avoided the term malpractice. I wonder why? Is that how you hide your errors in government supported research?"

At this point, Congresswoman Sally Andrews requested permission to ask questions. The chairman imperiously nodded his assent. Sharing the spotlight with a second-term black Congresswoman couldn't be bad for his image and there were appointments in his future to be considered. Initially, I was quite grateful to her, as I had no good answer to his question.

"Dr. Rogers, would you please describe the screening procedures used to select participants for your study."

"Yes. The protocol demanded that all subjects be HIV positive and had been so for at least two years. All should have had at least one year of medical therapy and should have demonstrated that such treatment was ineffective in reducing the HIV virus in their system. In other words, standard therapy was ineffective and each individual had a high probability of dying of complications from AIDS if the experimental treatment was not effective. Each of the subjects was individually interviewed with follow-up documentation from a licensed physician. No subject was allowed to have any other major chronic medical condition, unless it was secondary to HIV."

"Okay, so where are the questionnaires from these two subjects? Where are the physician's reports?"

"I don't know."

"Why is it that only these two subjects have these items missing?"

"I don't know."

"You seem to have a very selective memory, Doctor."

My immediate response was to rise out of my chair and tell this skinny broad where to get off. I was half standing when I got control and realized that this sort of behavior would only get me into deeper trouble. I took several deep breaths, relaxed my clenched hands and then reseated myself.

"I cannot comment on things that I did not supervise. I regret that I failed to monitor my subordinates more closely, but I don't think that justifies your implication of any sort of impropriety on my part. I have developed a biological agent that eliminates HIV in over sixty percent of subjects. I think that one should look at the results of my work instead of my deficiencies as a supervisor."

"And the results of that work include two dead individuals."

"But, those individuals died from complications attributed to AIDS. All of these subjects were likely to die if my treatment was ineffective. Why pick on two who did die?"

"Doctor, that is very simple. You were responsible for warning all subjects of the dangers of your procedure. The lack of documentation suggests you were criminally negligent in your oversight of your subordinates and their failure to insure all subjects gave informed consent."

This inquisition continued for hours. Somehow the lack of a few documents made me responsible for the death of two individuals. The fact that these HIV individuals were likely to die in any case if the injection was ineffective was ignored. The fact that I had documentation for every other subject, more than 185 people, was ignored. The loss of my grant was a forgone conclusion. What I hadn't expected were the trials conducted on the front pages of the public press—all of which found me guilty. This publicity was followed by criminal charges which were then followed by the lawsuits filed by the families of the dead subjects.

The criminal charges came rapidly, but all were dismissed by the judges. They all agreed that there was no basis for any of the criminal suits, since the coroner's reports indicated that the individuals died of complications resulting from AIDS and could in no way be directly attributable to the experimental treatment. The dismissal did not come in time to prevent my reputation from being totally ruined by the media. Nor was there much publicity given to the judge's decision exonerating me. I was continually portrayed as preying on poor, sick, defenseless individuals. I was a mad scientist with no regard for human life. Dr. Frankenstein would have received better press than I did. Somehow, my goal of finding a cure for HIV was totally ignored. The overwhelmingly positive results of my second test group were also totally ignored by the press.

According to my lawyer, Randall Simonides, the lawsuits were basically nuisance issues. He settled both suits out of court for less than $100,000. My insurance through SynthGen paid for almost all of the settlements. Unfortunately, I now had no income, my lawyer wasn't free, and neither were court costs. So after all was said and done, I had to sell my house and almost every thing else that I owned. In the space of less than two years I had moved from being a respected scientist, financially very well off, with a home, car, boat and a nice retirement savings account to a near penniless individual. I had moved into a tenuous state unfamiliar to me. I couldn't remember the last time I had to worry about a place to stay, how to buy food rather than simply ordering it from the market, much less how to look for a job.

Chapter 2

The two of them sat there facing each other. John, the older of the pair, grasped his drink as though he could crush it. He was in his 50s with a receding hairline and a strong, determined chin. His eyes appeared to vary between a light blue and a light green depending on the light. Currently, they were partially closed. His camel hair sports coat was unbuttoned and his white-on-white shirt was wrinkled. His free hand played with his British Guards tie, rolling and unrolling it.

"I just don't understand how he could do it to me," he said. "I just don't understand."

Larry simply looked at him, having heard this refrain many times during the past week. Larry was the pudgy one of the pair. His chalk striped suit looked as though he had slept in it and his pale blue shirt had more than its share of stains from ink, lunch, and a variety of other foreign materials. He was so short; he looked the Abbot of Abbot and Costello.

"You can complain to me all you want, but that isn't going to do you any good. It won't solve your problem," Larry stated matter-of-factly. They had known each other for a couple of years. Their wives had met at a Spa and liked each other, so they had started to do things as couples. John had offered Larry some on-the-job help which moved him up in the organization. He'd never get to John's position, but he made a comfortable living with lots of benefits. He felt he owed John something, but wasn't quite sure what or how he might pay the debt.

"But he promised me that if I made the Bennington deal, I would be next in line for a vice-presidency. I sweated blood to get their signatures on the dotted line. I worked my tail off for more than two months to put that deal together. It's just not fair."

Larry simply shook his head. There was nothing he could do or say which would change things. Peter Stanford ruled VYRO Solutions exactly like a king might rule his country. Everyone did things his way or they were no longer employed. Larry had to admit that Peter was effective. His company was making more money than anyone had predicted. His product was light years ahead of anything the competition could produce and his ability to sway the various government entities to buy his product and no others was nothing short of magnificent.

His personnel were well paid. Company benefits were excellent. The equipment was top of the line. As long as you toed the company line, you were in clover—no, change that—you were in cashmere.

John had been told that he would be next in line for a vice presidency, if he made the Bennington deal. He made the deal, but Peter was unhappy with some of the terms, so no vice-presidency. There was no arguing about fair or unfair, good or bad, black or white. What Peter said was what happened. Larry wished he could say something that might help John accept the fact that Peter had gone back on his word and John had no choice but to live with it, but he couldn't think of a thing to say.

"You know, there ought to be something that could be done to that son-of-a-bitch. I have worked for him for almost three years, making this company one of the biggest bio-medical outfits in the world and he treats me like dirt. What do you think, Larry, is there some way to make him change the way he treats me?

"John, let me ask you something. You direct an entire department; your salary is well up into the six figure range; with bonuses, you make over a million dollars a year, your stock options have made you an extremely wealthy man. Why can't you live with all that? What other company could give you the same payoffs as VYRO Solutions? You just have to understand that Peter's management style isn't one that makes his employees particularly happy. On the other hand, it does make them wealthy."

"I know all that, but I still feel like I have been misused. I worked my tail off for everything I have received and I think I have done a damn fine job. There is no good reason for denying me a vice presidency."

Larry grimaced and said, "Have you talked to Peter about it?"

"Of course I tried, but that didn't do me any good. His majesty was unsatisfied with a couple of minute issues in the contract and that was enough for him to deny me the vice-presidency."

Larry stood up. "I am sorry, John. I understand how you must feel, but I have to get home. Janine will be waiting dinner. I hope you can learn to live with this. You have a great career here and I'd hate to see you do anything to mess it up."

"Thanks, Larry. I can always count on you to support me. I think I can learn to live with not getting a vice-presidency. I wonder if Peter can?"

Chapter 3

Helen sat in front of her vanity. She looked at her appearance in the mirror. She was only thirty-two and looked at least five years younger. Her bright green eyes were set off by a slight tan, which also accented her red-gold hair. Her face was unlined and according to most men was absolutely stunning. She stood up, opened her robe and looked at her body in the mirror. Pert breasts, slender waist, perhaps the tiniest bit hippy, but all in all a very nice body. What was wrong?

She had been married to Peter for less than two years and she knew that he had already had several brief affairs. She tried to remember back to when she had been a pool typist, then a secretary, then his secretary, and finally his personal assistant. He obviously thought she was skilled, since Peter had a near zero tolerance for inefficiency or stupidity. She sometimes wondered why he had married her, but she thought about all the times he had taken her to affairs with influential politicians, thrown parties for major businessmen, or had intimate dinners with people he wanted her to influence. Yes, she still worked for him, just in a slightly different capacity with a few fringe benefits thrown in.

She was good at influencing people. She knew all the cold facts and figures, but could combine these with charm and wit. She remembered when Peter had invited the Premier of France to dinner. Her high school French had enchanted him. He had kissed her hand more than a half-dozen times and told her innumerable times how lovely she was as he leaned over her gown to look down at her breasts. She remembered that his vote was critical in the approval of Peter's HIV drug. And, after that dinner, she was sure that they had it.

Why had she married Peter? She had to admit she was intoxicated by his interest in her, by his willingness to share some of his power and influence, and, quite frankly, he was a good-looking man. He was also quite selfish, authoritarian, and could be extremely cruel when things did not go his way. She could divorce him, but then there was the prenuptial agreement. Yes, she could divorce him, but she would come out of the divorce with some clothes and jewelry and nothing else. She also knew that if she tried to divorce him, he would do his best to make sure she would be unable to find any but the most menial jobs.

She could take lovers like he did, but that wasn't what she wanted. She wanted to be loved for herself, not for the skills she brought to the business. Well, she had no one to blame, but herself. She had been thrilled with each promotion, and ecstatic with the offer of marriage. Enough of this intellectual masturbation; she needed to do something.

Failing to come up with an immediate solution, she decided to dress and go to her office. She took off her robe and walked nude to her dresser. She selected a Victoria's Secret lacy black bra and matching panties. As she put them on, she smiled. They made her feel sexy and that was a good feeling. She selected a pair of gray, tailored slacks and a crimson colored, raw silk shirt. Slipping her feet into a pair of low-heeled black leather sandals, she walked out of her bedroom and downstairs to her office.

When she got to her office, she looked around the room. She had to admit, Peter brought the best. The teak desk had come from Denmark and probably cost more than most of the employees at VYRO Solutions made in a month. She didn't know where the ergonomic chair had come from, but had to admit that it was one of the most comfortable work chairs she had ever sat in. Her desktop computer was less than 6 months old and was continuously updated by the computer maintenance staff at VYRO Solutions. She had a laptop computer as well, but generally only used it when she went on business trips.

She sat down, looked around the office, and decided that there was nothing she wanted to do in here. She need to talk to someone and that someone had to be Ruth. She picked up the telephone and called Ruth, her best friend.

"Hello, Ruth. I need someone to talk to. Could we meet somewhere for coffee?"

There was a brief pause, and then Ruth said, "Sure, Honey. What's wrong?"

"I don't want to talk about it on the phone. Where do you want to meet?"

Ruth replied, "Lets go to the cute little place down the street from Powell's Books. I can't remember the name, but you know the one I mean, with the very retro tables and chairs, and the really good-looking waiter."

Helen had to smile. Ruth was forever judging places by the good-looking men who worked there. It was strange. She was happily married, but she loved to flirt. Her husband seemed to have no difficulty with her flirting and she always limited her actions to flirting.

"Okay, I know where you mean. I'll leave in a couple of minutes and meet you there."

"Oh, Honey, take your time. It will take me a few minutes to get myself organized to go out."

"Okay, Ruth. I'll just wait for you there. Bye."

"Bye, Honey.

Chapter 4

I found out that an investigation, even without a conviction, led to more than a loss of income and reputation. Suddenly I was a pariah. People who had been professional associates for years could not find time to see me. I was no longer invited to any professional activities. Friends found it uncomfortable to be around me and subtly let me know that I was no longer welcome in their homes. I left the comfortable, secure life I had known and now was forced to venture into the unknown.

My first issue was a place to stay. I hadn't rented anything for years and had no idea of the costs involved. I looked through the newspaper and found that most of the places that sounded nice would deplete what little money I had in no time at all and that was only if I could avoid those little conveniences such as food and clothes. I sat down with my calculator. With the SynthGen logo, it wasn't in much demand and no one objected to my keeping it.

After a great deal of calculating and some major concessions from my previous lifestyle, I found a room to rent. It was semi-furnished with a bed, a low table and several pillows, but no chairs. It even had a tiny microwave oven and a mini-refrigerator, but it cost less than $350 a month. I could have found something for even less, but I insisted on having a toilet in my room even if it was only in an alcove separated from the rest of the room by a curtain. The building was old and in an unfashionable part of town, but the room was comparatively large and had recently been painted.

After signing the rental agreement, I bought some towels and utensils at Goodwill, then went to Albertson's to buy toilet paper and the other mundane necessities of life. These tasks completed, I retreated to my room and set up housekeeping. The next step was to find a job.

I had no idea where to start looking or what I could put on an application for experience. I went to the unemployment office and told them I would take anything. That's what I got! It had taken a major effort to swallow my pride to apply for a position bagging groceries. I had to deal with 20 year olds telling me what to do and offering rather negative opinions regarding my skills, dress, attitudes, and "customer responsiveness.". But, I had swallowed my pride and learned to keep my eyes on the floor and my opinions to myself. I had also worked in a car wash, swept floors, washed windows, gathered signatures for political issues, delivered handbills in a variety of neighborhoods, and bussed tables in a cheap restaurant. My self-esteem bowed to my needs for food and shelter. This was a part of life I had never experienced before. and it changed me in ways I am not sure I can begin to describe.

After almost three years of struggling, I finally found work as a pharmacy technician. Thankfully, on the job training was provided, as I hadn't yet taken the State pharmacy technician licensing test. While the test certainly demanded less skill than a virology researcher, there were lots of procedures which I had never learned, some technical terminology and a number of things once learned, but now long-forgotten.

I was finally making more than minimum wage and actually had some benefits. This was a major improvement over all of the jobs I had taken previously just so I could eat and have a roof over my head

Previously, I had worked 10 to sometimes 14 hours a day, usually working two jobs, often seven days a week. I worked to make enough money to eat and pay for the most basic necessities of life. More importantly, I also worked to occupy my time so that I did not have to think of what had happened to me. When I returned to my small rented room, I was often so tired that a quick microwave meal was followed by totally exhausted sleep. This sequence was repeated day after day until the pain of what had happened to me faded into a blur of mindless work, long commutes to work on foot or by bus, tasteless meals and then horror-filled dreams instead of peaceful sleep.

Time passed and the intensity of the dreams slowly decreased. The pharmacy job had a few intellectual challenges and I was allowed to study the prescription drug interaction report forms and could occasionally offer information which wasn't included in the pharmacy drug interaction software. I had to pretend that it came from additional reading I was doing rather than any information I already had. A secondary advantage of the job was that it paid enough to allow me to work only one job. I was basically a clerk, recording incoming prescriptions, counting pills, checking that the pills corresponded to the prescription, placing them in the appropriate sized plastic container and affixing the computer printed label. I was also responsible for assisting with incoming orders. It would sometimes take half a day to unpack everything, check what we received against our orders and then to appropriately shelve or refrigerate everything.

It certainly wasn't an intellectually challenging position, but the need to be accurate 100% of the time placed just enough pressure on me to make sure I attended carefully to each task. The requirement to wear a white shirt and tie were new to me as in previous jobs I had usually worn jeans and some sort of pullover shirt. I remember feeling somewhat foolish as I looked over ties in the St Vincent DePaul thrift store, but I bent to this requirement as I had bent to all the other requirements of all the other jobs I had in the past.

The job also gave my first health insurance in well over three years. I had been very lucky in the past. I had never had an illness more debilitating than the common cold. In my job in the car wash, I had cut my hand on a ragged piece of metal and had to be taken to the emergency room, but since I was basically indigent, there was no charge. If I had a cold or the flu or any other common illness I went to work, because if I didn't show up, I didn't get paid.

I finally had paid days off. I used the time to walk around the city. Portland has some beautiful parks. Washington Park quickly became my favorite, possibly because of its Japanese Garden. I learned to enjoy some of the simplest things in life. I had always been too busy to watch flowers grow and bloom, to notice the changes in the seasons, to appreciate the feel of the rain on my bare head, or to listen to the birds. Portland is a very pretty city. I loved the Spring when literally hundreds of thousand of bulbs would bloom producing a riot of color almost everywhere. Even the trees bloomed, with white, pink, red and purple flowers.

Portland also has one of the best commuter transit systems for a city of its size. I could get anywhere I wanted to go within a few blocks on one of the numerous buses or the light rail system.

I was finally even able to move to a small apartment. It may not seem like much to most people, but having my own shower was a substantial step up in status. I bought some used furniture at the St Vincent DePaul thrift store nearest me. I even talked one of the fellows into dropping the stuff off at my apartments as I had no other way of getting it there.

I had a bed, a rebuilt mattress, a small table and two chairs. My kitchen equipment now included a stove, a microwave and a full-sized refrigerator. I even went so far as to invest in a small used television set. Tube-based sets were being rapidly replaced with solid state equipment and were no longer in demand, so they sold for practically nothing in many second hand stores. I paid $7.50 for a 13-inch set. I couldn't yet afford any living room furniture so I furnished my living room in a 1960s motif with cheap pillows all over the floor.

Chapter 5

I visited the library on a regular basis now. I had learned how much cheaper it was to read in the library than to buy newspapers, magazines, or even second-hand books. I also learned to use the library computers to search the internet. It was at this point that I came across a newspaper article in the library. The article talked about a new treatment for HIV produced by a company called VYRO Solutions. I read about their developing an effective treatment AIDs. It said that 60% of the individuals who received the inoculation prior to becoming AIDS-positive never became AIDs positive. Some 90% of the individuals not receiving the inoculation did become AIDs positive. Since the treatment was a single inoculation, I was quite curious and wanted to find out more.

I was floored when I found that the CEO of VYRO Solutions was Peter Stanford. I knew he had no real research skills and certainly didn't have the scientific background to develop anything associated with HIV. I devoured the available scientific journals in the library. Peter claimed he had developed the cure. He obtained a grant, did animal testing and then a human trial. The results of the human trial were so impressive that the FDA granted him the right to produce and sell the drug almost immediately. The drug was phenomenally expensive, but since it was a single inoculation, insurance companies would rather pay for it than the much, much more expensive long-term care associated with HIV. Peter was reported to be a multi-millionaire and would soon be even richer as he expanded overseas. This had to be my anti-viral agent. Peter has gone ahead and gotten permission to continue my work. Obviously, he had changed the name of the company to prevent the bad press associated with my fall from grace from harming it.

I needed to get in touch with him. I was so excited. I could be worth millions. I could stop living in a cheap apartment and eating only microwave meals. At the same time, I wondered why he had never attempted to contact me. Wait! That thought was unworthy of me. If I was trying to find a person who had slipped out of public sight as quickly as I had, how would I do it. Certainly, I'd put no ads in the newspapers. I wondered if all the jobs I'd taken as a day laborer, to keep my name off any paperwork, could have contributed to his inability to find me. I had no phone, no driver's license, and until recently, no permanent address. How could he find me? I had effectively disappeared. No wonder he had never contacted me.

Perhaps, a part of the issue was due to my personal efforts to remain hidden. I used my correct social security number only when required to do so, but used Frank Rogers as my name. This was legal since it was my name (Karol Franklin Rogers), but would certainly tend to confuse most simple computer-based searches for me.

After my initial exposure to the investigative press, I had learned to be very cautious. I wouldn't want to damage the reputation of the new company by going public with my association with Peter. I had to figure out how to contact Peter and let him know I was still alive. I was sure that he'd be interested to find out where I was so we could figure out ways I might help the company and share in some of the profits. I had to temper my excitement. I had to be circumspect.

It would not do for me to meet with Peter in public. I needed to contact him, but very cautiously. I found the newspaper that first caught my attention. They offered no telephone or fax number, no e-mail address, and only that it was a Portland, Oregon company. No problem. Even though I had no telephone, I could get a Portland telephone book and look up the telephone number and address of VYRO Solutions. Finding VYRO Solution's phone number was equally easy, but the only address listed was Research Square. While I had lived in the Portland area for years, I couldn't remember any place called Research Square. There was no zip code listed so I couldn't be sure that it wasn't in any one of a number of small towns that had been absorbed into the Greater Portland Area.

I lived just a few blocks away from the Portland Metropolitan Light Rail (MAX) line in Gresham, close to the Gresham High School. I could take this line into central Portland. I decided to call and to obtain the address over the phone. But this turned out to be more of a challenge than I expected. I had no phone, so I planned to get enough change to use a pay phone. It could be a long distance call, but I would be prepared. I got change for a $10.00 bill at the Albertson's where I worked. What I had forgotten was that the popularity of cell phones had nearly eliminated the pay phone and those that did exist usually took credit cards rather than cash and, of course, I no longer had any credit cards.

I rode into Portland on the MAX light rail, looking for a pay phone. I stopped at the Washington Zoo and finally found one next to the zoo entrance. I deposited the correct amount of change, and dialed the VYRO Solutions phone number. A rather sultry-voiced receptionist answered and told me that the address of VYRO Solutions was One Research Square in Hillsboro. Hillsboro was just on the West side of Portland. I recognized the general location and could probably get close to it on the Light Rail. Then the receptionist told me that all mail was directed to their post office box 1270 in Hillsboro, area code 97123. That was even better. A post office box was truly anonymous. I could write to Peter and no one, but he would know. That would give him time to figure out how best to contact me.

I wrote Peter, describing in detail all that had happened to me since the investigation. I asked how he had managed to save the company and how he had developed my anti-virus into an FDA approved vaccine. I told him my current condition and asked if I might have an advance on my share of the profits as my current economic condition was a bit Spartan.

Weeks passed and there was no response. Then I thought about my old habits of dumping mail on my desk until I had free time and then trying to go though weeks of mail in an hour or so. I thought that it would be a good idea to write again, just in case some secretary had misfiled the first letter. I did so and waited.

Just a single week later, I received a letter from Knowland, Samuels, and Robertson, Attorneys at Law. They informed me that I had no claim to the property or to the intellectual rights of the VYRO Solutions Company. While some of the basic research was based on my ideas, that information was public knowledge. The current vaccine was developed under the supervision of Peter Stanford and all patents were in his name. They enclosed a copy of check made out to me for $100,000.00. In order to cash the check, I must sign a form releasing "any and all claims" to the vaccine, the intellectual property rights of the company and a bunch of other lawyer jargon.

Initially, I was baffled. I found it hard to believe that Peter would refuse to acknowledge my contributions to the development of the vaccine. Perhaps, my letter had been intercepted by some mid-echelon bean counter who simply wanted to get rid of me without bothering Peter. I knew about people like that. They sucked up to their bosses by trying to personally claim benefits directly due to others. I needed to contact Peter directly. I was sure that once he heard my story, he would do his best for me.

On my next day off, I got on the MAX Light Rail at the Gresham stop, just west of the tiny Cedar Park. It was about 14 miles to Hillsboro, but only a half-hour train ride. I got off at the 12th Street SE stop. It was a short walk from there to One Research Square. It was a fairly imposing building. I walked through the plate glass doors and into the marble entry. I looked for the building directory and found that VYRO Solutions occupied the top three floors, with Peter's office listed as 2001. I took the elevator to the top floor, exited into a marble hallway, and looked around for Peter's office.

I found the office of the CEO, but was immediately intercepted by a secretary. I didn't recognize her, but then I hadn't seen anyone I recognized from the days I worked at SynthGen. She introduced herself as Sheila and said she was a temporary receptionist. She told me that I'd need an appointment to see Dr. Stanford. I told her who I was and what I wanted. She smiled like she recognized me and said she would see what she could do. She asked me to wait and she would contact his personal secretary immediately. At last I was getting some action.

As she walked away, I finally noticed that she was attractive, with fiery red hair and a figure that looked extremely trim. I was surprised by my observations. It had been years since I had really noticed a woman. Perhaps, this marked another major change in my life.

Peter's private secretary, a rather dried up prune of a woman, whose gray hair was up in a bun at the top of her head and who was dressed in a dull brown outfit that struck me as having the same exciting characteristics as the Sack, so popular in the 1970s. Her shoulders were hunched forwards as though she were trying to make herself smaller. This, unfortunately, did not affect the way she spoke to me. In the briefest of terms, she told me I would have to wait and showed me to a very up-scale waiting room.

The very modern-looking chair I chose was surprisingly comfortable and there were a large number of magazines as well as a report on the company scattered on the table tops. I started reading the annual report, as I wanted to know what VYRO Solutions had accomplished. I wandered through a morass of financial data without finding anything that told me what I wanted to know. How had Peter saved the company? How had he perfected my vaccine? I did finally come across one interesting bit of data: the company's sales had been in excess of $380,000,000 last year. Never in my wildest dreams did I realize my research could have produced such a fantastic reward. Even with all the costs associated with producing the vaccine, the profit was over $15,000,000 in just one year. This was staggering!

I was off into fantasyland. What would I do with millions of dollars? I thought of houses and cars, nice clothes, and the ability to dine out once again. God, how I longed for all of that. I floated off in this imaginary wonderland, but was interrupted by a strange guttural sound. I looked up to find someone clearing her throat. It was the Prune motioning me toward a door. She had a somewhat lopsided smile, or perhaps a grimace, on her face as she opened the door. Her thin lips were pressed so tightly together, they almost vanished. As I passed by her I got the scent of rotting blossoms and wondered why anyone would choose to wear that as a perfume.

I was ushered into a large, well-decorated office. I walked on a plush carpet that looked more expensive than the entire home I had once owned. Behind a desk that looked like it had been carved directly from a massive black walnut tree, stood a thin, bespectacled man in an obviously tailored, pinstriped suit. The suit looked expensive, but somehow failed to quite hide his sagging belly. His eyes were the color of mud and his pursed lips suggested he had just eaten something very sour. His salt and pepper toupee was just slightly askew, giving him a rather ridiculous appearance. His skin was the very pale white you expect to see on a corpse. All of these characteristics were high-lighted by the sunlight coming in from the huge plate glass window to his side. His manner seemed pompous even before he uttered a single word.

"Mr. Rogers?'

"It's doctor, actually." I usually don't demand the title that goes along with the Ph.D., but this fellow irritated me. I'd asked to see Peter and here I was facing some functionary.

"My name is F. Downing Robertson. I am Head Legal Counsel for VYRO Solutions. I assume you are here in response to our letter."

"Well, you assume wrong. I am here to see Peter Stanford."

"That will not be possible. Dr. Stanford is quite busy and he has instructed me to handle the matter of your request."

"My request? I don't understand. Peter and I started this company. We are equal partners. I am simply here to talk to Peter about our company and ask him some questions about how he managed to salvage my work."

Pointing his index finger at me like a knife, Robertson said, "Dr Rogers, you are wrong on several counts. First, you and Dr Stanford were partners in SynthGen. SynthGen went bankrupt following your investigation, criminal prosecution and civil trials. Mr. Stanford bought the assets of the company and formed a new company, VYRO Solutions. A company, incidentally, of which you have no part. Secondly, your claim to the treatment currently employed by VYRO Solutions also lacks merit. Yes, you were responsible for some of the preliminary work on which our current treatment is based, but that work was published and is part of public knowledge. The current treatment is an outgrowth of that preliminary work, but being based on unpatented, public knowledge, you can have no claim to it."

"This is wrong. It was my work that developed the treatment."

"No, your published work was part of the basis for the development of the current treatment. That is why Mr. Stanford offered you $100,000.00 even though he had no obligation to do so. I consider it a more than generous offer and, were I you, I would take it."

It seemed impossible, but I was being told that I had no claim to the treatment I worked on for years and had invented and was being shunted off with a pittance compared to the company profits. Arguing with this lawyer wasn't going to get me anywhere. I needed a lawyer of my own.

"I'll need to review your offer with my lawyer," I managed to mumble. "I'll get back to you." I turned and practically stumbled out of the office feeling completely overwhelmed.

The Prune gave me her smile or grimace, depending on how you interpreted it. She handed me off to Sheila, like someone scraping off dog feces from their shoes. I was too numb to even respond. Sheila smiled at me as I walked though the door into her outer office. "I'm sorry. I read the summaries of some of your earlier work and know how much this company is based upon your research. I wish there was something I could do, but . . . ." I was so stunned I even forgot to thank her for this small kindness. I stumbled to the elevator and sometime later found myself on the street near the MAX light rail stop.

Chapter 6

John nodded, apparently deep in thought. Perhaps there was an answer to his disappointment at not receiving the vice-presidency. Perhaps Peter had not heard the last of this issue. He stood up, brushing invisible crumbs from his shirt, paid his bill, grabbed his raincoat from the coat rack, and walked out of the bar. He was convinced that he should do something that would make Peter acknowledge that he had done a good job and protect others from receiving the same treatment.

He walked to his car, oblivious to everything around him. He attempted to open the car door, but he had forgotten to unlock it. He took the keys from his pocket and punched the remote button to unlock the doors. He got in and fastened his seat belt. He sat there for several minutes thinking and then shook his head. He had to pay attention to what was going on around him or he'd never make it home safely. He looked at his rearview mirror and decided there was room to merge into traffic. A loud honking horn told him he was still not paying enough attention.

He took a few deep breaths, looked into the rearview and side mirrors and carefully pulled into traffic. It was lucky, he thought, that he had driven this same road so many times over the past years as he could do it almost automatically. A bit over an hour later, he arrived at his house. He didn't really think of it as home anymore. Since Vicki had left him, it was just a place to sleep, watch TV, and, occasionally, eat.

He remembered her last words to him, "You chose Peter over me. I hope you are happy with him." Couldn't she understand that all the time he spent was to make a better, more secure life for both of them? Now he had no wife. He had no vice-presidency. What was he supposed to do? There didn't seem to be much point. All the things that he had worked for seemed to be vanishing as though in a mist.

As he pulled into the garage, he thought back to the time he and Vicki first saw the house. They had just come to Portland to look around at housing. The real estate agent took them to Beaverton and showed them Corrine Heights. The houses were so impressive, sitting on acres of beautifully landscaped land, with views of the water. Vicki fell in love with this house almost at first glance. It had fireplaces in the living room, the master bedroom, the deck overlooking the water, and in the game room. It was bigger and a great deal more expensive than their previous house, but Vicki was so taken with it, that he decided they'd buy it. It took some major financial adjustments because along with the house had to come a gardener and a maid, but part of VYRO Solutions employment package was an agreement to cover 50% of the down payment for any house purchased in the Portland area.

When they had closed the deal and moved in, they seemed to rattle around in a near empty house, but Vicki found several furniture stores that could supply the type of furniture that went with the house. Within a couple of months, the house began to take on a more lived in appearance. Vicki quickly made friends with several of the neighbors, joined a spa, volunteered at a local children's center, and became active in the Susan Koman breast cancer movement. She was busy. He was busy. They seemed happy.

He sat, wondering how things had gone wrong and what he should do now. He didn't understand what had gone wrong. He loved Vicki, but clearly he had screwed up in some massive way. Finally, he unclipped the seat belt, opened the car door and went inside. The cleaning lady had left the entryway light on. He walked through and turned on the kitchen light—she had left him a note.

The agency she worked for was about to raise rates again, he was out of milk, no newspaper had been delivered again, and she suggested he change dishwasher detergent as the one she had been using seemed to be causing some sort of build-up in the dishwasher. She also wished him a good night. John leaned on the counter and laughed. This was unreal. Here he was worried because his wife had left him and Peter had refused to give him a vice-presidency he had earned, when all that was really important was that he was out of milk, had no newspaper, and needed to find a new dishwashing detergent. He shook his head and headed for the liquor cabinet.

A good jolt of Scotch wouldn't solve any problems, but certainly would make him feel better. He wondered when Vicki would file for divorce. He had plenty of money, the house here in Portland as well as a condo just outside Miami. They had no children, one dog, and had three cars. Unless she was totally unreasonable, he would still be able to live a fairly comfortable life. That, he thought, was an issue that could wait. He couldn't do anything until she filed.

Waiting until Vicki filed for divorce was a really stupid idea, he thought. He loved Vicki. Perhaps it wasn't the all-encompassing adoration he felt when they were both in their 20s, but he felt comfortable with her. He liked doing things with her. He liked simply being near her. Why, he wondered, was he so complacent about losing her? He had to admit, he had spent so much time on VYRO Solutions work that he had badly neglected her. She should have understood why he did it.

He sat in the soft brown leather recliner Vicki had bought for his birthday a couple of years ago. He wished he'd listened to her and converted the fireplace to gas rather than letting it burn wood. He'd like a fire tonight, but he was damned if he was going out in the rain to get wood. He'd thought about bringing wood into the garage so that he'd have dry wood whenever he wanted, but somehow he had never gotten around to doing that.

Vicki had even taken the dog. Not that he'd been terribly found of the strange little mutt, but it would have been nice to have his warm little body climb up into his lap tonight. He pulled off his tie and opened the top button of his shirt. There, now he could breathe. He remembered when Vicki took him to the men's store to make sure he bought clothing which reflected his position at VYRO Solutions. He probably would have continued to buy wash and wear slacks and clip on ties without her influence.

He sat there, nursing his scotch, musing about how unfair life had become when he decided that it was time to turn things around. He needed to talk to Peter to determine what it would take to get that Vice-presidency. He was sure that with his sales skills, he could come up with some sort of deal that Peter would accept. After all, he was still a valuable member of the team and he was sure that

Peter understood that. Perhaps, he could look at some of the other contracts that Peter wanted. He wasn't sure what they might be since he had been working almost 18 hours a day on the Bennington deal. The Bennington Company would be supplying some of the needed reagents for the process of producing the HIV drug. He thought he'd made a great deal since they supplied the reagents at cost, plus a mere 2 percent of the after-tax profits. It seemed fair that the more money VYRO Solutions made, the more money Bennington made. Clearly, Peter didn't see it that way.

Perhaps when he'd gotten his vice-presidency, Vicki would see that all the work had paid off. John felt that if he could only get that vice-presidency, things could work out between Vicki and him. He just needed to deal with Peter!

John finished his scotch and got up from the chair. He went to liquor cabinet to pour another drink. He took off his coat and tossed it on the little couch. Vicki had always hated when he did that, but he knew the maid would collect it tomorrow and send it to the cleaners, along with his slacks and shirt.

He walked up the stairs to the master bedroom and turned on the light. The king-sized bed was immaculate as usual. After a few moments, he decided that there was nothing he could do tonight, so he'd watch a little TV and he'd get a good night's sleep for tomorrow.

He slid under the covers, pushed the pillow up against the headrest, sat up, and turned on the TV with the bedside remote. He took another swallow of his scotch and listened to CNN. It seemed like nothing ever changed. There was a war somewhere; elsewhere people were dying of some disease or another; someone had been shot; drug use was on the rise; and some Hollywood celebrity was caught in bed with another woman. He'd look at the paper in the morning, if it came. He shut off the TV and picked up one of the paperbacks from the bedside table.

He remembered when Vicki took him to the used bookstore and he got 10 used paperbacks for less than the price he would have paid for one new hardback. She said that it might relax him on some of the longer plane trips, since even first class becomes a bit boring after a while. He had started several, but had never finished one. Perhaps now, with more free time on his hands, he could actually read one from start to finish. The paperback he chose was an adventure story by some guy named W.E.B. Griffin, named *A Call to Arms*. He remembered it had something to do with war and Marines, but other than that he couldn't remember a thing about it.

Chapter 7

Helen hung up the telephone, went back to the bedroom to pick up her purse, her coat, and her car keys. She wasn't going to use their driver today. Her little BMW roadster was in the garage. She slid in the car, opened the garage door, and backed out. She told the built in GPS the address of Powell's Books and then mindlessly followed its directions. Across the block from Powell's Technical Bookshop there was metered parking that accepted credit cards. She pulled into a slot and parked the car

She locked the car, and walked toward the little café. She was less than half a block away when she realized that it wasn't the same café anymore. The owners had sandblasted the front to show the original bricks. The interior was now booths instead of tables and the walls were painted a soft yellow. It was now called The Mandela. Helen wondered if the same good-looking waiter would be there. If not, Ruth would certainly be disappointed. Helen smiled. That was the first humorous thought she had had today.

She walked in and stood by the sign which said 'We would be pleased to seat you.' That seemed to be a much friendlier way to say 'wait to be seated. A young lady with piercings in her nose, lips, and left eyebrow approached her. Her hair was cut so that the left side was much longer than the right side; the longer side was red and the shorter side purple. To Helen, she looked bizarre, but so did a lot of youngsters today.

"May I help you?"

"Yes," Helen replied. "There will be two of us."

"Would you like a booth by the window or would you prefer something further back?"

"By the window is fine." That way, Helen thought, she'd see Ruth coming. She wondered what Ruth would think when she saw the young lady instead of the good-looking waiter she expected. She put her purse and coat on the seat and then sat down, herself. There was no menu and she looked toward the young lady who was disappearing into the back. She looked around the room, finding only two other booths occupied. She expected the waitress to return with water and a menu, but that didn't happen.

She noticed that the menu was written in chalk on a blackboard hung above the register. The menu looked as though someone studying calligraphy had written it. It was decipherable, but it took a bit of concentration. There was a lot of organic this and organic that. She saw six different varieties of coffee and about ten different varieties of tea. Ruth was somewhat of a coffee snob, so she would enjoy having those choices.

Just as Helen was about to give up waiting for the waitress, Ruth walked in. The waitress walked up to her and Ruth pointed toward me. The waitress walked her over to the booth.

"May we order now?" Helen asked.

"Certainly. Besides our usual menu," she tossed her head toward the blackboard, "we have two organic soups today: pumpkin and soy milk or a farmer's market special"

Ruth couldn't help herself. She had to ask, "What is the farmer's market special?"

"It's a wide variety of vegetables from the farmer's market, sautéed in rapeseed oil and then blended into a vegetarian broth."

Ruth said, "Lets start out with two coffees. Which ones are fair trade?"

"All of our coffees are fair trade," the waitress responded, apparently somewhat offended.

Helen couldn't care less about organics and coffee. She wanted to talk. She said, "Bring us two cups of your very best coffee. We'll decide on anything else later."

Ruth looked a bit surprised that she was prevented from her usual coffee evaluation and looked askance at Helen. "What's the rush, Honey?"

"Ruth, I need some advice. I just don't know what to do. You know that my marriage to Peter is a farce. He sleeps with anyone he wants. He totally ignores me except for work related issues. I don't know how much longer I can deal with this and you know about the prenuptial agreement." Tears were beginning to form in Helen's eyes and she quickly pulled a tissue from her purse and blew her nose after wiping her eyes.

"Oh, Honey, I am so sorry. Please tell me how I can help."

"I don't know that you can." Helen proceeded to tell her about the travesty of her marriage. She described the only true conversations she had with Peter as those related to the business or someone Peter hoped to influence. Helen talked about the total lack of intimacy. Tears began to fall more rapidly and her misery seemed to defy any possibility of relief.

"Helen, look at me. There is an answer to every problem. Hank taught me that. Let's look at some possible solutions. First of all, I assume that a divorce would leave you pretty much penniless."

"Ruth, you know that's true and you know that Peter would do his best to prevent me from getting any sort of job where I might make a reasonable living. I think he would hound me or have some of his hirelings hound me until the day I died. I have my clothes and some jewelry, but that's all that is mine according to the prenuptial agreement."

"Oh, Honey, I know you must feel terrible. I have watched you try to make things work with Peter and knew it must be tearing you apart. I have spent some time talking with Hank to see if there was something we could do to help you."

"Ruth, you are such a treasure. I don't know anyone else who would worry so much about another person."

Ruth sat up a little bit straighter, scratched her head, and then said, "I think I have some possible solutions, but you have to consider each on its own merits. Number one: you take whatever money you have and start investing in your own name. That will take some time, but eventually, it will guarantee you a reasonable income. Naturally Hank will help. Number two: start actively stealing money from Peter. He doesn't do everything by credit card and you can ask for money for 'female things.' Over time you can build up quite a nice nest egg. Hank can help you invest or hide the money. Number three: You can divorce Peter and accept the fact that you'll be poor until you can find a good job. Given your skills, I it shouldn't be too hard to find a reasonable job unless Peter actively tried to prevent anyone from hiring you. Number four: You could try to threaten Peter with information about his affairs and his treatment of other people, like that nursing student you told me about. And finally and most radically, number five: You can kill Peter and inherit everything he owns.

"What?" Helen gasped. "You are suggesting I kill Peter?" Her face blanched to a deathly white. "What sort of idea is that? I am not a murderer. I won't consider it."

"That's only one option. I suspect that if you rendered him incapable to running the company, that would produce about the same result, although I suspect there would be more legal complications and more people trying to grab a piece of the pie."

"Wait a minute. Let's back up. You are seriously suggesting that I consider killing a human being?" She raised her hands as though she was fending off something terrible.

"No, I'm saying that's one of your options. I agree that killing Peter is somewhat drastic, but its an option to consider."

Helen was momentarily speechless. She had been aggressive, perhaps occasionally even somewhat ruthless, in business negotiations, but to kill someone—that was ridiculous. She wasn't very religious, but she had always considering killing was a sin.

"On the other hand, you could wait until he divorces you and you end up with nothing," said Ruth sternly.

Helen swallowed hard. She had considered her divorcing Peter, but not the converse. If he divorced her, she'd end up with the same nothing as if she divorced him. Peter had a habit of discarding personnel who no longer served his needs. When would she fall into that category? This was more serious than she originally thought. Somehow the thought of being *discarded* like a piece of trash made her feel unclean. This wasn't something she had thought of and it made her feel even worse.

At that moment, coffee arrived. Helen took a sip as she tried to think about her options. Peter had succeeded in obtaining the European rights to sell his HIV drug. He was negotiating with Russia, India, and China. But after that, who would he need to persuade to buy his product? No one important. At that point she'd lose her utility to him. What would she do then; she'd no longer have a choice.

"Helen, what's the matter? You have gone completely pale."

"I guess I just realized that I am not necessarily the one who'll make the decision. I have to consider how quickly I need to do something before I am left penniless and on the street. Jesus, I am scared. I don't know what to do."

"Okay, Honey. I understand, but you'll never be left on the street. Hank and I would welcome you into our house in a minute." Ruth considered her next statement carefully. "If I were you, I'd consider all my options carefully. Don't dismiss option five out of hand. It is radical, I agree, but that would remove any possibility of revenge as well as make you a very wealthy woman."

"Ruth, I don't know. I don't think I could kill another human being, even Peter."

Ruth starred into space. What sorts of suggestions could she offer Helen? Peter has used her to expand his business. She has been an integral part of his marketing. What did she have to show for all that work? When she worked for him as his assistant, she was paid a salary, given health benefits, time off, etc. What benefits were there in this so-called marriage?

"Honey, I think you need to sit down and consider what Peter owes you. You can try to accumulate some money and invest it, but I don't think that will net you very much before Peter decides you are no longer useful to him.

"You can always ask him for money or stock in the company as a statement of appreciation for all your work. What's the likelihood he'd give it to you? What do you think even asking him would do to your status? Do you think that requesting money or stock might suggest that you wanted to be independent of him? What would he do then?"

Helen hung her head, defeated. "Ruth, I just don't know. I doubt he would give me money or stock in any significant amount. That just wouldn't be an option. I'm going to have to think about this. I just need some time to think. I just can't make any kind of decision on the spur of the moment." She kept repeating her need to think as though it was some sort of mantra.

Suddenly, Helen paused. She sat there like a statue, unmoving. She hadn't heard any of Ruth's ideas before hearing them this morning. She have never considered Peter divorcing her and what that would mean in terms of her ability to support herself. Peter needed her help to win over the few remaining major players in the world facing significant HIV problems. What would happen when that was accomplished? Would Peter throw her out as something used, but no longer valuable? She didn't like that picture. She didn't think that she could kill anyone, but what her alternatives. She had no ideas and that scared her, scared her a lot.

There were too many things rushing around in her head. She couldn't focus on any of the options. Things seemed to be a blur, whizzing through her brain like an express train. She kept repeating "Time, that's what I need."

Ruth sat, sipping her coffee, allowing Helen to consider her options. This wasn't something she wanted to push on her. On the other hand, her disgust with Peter knew no bounds. He was everything she hated. He used people and then discarded them without a thought. He punished anyone who didn't adhere to his company line. He was a cruel, vindictive monster. She remembered how he had manipulated Hank into a contract and then penalized him when he couldn't reach the outrageous requirements. She thought of the people she knew who had experienced Peter's wrath. So many of them were left damaged, economically, emotionally, and socially. Ruth detested the man, but could never figure out anything she could do about it.

She would help Helen. Peter needed to be stopped. He had hurt too many people. He shouldn't hurt anyone else. The question was how she could help.

"Honey, why don't you come over to my place? We can sit around the pool. I can make some drinks and we can talk all day."

"That sounds nice, Ruth, but today is the day I volunteer at the nursing school. I am trying to help a student get the courses she needs after she was fired by Peter and then beaten up by someone. I am hoping to find her some sort of job so she can continue to pay for her education."

"Helen, don't you think it would be wiser for you to worry about yourself first?"

"Oh Ruth. I don't know. The nursing school gives me something concrete to do. Something that isn't associated with VYRO Solutions. I can't just sit around and think about what to do with Peter. I'd go nuts. I just need some time to deal with something other than Peter."

"Okay, Honey. Why don't you go off to the Nursing School and then call me when you've finished for the day. We can talk about what you want to do at that time."

"Ruth, you are such a good friend. I don't know what I'd do without you," Helen leaned over and hugged Ruth. "Thank you so much for being my friend." Helen failed to notice that Ruth now had tears in her eyes.

Helen opened her purse to pay the check, but Ruth stopped her and told her she'd take care of it.

"Perhaps, you need to think about saving starting now."

"Yes, you're right. Thanks again. I'll call you when I'm done at the nursing school." Helen left the restaurant and slowly walked to her car. It was misting heavily, but she didn't seem to notice. She got in her car and drove to the nursing school still trying to figure out what she should do, but no answers came.

Chapter 8

I didn't know how I could afford a lawyer on what I was making as a pharmacy trainee, but I had seen TV programs where lawyers took cases for part of the settlement. That seemed to be the best way to proceed. Now I simply needed to find a lawyer that was familiar with this type of civil case.

I went back to the telephone book, but there seemed to be thousands of lawyers listed in the Yellow Pages. How in the world did one pick one that knew what he was doing and would do it on a contingency basis? I went on line with the library's computers, but that was no help. There were still hundreds of lawyers, each stating that he or she offered better services for less money than any of the competition.

I had learned 'contingency basis' from TV. I contacted Randall, who had been my lawyer during the civil suits. He was unavailable, but his secretary gave me two names to contact after I explained what I was after: Larry Wilson and Hideo Sakura.

I looked up both of them in the telephone book. Neither had an ad in the yellow pages, which suggested they weren't big time. I looked them up on the internet, but only Larry Wilson had a web page and that only said he was a lawyer. I called each to make an appointment to discuss my case.

Wilson could see me in two days, while Sakura couldn't see me for almost a week.

I met with Wilson in his office: it was on the third floor of an old office building. His office was cramped and all the furniture looked fairly new, but cheap. Wilson was a rumpled looking man of about 50. He was about my height. His face was lined as though he had worked out of doors, but his complexion was too sallow for that. He wore a pair of light tan wool slacks that had seen better days, but sported a bright new-looking Pendleton shirt. The effect seemed a bit casual for a lawyer, but who was I to judge. He ushered me to a wooden chair next to his desk. This was a far cry from the office of F. Downing Robertson. He apologized for his secretary's absence. He explained that she was out of the office hand-delivering some paperwork to the courts. I wondered where her desk was, but dismissed that as inconsequential.

I described the situation starting with my development of the anti-virus, moving through the investigation, my fall from grace, and my attempts to contact Peter after I had learned about VYRO Solutions. I described the offer F. Downing Robertson had made me and told Wilson that I thought it was an insult. When I was finished, I asked him what he thought.

He gazed down at his desk and said, "I don't want to disappoint you, but this isn't the sort of a case I can take on a straight contingency basis. You see cases like this can take years to actually bring to trial and court costs, filing fees, and researchers have to be paid. I can see my way clear to placing my fees on a contingency basis, but I will need at least $5,000 for the direct costs involved in initiating your case."

I stammered, "$5,000. I have barely a tenth of that saved."

Wilson looked at me and stated flatly, "Then I am afraid that I can not help you. If you can save up the money, please come back and see me again."

I walked out of that office with no idea of where I could get $5,000 or how long it would take me to save that amount. I must have walked aimlessly for hours and wound up in a part of town I was unfamiliar with. As luck would have it, I looked around and found I could see the top of the VYRO Solutions building. I was only a few blocks away from where I had started. I walked toward the building to get my bearings and find the Max light rail station to catch a train home. A glance at my watch showed it was 5:15 which explained the exodus of people from the VYRO Solutions building.

Chapter 9

"Dr. Rogers?"

I turned around to find Sheila waving at me from her silver Toyota. I hesitated and then waved back. She drove up along beside me and asked if I needed a ride home. I wasn't sure whether to accept or not. Could this be some sort of gambit on Peter's part? Even if it was some sort of gambit, I needed a ride home, so I agreed and got into her car. We were both cautious about what we said so there was mostly silence on the drive to my apartment.

When we arrived at my apartment building, I apologized for my suspicious behavior and thanked her for the ride. I invited her inside, but she demurred and said she didn't know me that well. I almost laughed at this expression of modesty, but thought better of it.

"Would you care to have a cup of coffee at the coffee shop on the corner?" I asked.

"That would be nice," she said.

What in the hell was I doing, inviting one of Peter's employees to coffee? She could be setting me up for almost anything. Yet, after years of being alone, I was intrigued that this very nice looking woman would agree to have coffee with me. I wondered what she was after. She parked her car and we went inside. I noticed an outdoor table in a protected corner of the shop. I asked her where she would prefer to sit and what she would like to drink.

"I'd love to sit outside. I really don't like coffee very much. I'd prefer a cup of tea."

Again I became suspicious as I don't care for coffee, but do like tea. I was sure that my preferences were known and wondered if she was somehow trying to get close to me to make sure that I wouldn't cause trouble for Peter.

"What type of tea would you like?" I asked.

"What I'd really like is Lapsang Souchong, but I am sure they don't have it here."

This was more than a coincidence. Lapsang Souchong was my favorite tea and was definitely not a preferred tea by most people. How could she have known what I liked?

I walked up to the counter and asked if they had Lapsang Souchong. Somewhat surprisingly, they had it. My head was beginning to spin. Here was this very pretty young woman accepting my offer of a drink, volunteering that she liked a unique tea that I liked, and that tea was available at this neighborhood coffee shop. This was too many coincidences. I began to consider the possibilities that she had been sent to trap me. Trap me for what purpose? Trap me how? Was I becoming so suspicious that I viewed everyone as plotting against me? Then I thought that even paranoids could have enemies.

"Sheila, I need to ask you some questions. Please forgive me if they seem insulting, but I have just been told that a research project I worked on for years produced a fantastic product which is no longer mine. I have no way of obtaining the recognition, the money or the status I once had and I have become very suspicious of the motives of other people. Why did you offer me a ride?"

" I read summaries of some of your papers during my nursing studies and think that you got a lousy deal. Your last study provided the entire basis for Dr. Stanford's HIV drug. I felt you were being treated very unfairly."

I looked into those emerald green eyes and wondered if I had found someone who actually believed I was innocent. Someone who thought of Peter as a villain rather than a hero. 'Whoa, put on the brakes!' I thought. All of these coincidences are just a bit too neat and convenient,

"Sheila, I don't want to seem ungrateful, or a boor, but you work for Peter and I wonder why you'd even associate with me. That surely couldn't have a very positive impact on your job."

"Dr, Rogers. Karol, may I can you Karol. Dr. Rogers seems so formal."

"Certainly," I responded.

"I heard a good deal of the reactions from the upper management staff when your letter arrived. The talk concerned how to deal with you so you didn't cause any trouble. The suggestions ranged from fairly annoying to rather deadly. One individual even proposed getting rid of you permanently. After all they had done to you, I wanted to warn you to be careful."

"I plan to be, but I want to thank you for your concern. It has been so long since anyone cared anything about me. I must admit I am surprised that this would come from someone working for VYRO Solutions. Sheila, tell me how you ended up working for VYRO Solutions."

"It's very simple really. I needed money to continue school. I applied for all sorts of positions, but almost all of them wanted someone who could work a 40 hour week. Several of the others seemed more interested in looking down my blouse than in any skills I might have. And almost none of them were interested when I told them about my needing to do some schedule switching each semester."

I wanted to go on talking to her, but I didn't know if she was married, engaged or otherwise spoken for. It had also been so long since I had just chatted with a woman that I wasn't really sure where I should go with the conversation. What does one talk about with a very pretty woman? I was clearly very out of practice and, to be honest, I was never very good when I was in practice.

"Sheila, this is going to sound a bit lame, but I'd, uh, would like to get to know you a bit better. Anyone who'd risk their job to let me know that I might be in danger is someone I'd like to get to know better."

She smiled and showed off a set of dazzling white teeth. Her lower incisors were just the slightest bit crooked which just added a bit of cat-like appeal. Luckily, the waiter came with our teas and prevented me from saying anything else which might damage the relationship before it started. He asked if we took sugar or cream. Sheila asked for Splenda. This was beginning to seem truly weird. She liked tea rather than coffee; Lapsang Souchong rather than some herbal tea and used the same sugar substitute as I did.

"Sheila, do you realize that you have expressed a preference for the exactly the same things I wanted? I don't care for coffee. Lapsang Souchong is my preferred tea and I always take it with Splenda. Doesn't that seem a bit strange to you?"

"Yes, it does, but having things in common is the best way to start a friendship." She smiled again and this time I joined her. Perhaps this wasn't any sort of set up.

"Would you tell me more about you?"

"Let me see. Where should I start? I am 29 and have been so for several years," she smiled to let me know this was a joke. "I was a mediocre student through high school. I didn't date at all because my face was almost always broken out and usually infected. I was severely scarred and I was embarrassed to have people see me. My face was so bad that jobs requiring that I interact with the public were simply out of the question for me. I didn't know what I wanted to do with my life. I wasn't excited about any career I could think of. My parents were really good about supporting me in whatever I wanted to do. Dad was middle level management in an insurance company. He offered to let me train to do actuarial work in the company he worked for. Mom was a special ed. teacher. She invited me to work with one or more students from her class. She'd help me to learn enough to tutor in a variety of areas I tried both, but found I wasn't interested enough in either area.

"When I was 19, my father suggested that I talk to a dermatologist about my face. He was very aware just how up tight I was about my face. The dermatologist I talked to told me about several options for treating my face. Most of these options were pretty scary to a 19 year old. When I got home, my parents sat me down and talked to me very bluntly. They told me that they recognized that my feelings about my face were the biggest impediment in doing anything with my life. They would cover the costs of any of the treatments that the dermatologist recommended. They also said that their insurance covered me until I was 21. Even after that they would try to do whatever it took to make me as comfortable with my body as they could. Mom and I ended up crying and I decided then that I had to **do** something.

"Two weeks later, a very frightened 19 year old showed up at the hospital to talk to a plastic surgeon. She laid out the various possibilities, risks, and problems. Finally, she recommended a series of surgeries. The procedures would require a minimum of 5 months and there was no guarantee that I would like the final result, but the odds were in my favor. I sat up for hours, holding Zippie, my little miniature rat terrier, wondering what I should do. Zippie nuzzled me and licked my hand. I knew she would love me regardless of what happened. I walked into my parents' room and told them I would follow the advice of the plastic surgeon.

"Three weeks later I was in the hospital on a gurney on my way to surgery. Mom and Dad had come and wished me the best. They even let Zippie climb up and lick my face. A few hours later I was back in my room with my face covered in bandages, feeling terrible and hoping that I hadn't made the biggest mistake in my life. It was almost three weeks later before I was allowed to see the results of the first surgery. It was pretty awful. I cried myself to sleep as they prepared for the second surgery. Surgery after surgery and then the terrible wait before the bandages came off.

"The last surgery with lasers produced a dramatic change. My face was smooth. I studied my face in mirrors, looking for any trace of the severe scarring. I couldn't find even one pimple, much less a scar. I wasn't sure what I should do at this point in time, but I realized that my life had changed. I was going to have to learn a lot and quickly. I was now pretty and I had no idea how to act. Needless to say, I made plenty of mistakes, luckily none of them fatal or even crippling.

"I think that after seeing what medical science did for me, I wanted to do something along those lines. I doubted that with my grades I'd ever get into medical school, but I did think that I might be able to get into a nursing school. Things were looking up and then Dad came home with the news. Mom was in the hospital. She had a very aggressive form of breast cancer. The doctors planned to use radiation and chemotherapy even though there was very little chance either would do much good. Mom refused both treatments. She wanted to spend what little time there was with her family without the appalling side effects that those treatments produced. She died just two weeks later.

"I had always thought of Dad as a very strong man, but Mom's death hit him very hard. He sat around the house, usually looking off into space. He was given compassionate leave from his job, but even when he had used up all his compassionate and sick leave as well as all of his vacation time, he seemed unable to bring himself to return to work. He spent a great deal of time in front of the television, with Zippy in his lap. I tried keeping things up around the house: paying the bills, fixing meals which he usually didn't eat, even to arranging Mom's funeral. I had to nag him to clean himself up, to shave, and to change clothes. Finally, I had to sit him down and talk about finances. He was no longer receiving a paycheck and the savings they had accumulated were rapidly being spent. I asked him directly what he wanted me to do. He just looked at me and shook his head.

"I told him things would have to change. He needed to add my name to his investment accounts. I also had him add my name to the car and house titles. I started canceling things we no longer used to try to stretch the money as far as possible. The magazines, memberships in the country club, the premium satellite TV, the cell phones—all had to go. I also told him I was going to sell Mom's jewelry. He didn't even object to that.

"I was trying to figure out how I could go to nursing school, make enough money to afford tuition, take care of Dad, and manage the daily expenses for Dad and me. I tried to tell him what I what I was planning on doing. He signed all the forms which gave me control over all the property, but I wasn't sure he understood what he was doing. I tried to get him to tell me what he wanted me to do, but he only offered me a faint smile, patted me on the hand and said I was doing the right thing. He patted Zippy and turned back to the television set.

"Later that same night, he came into my room. He thanked me for everything I had done for him. He said it was time for him to do something, so I could get on with my life. He hugged me tightly, kissed me on the cheek, and said good-night. Somehow I missed it.

"When I awoke the next day, it was to two Sheriff's officers, knocking on the front door. They said Dad had missed a turn on his way to the coast and his car had gone into the Columbia River. He was dead and I was alone. I had some aunts and uncles back East, but I barely knew them. He had decided he couldn't go on, but wanted to leave me without the burden of taking care of him. Taking care of him, the house, and the bills for months probably gave me the edge I needed not to collapse. I was terribly sad, but I knew I could go on.

"He had two life insurance policies: a big one, worth $5 million, with the company and a smaller one he and Mom had taken out for $50,000. The former would not pay since they maintained that Dad had left their employ when all his leave was exhausted and he refused to return to work. The second one did pay. It covered all outstanding bills and left me with a small nest egg that I could use to help pay my way through school. I sold his second car and put the house up for sale. The market for houses in Portland was grim, with unemployment still hovering near 11%. By the time the realtor and the mortgage company were paid, I received less than $20,000 from the house which had sold for over $450,000.

"And that pretty much takes us to today. I am working and going to school and I haven't told anyone as much as I have told you in the last hour. I don't know what came over me."

I replied, "I guess I am a good listener, Sheila. You have certainly had it rough as well. How did you happen to choose VYRO Solutions?"

She smiled, "It was an accident. I was going to apply for a part time job in an insurance company on the 11th floor of the VYRO Solutions building. I wasn't paying attention to the elevator and got off on the top floor. I walked up to the reception desk and told them I was here to apply for the job. The woman behind the desk said she didn't even know it was advertised yet, but would let me talk to Human Resources. Twenty minutes later, I had a job being a part time receptionist."

"How do you like it?"

"I don't, really. Dr Sanford is one of the most arrogant men I have ever encountered. He is rude and overbearing to everyone. I have never met a more hostile person. I am lucky that I seldom have to encounter him. On the other hand, the job pays well and they let me adjust my hours to meet my nursing schedule every semester."

She glanced down at her watch. "It is almost 8:00. I can't believe we have sat here for two hours. I need to get home. I need to take care of ZippyII and I have a lot of studying to do."

"Sheila, would you let me call you up to get together some time . . . . nothing fancy, a movie, a pizza . . . . something like that." I was practically stammering and felt like an idiot. How long had it been since I'd asked a girl, check that, a woman, out on a date? I wasn't sure what to say or what to do at this point. I almost wanted to look down and see if my zipper was zipped or my shirt was sticking out of my trousers.

"That would be nice. Let me give you my phone number"

She wrote it down, stood up, shook my hand, and walked to her car. I didn't have the presence of mind to even stand up and wave good-bye. I felt a flood of emotions, mixing embarrassment with joy and feelings of stupidity underlying both.

Chapter 10

I felt warm. comfortable, and more than a little excited as I walked back to my apartment after my tea with Sheila. Slowly the gloom that followed my meetings with F. Downing Robertson and Larry Wilson returned. My only hope now was Hideo Sakura. I don't know why I couldn't focus on Sheila, but all my thoughts were focused on Peter, VYRO Solutions, and getting what was due me. I put a frozen dinner in the microwave, but was so angry, I couldn't eat it and just threw it in the trash. I tried to sleep, but just lay in bed for hours. When I finally did fall asleep, Peter appeared in my dreams mocking my attempts to get credit for my discovery. I awoke thoroughly exhausted and stumbled through the tasks of getting ready for work.

Luckily, the next day was an inventory day and we had to work until all the drug counts balanced. I had no time to think about anything else. By 5:30, we had matched all inventory, paid orders and placed orders, except for one container of diabetes test strips. All of the employees were told to return to the stock room and find it. Sometime after 8:00 pm someone remembered that the missing container of diabetes test strips had been tossed because they were out of date. Sid, the head pharmacist, read the entire staff the riot act for failure to record the destruction of the test strips.

I was home by 9:30 pm, but was completely worn-out. I threw off my clothes to land wherever the spirit moved them and fell into bed. I must have been asleep the moment my head hit the pillow. Unfortunately, it was far from a restful sleep as I relived the investigation over and over in my dreams. When I finally awoke at 5:30 am, I was exhausted; my pillow and sheets were soaked with sweat, and my head was being squeezed between the hands of a giant ape. Two nights in a row of these dreams was wearing me down to the point I didn't know if I had any fight left in me.

I groped my way to the shower and stood, unmoving under the hot water, slowly recovering from the nightmares of the previous night. When most of the muscles had relaxed and the headache was down to somewhat more tolerable levels, I stepped out of the shower, toweled off and returned to the bedroom to dress. I glanced down at the bed which looked as though a fight had taken place among several cats. I simply tossed the covers back over the bed, turned away and put on clean clothes.

It was my day off and I decided I needed to get away from all this stress. I thought about calling Sheila, but there was no way I wanted to dump all of my anger on her. I ended up taking the Max rail to the Washington Park and wandering through the Japanese garden. I knew I shouldn't spend the $9.50 for the admission or buy a cup of tea at the teahouse, but I needed the calm that always comes with such a visit. The soft gurgling sounds of the running water, the wind whispering through with the pines, the formal stone gardens, and the bamboo bending slightly in the breeze calmed me. I sat on one of the stone benches near the confluence of several of the streams of water to enjoy the peace and tranquility of the location. I am not sure, but I think I drifted off.

When I looked around, most of the afternoon had passed and a rather large woman was shouting into her cell phone. She managed to totally destroy the serenity of the setting. I got off the bench ready to tell her how absolutely inappropriate her behavior was, but I realized that I needed to return home, eat and get things ready to return to work the following day. I also knew that the woman would take one look at me and dismiss me as a nobody. So, I gave her the finger, turned and walked out of the garden.

I took the light rail back home and was surprised at how much money I had spent in one day. After rent, utilities, and food, there was usually only ten or fifteen dollars left each week. I had used up more than a weeks worth of savings, with nothing to show for it. I swore to be more frugal in the future since the fortune I had imagined seemed to have vanished like the daylight. I was going to have a hard time taking Sheila out if I couldn't manage to put together a reasonable amount of cash.

Chapter 11

After several days of work, it was time to meet Mr. Sakura. I took an afternoon off and took a bus to his office. He met me at the door. He looked unprepossessing. He was perhaps 5'4," and must have weighed no more than 100 pounds. He had jet black hair combed down on both sides and the back. In front it was cut in the form of short bangs. He was coatless and his striped tie was askew. His huge glasses made his eyes seem very large.

"Welcome, Mr. Rogers. Come in. I hope I can help you." He made a slight bow as he waved me into his office.

Once again, I explained my case in detail, including my visit with Larry Wilson. Mr. Sakura had made a number of notes and he studied these for several minutes.

"Mr. Rogers, I fear what I have to say will upset you, but I must be honest with you. Your chances of winning this case are extremely remote. Morally and ethically, you are in the right, but the law recognizes only its set of rules. VYRO Solutions would be able to keep this case in process until any but a major firm would run out of money. I do not know why Mr. Wilson would ask for $5,000, as he must know as well as I that the chances of winning this case in the foreseeable future is essentially zero.

"I recommend that you consider taking the $100,000 as it is most likely the only money you will ever get from these people. I realize that is not what you wanted to hear, but it is the truth. I will not take your case because I think it very unlikely that either you or I would gain anything from pursuing this in a court of law."

"But then, what can I do?"

"Legally, you have few options and those have almost no chance of success. You can pursue this in court, or you can ask for a greater amount of money to release your claim. As I said, I can recommend neither of these options."

"So I have no real options?"

"Legally, that is true."

"Mr. Sakura," I pleaded, "what would you do?"

"As a lawyer, my only advice is to repeat that you accept the $100,000 and attempt to rebuild your life. While $100,000 may be far less than you deserve, it is a much greater sum than you currently have. It also has the advantage of having no legal fees associated with it."

I looked at Mr. Sakura. I had no idea what to say at this point. My dreams were a soap bubble which had unfortunately burst, leaving a faint trace of foul tasting soap on my face.

"Is there nothing more I can do?" I begged.

"Legally, I have given you your three options and once again my advice is to take the $100,000," Mr. Sakura replied. "Beyond that, I can offer no legal advice."

I stood up slowly. "Thank you, sir. You have been most patient with me. May I ask for your bill."

"There will be no bill as I was unable to help you. I wish you luck, Mr. Rogers and hope that you will not let this become an impediment to the rest of your life. You are still fairly young and can still have a successful life, even if not the one you had planned." He bowed as he showed me out of his office.

I walked out of his office into the afternoon. Surprisingly, it wasn't raining, although there was a solid overcast and a cold, wet wind was coming from the west. My depressed mood mirrored the weather. I was lost in an emotional whirlwind. How could I deal with this? It wasn't fair! I deserved the credit for the success of the drug. I deserved my share of the money that VYRO Solutions had been making. I deserved the public accolades for what I had done. But, I was powerless. How could I fight a company like VYRO Solutions? Mr. Sakura clearly indicated that I was almost certain to lose a legal battle and then only after years of protracted and expensive wrangling. I couldn't leave it like this, but I had no idea of what to do.

I walked for hours, finally ending up at my apartment. I went inside and turned on the radio. I sat down on the pillows I had in place of living room furniture, lifted my feet onto one of the pillows and laid back. My body tried to rest while my mind whirled. It was so unfair. My mind kept insisting there had to be something I could do. No answers came and I finally became so exhausted that I gave up and went to bed.

The following day I went back to work. My mind was still struggling to find an answer, so I tended to move through the day on automatic pilot. Luckily, I didn't make any serious mistakes, although I had to count several pill orders twice to get them correct. John, one of my co-workers, sensed I was having some difficulties and offered to help. I had years of experience learning how to accept help when offered and was more than grateful. With his assistance, I got through the day. I thanked him, politely refusing his offer to discuss my problems, and headed home.

As I tried to make myself relax and wondered what I could do. It seemed like all legal actions were closed to me. I did have the possibility of getting $100,000. That was more money than I could earn in years. If I invested it, plus my job . . . . Hell, wait a minute, I don't want to be paid off for my life's work with $100,000. Damn it, I deserve better. I sat up and started to think a bit more rationally. I had no real hope of getting any meaningful part of what I was owed me by VYRO Solutions. What options were open to me? I guess this was the point at which I began to consider revenge as an option. What sort of revenge could I obtain? I couldn't, no, wouldn't do anything to affect the efficacy of my drug—wasn't it ridiculous that I still considered it **my drug**.

After many hours fruitlessly considering options, I decided that the best course was to see if I could get some sleep so I wouldn't be such a disaster at work tomorrow. I needed to be done with all these emotional outbursts and start thinking more rationally.

It is said that sleep is an analgesic as well as a source for solutions to problems. So it was for me. I determined that I could do nothing to directly effect Peter's responsibilities to me, his position at VYRO Solutions, or the money I was due. This brought a certain amount of peace of mind, although it still lacked satisfaction. What I wanted was a way to punish Peter for what he had done to me. My first thoughts were based on my scientific background. I could write articles that exposed what he had done. What would I say? Who would publish them? If I could get them published, who would believe me? If some believed me, what could they do to change the current state of affairs? Obviously, this required some thinking outside the box. I knew what I really wanted was revenge, but somehow I had to at least let Peter know that I knew what was happening.

I decided that it was time to distance myself from my problems in hopes that my subconscious would untangle all these conflicting thoughts and come up with some sort of reasonable solution. I needed a diversion and Sheila immediately came to mind. It had been over a week and I hadn't even called her to say hello.

I walked down to the cafe where we had had tea since they had a public telephone. I called, but got her answering machine.

"Hi, Sheila, its Karol. I was calling to see if you might be interested in doing something Friday night. I don't know the kinds of things you prefer, but a movie, a pizza, a walk in Washington Park are all great with me. I don't have a phone yet, so I'll call you back later."

I called Sheila two more times and got the answering machine each time. I didn't know what I should do at this point. Perhaps she was screening her calls and didn't really want to see me. Perhaps she had gone out of town, but she had said she didn't have any family or close friends. Perhaps she was having to work late, maybe she was at the hospital for some of her nursing training. I really had no idea of what to do or how to reach her. It struck me that I didn't even know her last name. I thought I'd trying calling her one last time.

Chapter 12

John had started the story, but before he was past the first chapter, he had fallen asleep. He woke up at 6:00 am. He felt groggy, like he hadn't gotten enough sleep. He remembered his dreams. They had been bizarre. First, there was some lady telling him to watch his step or he'd fall. He couldn't understand as they were both on the ground, but she kept saying it over and over. There was a second dream, or maybe it was the first and the lady was second. He couldn't remember. But whether it was the first or the second, it was equally strange. He was seated at an immense table. On the table were torn scraps of paper. It was his task to but them back together, but there appeared to be thousands and thousands of pieces. He couldn't recall anything more than staring all the pieces of paper, but it still made no sense to him.

He slowly got up and went into the bathroom and threw some cold water on his face. He stared into the mirror, wondering who that middle-aged man staring back at him might be. He splashed more cold water on his face and then, shook his head to clear it, grabbed his robe from the walk-in closet, and went downstairs. When he smelled the coffee, he knew that Alicia had remembered to set the automatic timer so it would be ready at 6:30. He thought he wouldn't mind paying Alicia more money. Perhaps he should ask her if she wanted to work full time for him. No, that wouldn't do. He'd be bogged down with more paperwork for withholding, Federal and State taxes, W-2s, paying for benefits . . . no, no, paying the agency and giving her a few dollars here and there to supplement that pay was the best way.

He was surprised that it had taken him almost 40 minutes to get out of bed and come downstairs. He briefly wondered what had taken him so long. The coffee was ready and he poured himself a cup of coffee, added sugar and diet creamer, stirred it and sat down in the breakfast nook. He needed to decide how to approach Peter. He was a salesman; he should be able to sell himself to Peter. Perhaps he just needed some time to carefully figure out his sales pitch. He'd take the day off and organize his thoughts. He'd need to call in to his secretary so she'd be aware he wasn't coming in and ask her to set up an appointment with Peter for the following day.

It was only 6:45, so he'd have to wait to call in. Perhaps he could fix himself some breakfast. He opened the refrigerator to see what was available. There was a loaf of organic bread, some sort of margarine substitute, egg beaters, a plastic container of no fat cream cheese, a lot of salad stuff, and a lone cup of fat free pudding. There was also a six-pack of some sort of fancy water and two bottles of organic root beer. He remembered his arguments with Vicki over the type of food which she bought. She insisted that he needed to look after his health. He thought food was something to be enjoyed rather than just being tolerated. He opened the freezer to see if there was something stored there that he'd enjoy. As he expected, there was more health type foods:

no bacon, no sausage, no eggs, no bagels, no full-fat cream cheese, nothing for a proper breakfast.

He decided that he'd get cleaned up and go out for a real breakfast. First, he took his morning pills for high blood pressure and high cholesterol. He'd been doing this for so many years, it was automatic. Then he walked upstairs to shower and put on some casual clothes. When he came downstairs again, he felt clean, hungry, and ready to get to work on his sales plan. He checked to make sure he had his wallet and car keys then walked to the back door leading to the garage.

"Damn it!" he said, turning around and walking back into the kitchen. He picked up his phone and speed dialed his secretary. Since it was before 8:00 am, he got the answering machine. He told her he wouldn't be coming in today and asked her to make an appointment with Peter for tomorrow. Then he remembered Peter was going to be gone for a long weekend, but he'd be back the first part of next week. He told her to make the earliest appointment she could get and told her that he'd probably be in tomorrow, but please tell anyone who called that he was busy and would call them back.

Okay, the work related stuff could be put on hold now and he could go out for breakfast. He thought of going to the country club, but decided that wasn't what he wanted. Some sort of coffee shop which served large breakfasts without skimping on the butter or using fat-free anything. He never went anywhere like that with Vicki, so he had no idea what direction to go. Wait one minute. The last time he had been on the Beaverton highway, he had seen several likely places and they weren't that far away.

He got in the car and started out down the driveway when he noticed the newspaper sitting on top of one of the bushes next to the front porch. Perfect, he'd have something to read while he ate his breakfast. He collected the newspaper, and drove out of his driveway. It took him less than 30 minutes and no more than two wrong turns to find the Village Inn. It looked like exactly what he wanted.

Inside, it seemed like a comfortable place with no fancy pretensions. The waitress told him to take any seat he wanted and she'd be right with him. He sat next to a window with the sun shining through onto the table. It seemed warm and cozy. The seats were plastic, but somehow they seemed comfortable. The waitress appeared before he had a chance to open his paper. She placed a glass of water in front of him and asked if he wanted coffee. He said yes and she poured coffee from an insulated plastic pot into a mug already on the table.

"Cream?" she asked. He nodded and she placed a silver colored pitcher on the table. Handing him a menu, she told him, "Take your time. Just give me a wave when you are ready to order." With that, she turned and left. That was certainly a lot different than the country club where they hovered over you, filling your water glass after every sip.

He studied the menu, a bit surprised at how inexpensive the meals were here compared to the places he usually ate. He decided on the 'Incredible VIB' where he could select four different items and pay less than $7.00. He carefully considered his options and then waved the waitress over.

"I'll have the VIB. I want the cheese omelet, hash browns, sausage links, and French toast."

The waitress made a few quick checks on her order pad, refilled his coffee mug, and went to the cook's window to place the order.

John opened his paper, added some cream and sugar to his coffee, and began to read. He was unsurprised to find out that the paper reported many of the same things he had seen on CNN. The Middle East was still a hot spot with fighting between various religious groups as well as fighting among different Moslem groups. He didn't really understand what the sources of these differences were. He wasn't particularly religious, but he thought that all of these people worshiped one God and thought that they argued over the most minute and unimportant points of ritual. He wondered if a good salesman could get these folks together and make them see that their differences were inconsequential. No, he thought, these were fanatics and fanatics don't respond to good sales pitches.

As he was about the turn the page, breakfast arrived. "Thank you," he said.

"Welcome," was the response as she left the table.

He cut off a piece of the cheese omelet and put it in his mouth. He could taste the butter it had been cooking in. He guessed it was not a gourmet omelet, but it felt great in his mouth. He sampled the French toast, the hash browns and the sausage links and found them all to be quite satisfactory. He concentrated on the food and didn't return to his paper until he had finished every last scrap on his plate. He finished the coffee in his mug and poured another mug from the insulated pitcher the waitress had left on the table. He added sugar and cream and re-opened the paper.

There it was. Page three toward the bottom. VIRO Solutions makes another deal to have its anti-AIDs drug sold abroad. The article went on to describe the hundreds of millions of additional dollars that would add to the company's bottom line. The author of the article suggested that Peter Stanford would soon be one of the richest men in the world.

The following paragraph described the fact that Stanford was cutting costs at the same time he was increasing revenues. The article went on to say that most of the cuts would be in management. Perhaps this was a hint as to why he had been denied his vice-presidency. Was this going to be Peter's excuse to get rid of him? John felt his wonderful breakfast become a lead weight in his stomach. The fact that the stock price had risen overnight and made him more than $50,000 wealthier did nothing to alleviate his concerns

The waitress came by to remove his plate and ask him if he wanted anything more. He hesitated and then asked if they had any cinnamon rolls.

"Yes, of course we do. Would you like a single or a four pack? We also have them to go, if that would interest you."

"Hum," he thought. "I'll have the four pack. He would have these to eat at home as he worked on his sales pitch for Peter. It would have to be really good. Clearly he wasn't just fighting for a vice-presidency; he was fighting for his job.

He waved the waitress over for the bill. It was less than $15.00, so feeling generous, he left a twenty dollar bill, took his paper, and left.

Now it was time start working on his marketing campaign for a vice-presidency. What was he to offer Peter? Perhaps the first thing would be to discover exactly what Peter's objection to the Bennington deal was. Somehow 2% of the company's profits to get some of the basic materials at cost didn't sound like a bad deal. There must be some other reason why Peter finds that portion of the agreement objectionable. Okay, that would be step one.

Step two should be a summary of his successes over the past three years of employment. He needed to think of the best way to present that information. Perhaps in the form of a graph showing the amounts of money he had brought into the company. Perhaps a simple listing of the successful contracts he had negotiated and which Peter approved. Perhaps both.

And what would be step three? Could he come out and directly ask what Peter wanted in order for him to get his Vice-presidency? That could be a bit risky. Perhaps he should frame the question in a less specific fashion. What sorts of actions are you looking for in a vice-president? No, that was a bit too direct. He'd have to think about that. He'd filled up a page with notes and thought that it was time to try one of the cinnamon rolls he had brought back from the Village Inn.

He made another pot of coffee, heated the cinnamon roll briefly in the microwave, and sat down to enjoy his treat. The cinnamon roll was delicious, the coffee was equally delicious and the sun coming through the window warmed him. It was really pleasant and before he knew it, he was asleep.

Almost two hours later he awoke to a cold cup of coffee and a small piece of cinnamon roll on his napkin. It was just after 1:00 pm. He looked over his notes and decided he should get to work filling out the information for step two. He had access to the company's computer from his home, so he swallowed the last piece of cinnamon roll, and walked to his home office. He spent less than three hours obtaining the information he needed and then another hour putting it in a format that would be easy for Peter to understand.

That meant the first two steps were completed. He'd need to think some more about the third step.

He poured himself a glass of scotch, added some ice, and sat down in his leather chair. Perhaps rather than asking what it would take to get a vice-presidency, he should ask what Peter wanted from him. That might open up a more revealing dialog. Perhaps, it would point him to what he needed to do to save his job. Yes, that's what he would do. He finished the scotch, changed clothes and went to the hot tub. He soaked for a long while thinking and refining his sales plans. He toweled off and went back inside. He redressed and returned downstairs. Pouring himself another scotch, he thought about having another cinnamon roll, but decided the scotch was enough and took another sip while thinking about his marketing plan. He thought he had actually reached an excellent conclusion and was considering his presentation when he fell asleep again.

When he awoke it was dark outside. He glanced at his watch. It was just short of 9:00 pm. Given what was available in the house, if he wanted something reasonable for dinner, he'd have to go out. He could go to the country club, but he didn't want to get all dressed up. Did he want to go back to the Village Inn? Why not? He had enjoyed breakfast—at least until he had read that article about VYRO Solutions. He was sure he could find something he would enjoy for dinner.

As usual, it was raining, but it was a nice soft rain and even with the windshield wipers on low, he could easily see the road. He returned to the Village Inn, without any incorrect turns this time. It looked unchanged from this morning except there was no sunlight coming through the windows.

Dinner offered some additional possibilities beyond those of the breakfast menu. He thought of the dinners he had while working on the Bennington deal. He'd have chicken sautéed in white wine and garlic. He looked at the menu again. There was no chicken sautéed in anything, but there was a petite sirloin steak. That's what he would have. He waved the waitress over and gave her his order.

"Would you like something to drink besides water?" she asked.

"Yes, I think I'd like a scotch."

"I'm sorry. We have a beer and wine license, but can't serve hard liquor."

John hesitated. He hadn't run into this before. Everywhere he had gone for dinner, hard liquor was always available. "May I see your wine list then."

"We don't really have a wine list. We serve Gallo Chablis and Gallo Hearty Burgundy."

John hadn't had any Gallo wines and wondered whether they were from a California, Washington, or an Oregon vineyard. He'd tried enough different things today; perhaps he should just stick with coffee. "I'll just have coffee," he said.

John hadn't brought anything to read with him and wondered what he should do until his soup arrived. It had been a very long time since he had eaten dinner alone. Then he noticed a newspaper which had apparently been discarded by a previous customer.

He wasn't sure of the etiquette in obtaining someone else's newspaper, but since who ever left the paper appeared to be gone; he saw no reason not to take it. It was the Wall Street Journal. Good, he'd be able to see what was happening on the street and perhaps could use some of that information in his sales pitch to Peter.

It was like a repeat of the CNN news program and this morning's paper. There was a war, disease, several shootings, a rash of bank robberies, etc. There was further news of a European common market agreement to purchase VYRO Solutions HIV drug. "Wow," he thought, that should really make the stock take off. A look at the New York Stock exchange listings told him he was correct. If he cashed in all his stock, warrants, and options, he'd be worth well over ten million dollars. That was amazing. He'd never thought he'd be that rich.

The bill came, he paid and left a 25% tip. As he walked out to his car, he noticed that he felt satisfied; something he seldom did when he ate the stuff Vicki wanted him to eat. He wondered how she would feel if he announced that this was the type of food he wanted. She could eat the health food stuff; he would eat things that tasted good.

He awoke the next morning feeling fine. He'd get cleaned up and get to the office early. Less than 45 minutes later, he was in the car and on the road. In the seat beside him was his briefcase containing the sales material he worked on yesterday. He wanted to put together a really great presentation for Peter. After all, this might be his most important presentation.

He parked in his reserved slot and took the elevator to the 21st floor. He nodded to his secretary as he went into his office. Sitting in his fancy desk chair, he spread out his sales plan over his desk.

First, there was step one. How do I find out what the basis for Peter's dislike of the Bennington contract? The easiest way would be to just ask him directly, but that wasn't usually a very effective technique. Peter could become quite irritated if he thought you were questioning his judgment. If that happened the rest of the sales pitch could go down the toilet. He needed to come up with just the right approach. He needed a cup of coffee.

"Mary, is there any coffee in the kitchen?"

His secretary gave her usual exasperated huff. "Yes, sir. Would you like me to get you some?"

"Please."

Mary went to the kitchen, got John's mug, filled it, added Nutrasweet, and powdered creamer. She really didn't mind this very unsecretarial duty since John was a pretty good boss as bosses go. He seldom demanded overtime. He was quite generous with time off for personal reasons and he never shouted at her like Peter did with his secretaries. She really wished he had gotten the promotion to vice-president and not just because that would raise her salary. Well, there wasn't anything she could do about it.

He carried the coffee into his office and set it on his desk. "Is there anything else I can do for you?" she asked.

"Mary, close the door and come over here and sit down. I want to use you as a sounding board. I am trying to find the exact reason Peter disliked the Bennington deal. I'd love to ask him directly, but you know how that would probably go."

Mary nodded, with a slight smirk.

"Do you think that asking him if he'd go over the contract and point out my mistakes would be a reasonable approach?"

"Possibly, but I think that I would preface that with an expression of some sort of apology for wasting the company's time and money and now having to redo the contract."

John leaned back in his chair and considered Mary's idea. "You know, Mary, that might just work. Since I am in Peter's doghouse I suspect he expects some sort of apology. Thank you. Thank you very much."

Mary rose from the chair and looked at John. It wasn't that he never complimented her or used her as a sounding board, but his thanks seemed a bit over the top. On the other hand, it was really nice to be appreciated, something that seemed in very short supply at VYRO solutions.

Okay, he had a reasonable starting point. He would apologize for the time wasted and the fact that they would have to re-negotiate the contract. Then he would move onto the question of what was wrong with what he had done. He'd need to think of a better way of putting that. How could he appeal to the man's unbelievable vanity? Perhaps, some sort of 'can you help me improve my performance' might do the trick. Just then, an idea came to him: *Peter, I am very sorry I disappointed you. I am very interested in regaining your trust and would appreciate if we could review the contract so that you could show me where I went wrong and what a better response might be.* That might do it. It had the correct components of fawning, a statement of Peter's superiority and a request for help from a skilled underling.

Perhaps he should try it out on Larry. At least he knew that Larry would give him an honest answer and would offer help if he could. That could wait until he finished part two.

He had a list of all of the contracts he had negotiated which Peter had signed off on. He needed a way to make the projected savings due to his negotiation skills clearly visible. He started down the list. Some of these would be easy. In situations where he had found a new supplier and reduced costs, the differences between old and new costs could be clearly shown on a bar chart. Susan or Cynthia, down in production, could whip that out in less than an hour. That should impress Peter. Perhaps his concern about losing his job was unwarranted.

Okay, that dealt with the easy part. What about the negotiations for new equipment? New equipment was always more expensive than the older stuff. How did he show saving there? Could he show what other companies had paid for the same equipment versus VYRO Solutions? He'd have to get access to a lot of fairly confidential records to be able to do that. Could he show that he had gotten better equipment for the same price? How could he quantify *better*? Perhaps, he needed to think a bit more about that one. Maybe he could ask Larry.

The last component might be the hardest. It involved superior service which could mean many different things. Shipping was costly no matter who you used, but what about errors, timeliness, and customer relations. No, he would strike that. Peter was a shark. He had a product everyone wanted, he didn't have to worry about customer relations. At least he didn't think he had to do so. So, how did he show he had improved shipping? He pulled up the contract on his computer. It stated number of allowable errors per shipment and, he smiled when he remembered getting this part into the contract, penalty payments for greater number of errors. In the first 3 months, shipping costs were cut in half while Worldwide worked to cut down their errors. By the sixth month, they were right on target so the penalty savings were gone, but the complaints and additional shipments were reduced to near zero.

With Worldwide, he'd show the cost savings for the first 6 months and after that the reduction in errors. It wouldn't make much of a graph, but it still might be impressive. He'd ask Cynthia about a visual representation. She was very good at that.

Packaging had initially been done in house. John had looked at some of the well-equipped packaging companies and figured out that VYRO Solutions could actually save money and time by outsourcing. He'd have to figure out the direct and indirect personnel costs, but it was more than the costs of outsourcing. They had been able to increase output by over 15% and a slightly improved percentage of undamaged packages.

He continued to work though lunch, now firmly committed to showing how much he was worth to the company. By 2:30, he had finished putting most of the material together. Cynthia could get some of the figures from personnel and she'd probably be able to complete the graphs before the end of the workday. He stood up and stretched. It had been a while since he had spent this much concentrated time at his desk, but he thought he was satisfied with the results.

He took the elevator down to 19 and walked into the Production department. He saw both Susan and Cynthia conferring over something on Susan's worktable. Walking over to them, he said he had a rush job,

Cynthia looked up at him and asked, "When isn't it a rush job?"

"I need some material to present to Peter on Monday morning. Basically it involves a few graphs, but I'd appreciate them looking very eye-catching. Can you do it?"

"Let's see what you've got and then we can tell you if its possible." Cynthia took the paperwork out of John's hands. As she read each one, she handed it to Susan. "This doesn't look too difficult. Do you want posters, 8 x 10s or something else?"

John thought for a minute, "Let's do 8 X 10s, but on a heavy backing."

"Okay, come back in 2 hours. It will be done and packaged."

John smiled at the two of them. "I can't tell you how much I appreciate this, Ladies. Let me know when I can do something for you. If you'd just leave it on my desk when you've finished, that would be great."

They all smiled, each knowing that there would be some sort of payoff in the future. The two women knew that John was a man of his word and he knew that they'd ask for something, probably something inconsequential, but he'd deliver. He'd deliver more than they asked for.

The weekend went swiftly. He ate, swam in the pool, spent some time in the hot tub, and actually finished one of the books Vicki had him buy. He kept going over the sales plan in his mind. He needed something to get his mind off work. He turned on the radio. The disc jockey announced that Mary of Peter, Paul, and Mary had died and that they would be playing songs from the trio.

John couldn't believe it. Mary was dead. He'd listened to that trio for decades. How could Mary be gone? He listened to *Where have all the Flowers gone* and realized he was crying. He had sung along with *Puff, the Magic Dragon* and *Leaving on a jet plane*. At least this had distracted him from his constant worrying about Peter, his job, and Vicki.

Why was he so upset about the death of a singer he liked, but didn't really know? He wondered what was wrong with him. This was silly. He was almost a vice-president of a multinational business. Why should he be crying over this woman? He didn't have an answer and that bothered him. He thought about some of the things that Vicki had said about his lack of compassion for other people and wondered if that what was making him sad. No, he was a businessman and his business was selling.

He needed to stop crying. He needed to focus on his meeting with Peter. That was the important thing. He went over his marketing plan. He smiled as he thought that he was the product he was selling. He rehearsed his speech to Peter and satisfied, poured himself another scotch. He turned on the TV and found AMC was replaying Captain Blood. He had always enjoyed the swashbuckling antics of Errol Flynn. It turned out that this Sunday was a series of Errol Flynn's films. He loved the way Flynn solved his problems so easily, usually by killing someone. He relaxed in his recliner and watched as Errol Flynn saved the woman, captured the ship, and defeated the pirates. Somewhere in the sword fighting, love-making, and scheming, he fell asleep.

Chapter 13

When he awoke, it was still dark outside with the soft whisper of rain. He glanced at his watch. It was just 5:15 am. Errol Flynn was still on the TV, but now he was a cowboy in the old West. John shut off the TV. There was plenty of time to get ready for work. He rinsed out the coffee carafe, filled the basket with a coffee filter and coffee, then started the machine.

He carefully selected the clothes he would wear, with an eye toward looking like the ultimate vice-presidential candidate: dark gray wool suit, with a very thin dark blue stripe running through it; a white-on-white shirt with French cuffs; and, finally, a crimson silk tie. He looked at himself in the mirror. This was a very important day. Yes, he was ready to face Peter.

Arriving at the office just after 8:00, he noticed that his presentation materials were neatly wrapped and stacked on his desk. He opened the packages and looked at the graphic representations of his efforts. Susan and Cynthia had done their usual exceptional job. The materials impressed him. Certainly they would impress Peter who was always looking at ways to cut costs and increase profits.

"Mary," he called through the office door, "Did you get a specific time for my meeting with Peter?"

"He said he'd see you first thing this morning, but he usually doesn't get in until well after 9:00. Do you want me to ask his secretary to buzz me when he arrives?"

"That would be great. Thanks, Mary." John relaxed back in his chair and glanced through the graphics

In less than 15 minutes, Mary's phone rang. She told John, "Peter came in early this morning, so I guess he'll be ready to see you any time now."

John gathered up his materials, placed them in his attaché case, and walked out of his office. He walked down the corridor to Peter's office. He nodded to Peg, Peter's secretary, and asked, "Is he ready for me?"

"I think so, but let me check." She opened Peter's office door and stuck her head inside. He said something John couldn't quite hear and Peter made an equally unintelligible response. "He has one quick thing to take care of, but go right on in," said Peg.

"Thanks," he smiled and walked into Peter's office. Peter's office never failed to amaze him. In addition to the very expensive Danish modern furniture, every wall was covered with awards and pictures of Peter with Very Important People. It almost seems like he wanted some sort of assurance that he was as important as he thought he was.

John sat down in one of the chairs in front of Peter's desk. Again, he noted that Peter's desk was slightly elevated, as was his executive chair. Anyone sitting in front of his desk would always have to look up at him. John thought that this was a rather silly affectation, but Peter was the boss and he could do pretty much what he wanted.

Peter finished signed a set of papers and returned them to a folder on his desk. He put down his pen, looked at John and asked, "Well, John. What can I do for you?"

Just as he had practiced, John said, "Peter, I am very sorry I disappointed you. I am very interested in regaining your trust and would appreciate if we could review the Bennington contract so that you could show me where I went wrong and what a better response might be."

"John, I was more than a little disappointed that you didn't think the contract through before you sent it to me. The two major flaws are that you gave them a portion of our profits, totally unrelated to anything they might do for us in the future. If we developed a more cost efficient method of producing our drug, they would benefit from out research, even though they had nothing to do with it. Do you see where I am going? You can't give away our profits unless you tie any increases in those profits to improvements in their services or materials. You didn't do that. Bennington could just coast on our skills and receive continual increases in income based on our profits. That's just not thinking the issue though.

"You also accepted their materials *at their cost*. How in the hell are we supposed to determine what their real costs are? Did you put anything in the contract about raw material costs, shipping costs, and production costs or do you think they might want to slide some overhead costs into what they charge us. I know that Bennington, himself, likes to spend several weeks every years in the Caribbean at some very exclusive resorts. Do you think that might become an item in the costs they charge us? You just didn't think!

"I know you spent a lot of time working out this contract and that, too, has me concerned. If it takes you that long to come up with such a flawed product, how can I ever trust you as a vice president? I need someone who will make much more rapid and accurate decisions."

While John recognized some degree of accuracy in these comments, he was becoming increasingly uncomfortable with their tone. There was nothing being conveyed which suggested that he would be given another chance to prove himself worthy of a vice-presidency.

"John, I know you've done some useful things for the company in the past and I feel we have rewarded you amply for those accomplishments. I suspect you are prepared to show me all sorts of facts and figure about what you have accomplished, but to repeat a hackneyed phrase, 'What have you done for me lately?'" We can't rest on our laurels. We need constant improvement. I am not completely sure you are up to that task."

"Christ," thought John, "was he getting ready to fire me right here and now?"

"I will be doing an annual review of your department in another few of weeks. I will expect you to be able to show me that improvements are taking place, that improved contracts are being negotiated, that less expensive materials and other resources are being uncovered, that you are finding contractors either willing to do the same quality job for less or to do an improved job for what we are paying now.

"John, I have made you a very rich man and I have high expectations of anyone in your position. If you have questions about your ability to meet my standards, it might be helpful to raise them right now!"

John slumped in his chair, stunned. He had been told that if he didn't show some sort of improvement in a few weeks, he would no longer have this job. Hell, he'd probably no long have any job with VYRO Solutions. He was speechless. His brain had turned to mush and he could no longer formulate a coherent thought.

"Well, John? Any response?" asked Peter.

"I . . . ." John stumbled. He quickly regained his senses and offered, "I appreciate your honest evaluation of my efforts. In my defense, the appendices to the contract specify that materials costs are based on raw materials, shipping and production costs only. No overhead charges are allowed. Quarterly reports are required which specify each and every one of those costs for each individual product."

Peter looked down at him and said, "Well, maybe you didn't make such a mess of that part as I had thought. I'll have to read the appendices more closely. What about the profit sharing component? You'll have to admit you screwed up there."

Peter was becoming red in the face and neck. It was clear he didn't like anyone pointing out mistakes he had made, especially when he hadn't bothered to read the one hundred plus pages of appendices.

John was becoming aware that if he said anything more, he would be likely to set off one of Peter's infamous tirades. He struggled to come up with something that might mollify Peter.

"I will go back and review the contract with your crit . . . . evaluations in mind. Perhaps, it might be possible to tie any profit sharing increases to services, processes, or materials improvements from Bennington."

"I'd suggest you do that quickly. I'd like to know that you have solved this problem before your department evaluation," demanded Peter.

John rose, "Thank you for your time, Peter. I'll do my best to improve the contract based on your recommendations." He turned and walked out of Peter's office still carrying the packages of graphics.

He walked to his office, threw the charts and graphs on a chair, closed his office door, and sat down behind his desk. "Jesus H. Christ," he thought. "What a fucking bastard. He fails to read the entire contract and then shits on me anyway. Goddamn him." He was no longer looking to get a vice-presidency; he was only thinking about whether he could save his job. He wondered if it was worth it.

He remembered that with his stock, stock options, and warrants, he was worth more than $10,000,000. Of course that was before taxes and before splitting with Vicki. Still, he'd have more than $2,000,000 after taxes and divorce. That was enough to live on without working another day in his life. He guessed Vicki would get the Portland house. Didn't they always give the house to the wife?

He wished Peter was a more reasonable boss; someone who he could come to terms with. Unfortunately, the only terms Peter understood were his own. He decided that he'd break the problem down into components. There was Vicki. The outcome of that decision was not in his hands, although he might be able to affect it. There was VYRO Solutions and Peter. Did he want to work there? Was that decision still in his hands or was Peter simply setting him up to fire him? There was his money. Did he want to withdraw it and turn it into cash? That would avoid Peter trying to do anything with his options and warrants. Which was most important?

This was silly, Vicki was most important. He could cash out his holdings anytime. He could always find another job. He needed to pay attention to priorities. The reason Vicki had left him was that he spent too much time and effort trying to please Peter, when he should have been spending that time trying to please Vicki. He just hated the fact that after all he had done for VYRO Solutions; it appeared that

Peter was quite willing to fire him. Perhaps, he hoped to find someone cheaper; that would be just like Peter, damn him.

Forget about the job. Forget about the money. Concentrate on Vicki. He left his office, telling his secretary that he was leaving for the day and she should do the same. She looked at him with an unformed question, but he shook his head and marched to the elevator.

He drove home. As he opened the door to the kitchen, he heard Alicia humming to herself while she cleaned. "Hello, Alicia, I am home."

Alicia stopped sweeping and came into the kitchen. "Is anything wrong, Mr. Tanner?"

"No!" He paused, "Wait a minute. Yes, there are lots of things wrong, but I am going to start doing something to make then right. Do you remember where Vicki left the telephone number where she could be reached?"

"Yes, sir. I have it right here."

John looked at her and wondered how she happened to have Vicki's number immediately at hand, but that wasn't important. What was important was that he get in touch with his wife. He walked to the phone and dialed the number, noting that it wasn't long distance. Vicki hadn't left town.

"Hello,"

"Hello, this is John Tanner. I am looking for my wife Vicki."

"Hi John. It's Betty. I'll go see if Vicki's around."

Vicki had gone to stay with her friends Betty and Paul. They lived less than 10 minutes away. John knew and liked both of them.

"Hello, John," Vicki's voice was quiet, but then that was usual for her. "How are you?"

"Feeling rather stupid, thank you," he responded. "If you are willing, I'd like to sit down and talk to you."

"John, to be quite honest, I have been hoping you'd call. I didn't want to leave, but things had to change and this was the only way I knew to do something about it."

"It looks like Peter is setting me up to fire me. I am not totally sure that that isn't a good thing. I have been so focused on VYRO Solutions; I have forgotten what's really important. That's what I want to talk to you about."

"John, I'll be there in 15 minutes," and she hung up.

John was, to say the least, surprised. He'd expected he'd have to do some apologizing and maybe even some begging. He was happy he didn't have to do so. Vicki was a champagne drinker anytime she wanted to celebrate, so he put a bottle in the freezer in hopes it would get chilled quickly. He, other the other hand, would stick to scotch. He put out a champagne glass on the kitchen table, poured himself a small scotch, with water and lots of ice and placed it on the table as well.

He was trying to decide what he should do about Alicia when she walked into the kitchen. "Mr. Tanner, I will go home now, okay?"

"Certainly, Alicia and thank you."

Alicia smiled and walked out the front door. Men were so blind. Both she and Victoria knew that eventually John would come to his senses and call her to come home. Since she liked both of them, she was happy to see it finally happen.

John wasn't quite sure what to do with himself while he waited so he paced. He heard the front door open and called to Alicia to find out what she had forgotten.

"Hi, honey. Its me, not Alicia."

John ran to the front door and hugged his wife. She couldn't return the hug because her hands were full. She finally dropped her purse and raincoat on the floor and hugged him back. "I missed you," he said.

"I missed you, too," she said, lifting her face up for a kiss.

John kissed her and told her he had put some champagne in he freezer for her. "Let me open it and then we'll sit down and talk."

When they were both seated at the kitchen table with their glasses in front of them, John decided he needed to start the conversation. "I am so sorry I ignored you because of the job. I suspect that won't be a problem much longer." He told her about his meeting with Peter, the threatened department review, and the implication he'd be fired if he did produce something impressive in a matter of weeks.

"I think it finally hit me what a mean, vicious son-of-a-bitch Peter is. I guess initially I liked the idea of doing things which would get a life-saving drug to millions of people while I made a nice living for us. I just never fully realized how deep into Peter's trap I'd been falling. He was just using me like he uses everyone. I guess now that he has just about everything he wants in his grasp, he'll discard me like he discards others he doesn't need.

"But that may be a good thing. We'll have plenty of money. I can look for a job I can be proud of with people I respect. With any luck at all, I can find it here in Portland and we won't even have to move."

Victoria looked at him with a smile on her face. "I am so glad you finally came to that conclusion. I could see what that job was doing to you and I hated it. I don't care about the money or the house. They are nice, but what I really want is you and your arms around me. I tried to tell you, but you were so involved with the Bennington deal, you simply ignored me. The only way I thought I could get your attention was to leave" Victoria paused and then asked, "Are you going to quit or wait to be fired?"

"Oh, I am going to wait to be fired. It will give Peter a pain in the butt to have to actually have to tell me I am fired. He will probably do it by memo to avoid having to face me, but that means he'll have to put the reason for termination in writing. He will know that I could use that to get unemployment payments. That could increase his costs and he'd hate that. I guess at this point I'd like to do whatever would cause him the most irritation," he said with a grin. "I think I know what's important in my life and Peter isn't it, but you are.

"There are a couple of other things we probably need to discuss. While you were away, I ate foods you probably wouldn't approve of. And I liked them—a lot. I wonder if we could compromise on what's available in the house to eat and what we eat when we are out. I'll try not to comment about the foods you choose, if you won't comment about mine."

Victoria was startled. "I only tried to give you foods that would keep you healthy."

"I know, but I hated most of them."

"I didn't realize," she said tears forming in her eyes.

"Don't cry. We just need to talk a bit more rather than assuming things about the other person.'"

"I am sorry. I will try to talk to you more and make fewer assumptions. But Darling, your health is extremely important to me and I want you around for a very long time."

"I think I understand and I can appreciate your point of view, but perhaps we can do a bit of negotiation to allow me to eat things I like, but that are better for me."

"Okay. We'll work at it."

"The second thing is a minor issue, but it seems to upset you so much that I felt I needed to bring it up. There are times I come home and I am so tired, all I want to do is rip off my coat and tie and throw them anywhere. I realize this upsets you and I'll try to do better, but since Alicia picks them up and sends them to the cleaner when required, could you ease off a bit?"

"I'll work on it," she said, "but it really does annoy me. We have such a beautiful home; I don't like to see it spoiled by having dirty clothes strewn all over."

"One coat and one tie are *dirty clothes strewn all over*?" John demanded.

"Well, you know what I mean. It's messy and doesn't look good, especially if we have guests."

"Okay, I'll try, but I still think you could relax a little about it."

"Okay, I'll try as well."

John and Vicki starred into each other's eyes as if looking for some sort of ultimate truth. They both realized there was no such thing, but there was love and there was trust and it was up to them both to love and to trust. Vicki came in to John's arms and he held her so tightly that she knew he'd never let her go. He realized that this was what he wanted and Peter could go to hell, preferably soon.

Chapter 14

Helen started the car and was about to put it into gear when she realized she had forgotten to turn on the windshield wipers. She thought, 'I'd better pay more attention or I won't have to worry about Peter or anything else.' She drove to the college, trying to pay attention to the road, but thoughts of what she would do if Peter divorced her kept intruding. She'd have no place to live. Where would she get a job? Would she have to rely on her friends for things as basic as food? Peter would certainly not provide a recommendation. Who else could comment on her skills? Her friends might say nice things about her, but would that matter to an employer?

She parked and tried to turn her mind to the tasks she had at the college. She was supposed to help write some advertising material for the nursing school. That probably needed to be her first priority since they wanted it by the end of the week and she wasn't due back to the school until next week.

She walked into the cubbyhole provided for volunteers, glad that not more than two were ever on duty at the same time or they'd have to breathe in shifts. Opening her drawer in the desk, she took out the material the Dean of the School had provided. There were lots of facts and figures about percentage graduating, average salary amounts, demand for nurses all over the world, etc. It was about as dull and boring as reading ads for toilet bowl cleaners.

Helen sat for a minute and considered what her approach might be. What was the target audience? Who would be likely to consider nursing school? She had some ideas, but she thought she'd get some help from John. He worked at VYRO Solutions in contracts and was involved with marketing and advertising. She called, but was told he'd call her back later in the day. She told his secretary to have him call her at home.

She played around with several ideas then wrote a note to the dean, telling her that she would fax the completed paperwork by noon tomorrow. She collected the material in a folder and put it on the desk so she'd remember to take it with her. Looking at her list of tasks, she saw that she'd told Sheila she'd work on seeing if she could get her into classes which would allow her to graduate on time. Obviously, this was a task that she needed help with. She called the senior advisor and asked if she had time to see her. She did and Helen spent the next 90 minutes struggling with the advisor to put together a schedule that would work for Sheila. They failed. Helen knew she'd have to face Sheila and tell her, but not today. She could only face one catastrophe at a time.

She went back to the cubbyhole, picked up the folder with the advertising information and walked out to her car. She sighed and thought that at least for two hours she had been free of worrying about what would happen if Peter divorced her.

On the drive home, Helen kept thinking about all the things Ruth had said during coffee. Was she being vain? Was she being selfish? Was there some reason she couldn't go out and earn a living on her own? She was pretty and she was talented. Perhaps, she could consider working for one of Peter's competitors. They would probably have heard about her. Thoughts whirled around in her head, making it difficult to focus on any one of them for more than a few seconds.

"Damn it!" she said, pushing hard on the brakes. She had been so caught up in all her thoughts that she had nearly missed the turn off to her home. She slowed down and took several deep breaths. She was going to have to be careful if she wanted to arrive in one piece. She could do all her thinking once she was inside. When she arrived she went directly to the kitchen and pulled the vodka bottle out of the freezer. She poured herself a generous glassful and brought it back to her office.

She sat down, opened the folder, and took a drink. It went down smoothly. Too smoothly, she thought. This could easily become a habit. She pushed the drink to a side and started working on an opening statement. It should have something to do with humanitarianism, help giving, caring for others, but more than that.

The phone rang. It was John.

"Hi, Helen, what can I do for you?"

Helen explained her project and asked if he had any ideas. Naturally, he did and spent the next 20 minutes providing several formats for different audiences.

"You need to script for the audience. For high school seniors who are considering careers, you need the human caring component, but you also need the idea of being able to work anywhere in the world, making a comfortable living, and the range of things you can do with a nursing degree. For people leaving the Peace Corps or similar groups, a great deal more emphasis on helping people to help themselves, for religious groups, you have to stress the idea that this is God's work and you can bring your faith to many people."

Helen was rapidly scribbling all this information down on her yellow legal pad. She thought that John had just about written the whole thing for her. There would be three different ads, varying primarily in emphasis. She should be able to write it down and print it out in less than an hour.

"John, Thank you so much. You don't know how much this has helped me and the nursing school. I probably would have fussed for hours over this and not come up with anything as good."

"Perhaps you could tell your husband," John growled.

"Oh, I heard about him not giving you the vice-presidency, but I have to tell you that Peter hardly ever listens to me anymore. I am not sure my speaking up on your behalf would help or hurt you. I'll speak to him if you want me to, but I can't promise what the consequences might be."

John sighed, "Thanks for the offer, but you may well be right. I don 't want to do anything to make him any more angry than he already is. I am glad I was able to be of some help."

"Is there something else going on with Peter that I don't know about?"

"Yes, I get the distinct feeling he is about to fire me.

"John, you need to think about a lawyer. There are some conditions in the company by-laws where you'll lose your option rights if you are fired for cause."

John paused. He tried to catch his breath. He was not just faced with being fired, but also with loosing a substantial portion of the ten million dollar nest egg. He would not be poor, but this would amount to Peter robbing him of money he had already earned. He had to stop this. He quickly said, "Thank you, Helen. I need to go. Good bye."

"Bye, John," Helen said to a disconnected line

Chapter 15

"Hello, I am trying to reach Sheila."

This time I got an answer. "Hello." It was a man's voice deep and gruff. "May I have your name?"

"My name is Karol Rogers

What's going on? Who are you?"

"I am Detective Sergeant Williamson, Portland Police Department. May I ask what is your relationship to Miss Cartwright?"

"I am a friend. I was calling her for a date."

"Mr. Rogers, I am afraid Miss Cartwright has been injured. Can you tell me when you last saw her."

"Yes, it was about 9 days ago. We had tea together after work. What's happened to her."

"And can you tell me where you were this evening around 6:00 pm."

"I was at work. I work in the Albertson's Pharmacy on NE 18th at Glisa. I had to work late because we got in a large shipment that had to be checked, logged in and locked away. Would you please tell me what happened to Sheila."

"She was attacked and is currently undergoing surgery."

"Where?"

"At Legacy Mt. Hood Medical Center on Stark."

"Do you know when I can see her?"

"No," he said, "But if you have any information that might be relevant to the attack, I would appreciate it if you would come down to the office and file a statement."

"I don't know what I could offer, but if you think it could help, I'll come."

He gave me the address of the station and told me to ask for him when I arrived.

It was almost 9:00 pm and I was sure that visiting hours would be over before I could arrive at the hospital. I wanted to see Sheila, but didn't want to spend my time sitting in a waiting room. I decided to return to my apartment and call the hospital from work tomorrow.

I was at work early and had to wait for licensed staff to open the pharmacy. I put on my white coat and immediately went to work. By the time the pharmacist showed up and the pharmacy was open to the public, I had finished all of my pre-opening tasks and was dealing with the faxed prescriptions which had come in overnight. I got a nod and a smile from the pharmacist. I rapidly finished the remaining prescriptions and then asked if I might use the telephone to make a personal call about a friend in the hospital. Somewhat surprisingly, I got an okay and dialed then hospital.

"Hello, I am calling about Sheila Cartwright. She was brought in last night and had surgery. What can you tell me about her condition?"

I had to listen to the usual hospital rhetoric about how information could only be given to members of the immediate family. I told them I was her brother and said I would be in town by late this afternoon to see her. What they told me, chilled me! Sheila had been severely beaten and from the state of her clothing, rape had probably been attempted. She was still in intensive care, but would probably be placed in a standard room sometime today. I asked about visiting hours and was assured that members of the immediate family could visit anytime.

I hung up and thought about what I should do. I had some personal time, so I could leave now, but it might be wiser to save that for later, in case she needed help once she got out of the hospital. I asked if I could take off the extra time I had worked yesterday on the shipment that came in late. The pharmacist asked what was going on and I told him about Sheila. He told me to go now—no personal time would be taken from my account.

I had never seen this side of Sid, the pharmacist. He had always been the very rigid boss who expected everything to be done in his systematic way. He asked nothing extra and never gave favors. I'd worry about the why later. I thanked him, hung up my white coat and was out the door in about 2 minutes.

When I arrived at the hospital, I was extremely nervous. What would I say to Sheila? I had to remember that I was Karol Cartwright, Sheila's brother. How would she respond to that? What should I say? Damn, I was working myself into a frenzy when what I needed to do was calm down so I could be of some help to Sheila.

I walked to the information desk in the lobby and asked what room Sheila Cartwright was in. Surprisingly, the roof did not fall in on me and I was informed that she had just been transferred to 421B. "B" meant that she was in a room with another patient and that meant I needed to be careful about what I said to her. The young lady at the desk pointed me to the elevators and told me to turn right when I exited.

I got off the elevator, turned right and found myself near room 417. I walked a few yards further and I was at the door of room 421. I hesitated. I had met Sheila only twice. What was I going to say? I felt like an idiot, not knowing whether to go in or to get on the elevator and go back home. I sucked in a lungful of air and pushed open the door.

The patient in 421A appeared to be giving Methuselah a race for eldest and from the various tubes coming in, or perhaps out, of her was unlikely to be listening closely to any conversation I had with Sheila. I walked to the curtain separating the two beds and pushed it aside. My first impression was of a mass of white bandages. Then I focused on Sheila's face. It was so white, it seemed as though she had put on too much makeup. Her arms, her hands, her neck—everything but her face seemed to be covered in bandages.

"Sheila, its Karol. How are you?" What a stupid question for someone lying in a hospital bed with more bandages than the local Walgreen's Drug store.

She opened her eyes, blinked a couple of time and whispered, "Hi, Karol."

"Hi, Sheila. Is there anything I can get you.?"

Her hand came out from under the sheet and grasped mine. I don't view myself as any sort of Lancelot, but at that moment I was willing to take on a dragon for this lady. "Thank you for coming," she whispered.

I held her hand and wondered what sort of comforting thing I could say at this point. Boy, what a klutz am I. I just held her hand and looked into those beautiful green eyes. I didn't know what else to do.

"I was going to call you for a date," I said. Christ, what an idiotic statement to make to a person lying injured in a hospital bed. I had all the smooth of an alligator with hives.

"I mean that I was calling you when I found out you had been hurt." At least that statement had the virtue of being sensible.

"Karol, thank you for coming. I would liked to have gone out on a date with you, but I am so tired, I . . . ." she closed her eyes and was asleep.

I sat there, holding her hand for more than an hour when some technician came in.

"Please move aside sir, I have to draw a blood sample."

I started to release her hand, but she gripped me tighter and held on as though I was some sort of lifeline. "Use her other arm," I said in what I hoped was an authoritative voice.

I was so confused I didn't know what to feel. Here was the beautiful, terribly damaged woman that I barely knew holding on to me like I was her salvation. I was attracted and possessive and I don't know what. Damn, I had so many different feelings, I wasn't sure where I was coming from. I did know that for whatever reason, this woman was important to me.

The technician finished and left and I leaned over Sheila and said, "Its okay. Its all over."

Sheila said nothing, but gripped my hand even tighter. I don't know how long I sat there holding her hand. She eventually relaxed her grasp, but never let go. I thought I'd hold her hand forever, if that is what it took to get her through this.

The next morning the nurse came into the room. She smiled at me and said that she had to change Sheila's bandages and asked me to leave. I started to get up, but Sheila grasped my hand tighter and said, "No, please."

That did it! Nothing was going to move me. I leaned over her and said, "It's okay. I am here. I won't leave."

The nurse's smile disappeared as she pulled the sheet down and started to remove the bandages. I looked away as Sheila's bruises were exposed. It had been a long time since I had seen a woman totally naked and I had never seen one who had suffered such damage. There were huge bruises all over her chest, belly, thighs, and arms. I was amazed that one human could do something like this to another.

"I am going to have to roll her over to change the dressings on her side and back," the nurse told me.

"Sheila, the nurse can do her job easier if I let go," I whispered.

"No, please. Don't go."

I looked at the nurse as if to ask, 'what do I do?'

"If you help me move her, I can change the dressings and you won't have to let go of her hand. Right now, I think that you may be the very best medicine available."

I was beginning to feel like Lancelot again. I was the armored knight, protecting the fair maiden. The nurse's movements chased away my fantasies and I tried my best to help although I really didn't know what I was doing. After a year, or maybe only twenty minutes, the bandages were changed and Sheila was allowed to lay back in bed again. She relaxed her grip on my hand, but never released it.

"Sheila, my love (where in the hell did that statement come from? I barely knew this woman). I need to leave you for just a minute." Somehow a statement about the fact that my bladder was about to burst did not seem to be appropriate to this tender moment. "I will be back in a minute, I promise."

She relaxed her grip and I rapidly moved to the bathroom. Luckily, Lancelot did not have to remove much armor to relieve his bladder. Feeling several pounds lighter, I returned to Sheila's bedside and held her hand. She opened her eyes and smiled at me. Lancelot, hell! I was Apollo, the Sun God.

Apollo said, "Hi. How are you doing?"

"I hurt, but not so much when you are here."

Okay, I moved from Apollo to the God Zeus and was capable of *anything*. I couldn't remember when I had felt this way before. I was all powerful and would do whatever was necessary to protect this woman. It took only an instant to return me to reality.

"I need to pee," she said.

Oh, shit, what do I do? Where is Zeus, Apollo and Lancelot when I need them? I buzzed for the nurse and pretended to be perfectly calm. "The nurse will be here shortly."

The nurse came. I left. Several minutes later, the nurse said I could back in. Damn, it seemed like Zeus, Apollo, Lancelot, and I all had problems dealing with a woman's need to pee.

Feeling suitably chastened, I reached down and grasped her hand again. "I am here, Sheila." She didn't say anything, but held my hand. I don't understand it, but the warmth of her hand reached well beyond my hand. With my free hand, I pulled a chair close to the bed and sat down. If my holding her hand helped her, I was going to hold it forever—pauses for urination not withstanding.

Sometime later, Sheila opened those beautiful green eyes and said, "Hi, Have you been here long?"

"Not too long. Do you want me to get the nurse?"

"No, just stay here with me."

"Do you want to tell me what happened?"

"Not now," she said. "I am so tired; I don't want to talk about that now. Tell me what they day looks like outside. Is it sunny?" She drifted off to sleep as I started to answer her last question. Her grasp on my hand relaxed and slid away.

I looked at her sleeping peacefully and decided I could leave her for a moment or two. I went out to the nurse's station and asked if I could talk to the doctor who had performed the surgery. The nurse who had handled Sheila's need to pee was there and she told me that he had left the hospital, but I could talk to the resident on duty. I thanked her and told her that would be fine.

A few minutes later, a very tired looking young lady came up to me and asked who I was. Luckily, I remembered that I was now Sheila's brother. "I am Karol Cartwright. Who are you?"

She put a hand over her mouth to unsuccessfully hide a yawn and told me that she was the resident on duty. "What can I tell you?"

"Tell me what happened to Sheila."

She walked over to the nurse's station and pulled a chart from a rolling file cabinet. Flipping it open, she told me, "The patient suffered a large number of blunt trauma incidents to her chest, abdomen, arms, and thighs. While some of these could be attributable to a fall, others were more likely the direct result of a physical assault. There appears to be no permanent damage to any of the vital organs, so an eventual complete recovery can be expected."

I swallowed, braced my shoulders and asked, "I understand there was some question of rape."

"It may have been attempted, but as far as we can determine there was no rape."

I breathed out a sigh and said, "Thank you doctor. If its okay, I'll go back and sit with her."

"That's fine," she said muffling a yawn. She turned and walked off.

I returned to Sheila's room. She still seemed sound asleep. I sat in the chair I had pulled up to her bed and just watched her. She seemed so peaceful. Her face was unmarked and looked angelic as she slept.

I must have drifted off since I was awakened by an orderly bringing in a breakfast tray. Sheila was awake, but was doing nothing to sit up to eat from the tray. I rubbed the sleep from my eyes and smiled at her.

"Good morning," I said.

"Good morning," she responded quietly. "Have you been here all night?"

"Yes, but its okay. I got a few hours sleep in this chair. More importantly, how are you doing?"

She turned her head slightly toward me and smiled. It was a truly beautiful sight.

"Are you up for some breakfast?" I asked.

"I don't think so. I am not very hungry."

"How will you get better if you don't eat?" I asked.

"Okay," she said, "We'll share."

I have never been a devotee of hospital food. It has been my impression that they buy the most nutritious ingredients possible and then cook them in such a fashion that all the taste is removed. I studied the tray. It contained what appeared to be Jell-O, some sort of porridge, dry toast with an unidentified spread nearby, a small glass of what I assumed was juice and a cup of hot liquid, variety uncertain.

"What would you like?" I asked.

"I'll try the juice."

The orderly raised the head of her bed so she was nearly upright. When she waved her hand to signal him to stop, he did and said that he'd be back for the tray later.

She grasped the juice glass with both hands as though she didn't have the strength to lift it with one. I offered some supportive help and she took a few sips. She was about to put it back down, when I suggested that a few more sips might be a good idea. She looked at me and smiled, but did drink just a little more.

"Okay, now you," she said, pointing to the tray.

I was caught. I had a choice of a rather greenish-yellow Jell-O, a dish of some sort of porridge, or toast. I was no fool. What could you do to toast? I picked up a slice and took a bite. I have eaten all sorts of bread, but I had never encountered one which tasted as though its major ingredient was sawdust. I played the good sport, finished the bite and said, "I guess I am not that hungry either."

It was a very weak laugh, but she did laugh. We stared at each other for a while, not sure what to say. "If you don't need me now, I should go to work."

"I know. I'll be okay. Will you come after work?

"Of course I will," I answered.

I stood up, grasped her hand, and kissed her on her forehead. "Rest and get better, we have lots of things to do when you are well."

I can't be sure, but I think she laid back against the pillow and went to sleep again. I moved rapidly to get home, to get cleaned up and changed. I knew I'd be late, but I didn't want to push it any more than absolutely necessary.

As soon as I walked in to the pharmacy, Sid asked, "How's your friend?

"She's been pretty badly beaten, but the doctors say that she'll be okay in time. When I was there, she mostly slept. I'll be going back this afternoon after work."

"What is this girl to you, Karol?" Sid asked.

I didn't know how to answer that question. I wasn't sure what Sheila was to me. I liked her. I felt very badly about her being attacked. I was physically attracted to her. "She's a friend that I hope will become something more," I answered.

"Okay, Karol, leave when your shift is over, but I have people to cover the weekend so you don't have to worry about coming until Monday."

I usually had to work at least one weekend day every other week, so this was somewhat of a surprise. I thanked Sid and got to work. I passed on lunch so I could be sure I had everything done by the end of my shift. When 4:30 rolled around, I clocked out and was out the door on the way to the hospital.

When I arrived at Sheila's room, I was surprised to see she wasn't there. Methuselah, in bed A, still seemed to still be dead to the world, so I rushed out into the hallway to see if I could find someone to tell me what was going on. I almost ran into Sheila, being supported by a nurse and an orderly.

"What's going on?" I demanded.

The nurse told me that it was hospital policy to get patients up and moving as soon as possible. "It actually speeds recovery," she asserted, "but now we need to get her back into bed."

They returned Sheila to bed and I pulled my chair up to the side of her bed again and asked her the same question hospital patients must be asked a dozen or more times a day, "How are you doing?"

"I'm okay. I still hurt a lot, but the pain medication takes care of most of that. I still seem to be very tired, but I am very, very glad to see you. I got to call my girlfriend

Anita to take care of ZippyII, but other than that, about all I have done is sleep."

She grasped my hand and in less than a minute was asleep again. I stayed there, holding her hand for several hours. She was awakened by a young gal who came in to draw blood. She turned to me and said, "I am a bit surprised that you are still here."

"That's okay. I can stay as long as you need me. Has anyone told you when you can return to your nursing studies and work?"

"No," she said. "I have to contact the nursing department to see if I can make up the time I have missed. If I can't, I will have lost an entire semester. At least I don't have to worry about work. I was fired by Dr. Stanford."

"What? Why?" I asked.

"Apparently, he heard we had met and talked. He insisted on knowing what we talked about. I told him that we had talked about your work and my career goals. He became very angry and said that no one discussed what went on at VYRO Solutions without his permission. He fired me on the spot, told me to leave and that all my personal belongings would be shipped to my home. I was escorted out to the elevator by a security guard.

As I was leaving the building, a very large man grabbed me and pushed me into the parking area next to the building. He hit me and told me that if I knew what was good for me I'd keep my mouth shut. Then he proceeded to hit me and hit me and hit me." At this point she broke down and cried.

Damn it! Peter again. Devastating the life of someone who got in his way. I now had another reason to deal with him. This son-of-a-bitch was going to pay and pay hard!

I held Sheila's hand until she fell asleep again. I slept, rather badly, in the chair next to her bed and was only awakened by the orderly bringing breakfast again.

"What delicious treats to you have for us this morning?" I asked.

He smiled and said they had run out of caviar on toast points, but they had provided a delicious juice, two lovely poached eggs, toast, jelly, and a cup of tea. He was so entertaining that Sheila laughed and asked to have the bed raised so she could eat.

She drank the juice and played with the eggs, eating less than half of one. She tried a bite of toast, but even with Jelly, she had a similar experience to mine of the previous day and stopped with one bite. She took a sip of tea, made a face and put it back down on the tray.

"When I go out today, I'll get you some Lapsang Souchong and some Splenda."

"That would be really nice," she said. She had the bed put back down and said she thought she'd sleep for a while.

I left the hospital with a burning rage to get back at Peter, not just for me, but now also for Sheila. I wondered how many other people he had cheated or hurt to get what he wanted. I went back to the library. I found hundreds of stories suggesting reasons, techniques, outcomes, and consequences of revenge. As I read Poe, I envisioned walling up Peter as in the Cask of Amontillado. All of this was fantasy; none real. Then it became simple. I was in no position to ever get any financial or social revenge. But, there was another alternative. I could kill him!

Chapter 16

"John, this is probably not the best time for it, but there is something very serious I have to tell you."

"Okay," he responded, "What is so important?"

"Helen is thinking of killing Peter. Well, that's not totally accurate. Ruth called several of us together to help come up with a way to help Helen kill Peter."

"What in the hell are you talking about?"

Vicki then proceeded to tell John the entire story: Helen's pre-nuptial agreement, the probability that Peter might institute divorce proceedings after Helen had served his purposes, the possibility of Peter's revenge if she instituted divorce proceedings, and the likelihood of Peter eliminating any reasonable job possibilities regardless of who instituted divorce proceedings. John listened attentively, but kept shaking his head each time a murder scenario was discussed.

"Vicki, are you telling me that Helen is seriously considering murdering Peter? I don't deny he deserves it, but that like an awfully extreme solution, don't you think?"

"No I don't, John. I talked with Ruth and we discussed dozens of things that Helen might do, but none of them protected her. Helen is in a situation in which if Peter is alive, he can essentially bankrupt her and make her homeless. Oh, yes, she has friends who will immediately take her in, but where does that leave her. You know how vindictive that bastard is. He would do anything to make sure that he remainder of her life was as close to a living hell as he could manage."

John started to object and then realized that everything Vicki was saying was the truth. Peter would attempt to do everything in his power to eliminate every chance Helen might have to get a good job and enjoy a decent life without him. Of course, he expected Peter would attempt to do the same thing to him, but he had enough money, Helen didn't. He had a career history apart from his time at VYRO Solutions; Helen didn't. He had options: Helen didn't.

He struggled to come up with some reasonable alternative to murder. Murder was ridiculous. He thought we are all civilized people and civilized people don't murder each other. But all he came up with was an affirmation that killing Peter was the only way to protect Helen and eliminate any problems he and Vicki might face.

"Vicki, honey," he said, "It seems to me we are forgetting a very crucial point. How Peter is killed is a lot less important that making sure Helen isn't blamed for it. I would think that that is where the focus of our attention should be."

Chapter 17

Ruth put down the telephone. She had just finished talking to Lee Ann. Lee Ann would make five, including herself. That should be enough bright women to come up with some good ideas for Helen. She smiled when she thought how surprised Helen would be when this group met with her to share their ideas. She had better get busy getting things ready for their arrival.

She walked downstairs into the sunroom. There were plenty of chairs and the round, marble table would make an excellent writing surface for everyone. She went into the study, opened the supply cabinet and pulled out 5 lined tablets and 5 pens. She carried them back to the sunroom and placed them on the table. She considered a tablecloth and decided no—after all this was a working meeting. Drinks and snacks were the next issue. She had plenty of frozen hors d'oeuvres, but did she want to take the time to bake them. No, she didn't. Standard munchies would have to do. She pulled out bags of pretzels, potato chips, a bottle of pickled vegetables someone had given Hank, and a bowl of fruit. Napkins and small plates were next, plus a long fork for the pickled vegetables. All this was placed on the marble table with the pens and papers. What else? "Oh, my God," she thought forgot the drinks. Coffee would be no problem as the coffee maker was almost always ready to go thanks to Wu Lin. That had been a great catch; getting Wu Lin as a cook/housekeeper.

Wu Lin had arrived in the United States with only a small frayed red bag that looked like a reject from a rummage sale. She held a letter from her sponsor, William Gavin, which offered both housing and a job. It turned out that Mr. Gavin expected that her employment would include some sexual benefits. Wu Lin adamantly disagreed and the sponsorship was withdrawn. Without that sponsorship, she would be deported.

One of Ruth's women's groups heard about Wu Lin's case. Ruth investigated and then offered to sponsor Wu Lin herself; offering her both a place to live and a job. Wu Lin felt rescued from the edge of an abyss. She felt a debt of gratitude toward Ruth which she could never fully repay.

Since Alexandra was coming, Ruth knew she needed to provide something alcoholic. Alex loved fancy frothy drinks, but that would take too much time and would detract from the seriousness of the meeting. Perhaps a pitcher of martinis—no, Alex didn't like gin. Vodka martinis, that would do the trick!

Ruth went into the kitchen and mixed up a large pitcher of vodka martinis. She strained out the ice so it wouldn't get too diluted and put the pitcher in the refrigerator. Okay, was everything was ready? She looked around. Something was missing. Oh, yes, glasses and cups. She returned to the kitchen, got five cups and saucers and five glasses and placed them on a small table to the side of the marble one. Now, everything was ready!

"None too soon," she thought as the front doorbell rang. Before she could answer it, Wu Lin had it open and was welcoming Lee Ann and Sally.

"Come on into the sun room. You two are the first ones here."

"Good, I need a cup of coffee," said Sally.

"The coffees ready, the cups are on the table, and I forgot the cream and sugar"

Sally smiled, "I wouldn't worry. I take mine black. I wouldn't want to dilute the caffeine."

Ruth asked, "What can I get you Lee Ann?"

"Nothing right now. I'd just like to know what this secret conclave is all about."

"You'll have to wait until the rest get here," said Ruth.

The three of them sat down and chatted comfortably about all the things going on in their lives: their husbands, their children, and their activities. After a few minutes, with the mundane material out of the way, it was time to address the more important issues of the day.

"You know that Linda has been getting it on with the pool boy," offered Lee Ann.

"I'd heard that, but until I saw him, I didn't understand why. He's got muscles everywhere and he works in those tight little shorts. Mmmmm," uttered Ruth.

"I know for sure that Donald is doing it on the side. What's fair for the gander is fair for the goose," offered Sally.

"But doing it in your own house. That just doesn't seem too smart," insisted Lee Ann.

"Why, who's likely to interrupt them?" offered Ruth.

Just as Lee Ann was about to offer her thoughts, the doorbell rang again. This time Ruth was first off the mark and beat Wu Lin to the door. Opening it, she saw Victoria at the door and Alex pulling up in the driveway. She waited for Alex and then ushered them into the sunroom. She offered coffee and munchies, and then went directly to the topic.

"Okay, we are all here now. I called you together to help me come up with a solution for Helen. You all know her and I think you all know Peter."

A chorus of hostile agreements went around the table. "What are we going to do to that shit?" "Count me in." "I'd love to get back at that horrible creature." "I'd like to kick his butt."

"What kind of solution are you talking about?" interrupted Alex.

"I am not sure you know about the pre-nuptial agreement Helen signed. Anyway, it boils down to the fact that if she divorces him or he divorces her, she gets nothing. I am concerned that when he has no further need for her in his business, he will simply dump her. Since you all know Peter, you know how vindictive he can be. I suspect he won't stop with making her penniless, he will also do his best to see that she becomes unemployable," said Ruth.

There was a babble of verbal objections, agreements, and questions, until Ruth held up her hands and said, "Okay, but one at a time. We'll go around the table for questions or suggestions, starting with you, Alex"

"What sort of solution are you looking for? Knowing Peter, the pre-nup will be unbreakable. He has enough good lawyers to make sure of that. If you can't alter the pre-nup agreement, I don't see that you have many options."

Sally interrupted, "I am not sure I see it that way. I think that Helen could raise quite a stink about the way she has been treated during the marriage. If she went public with that, wouldn't that hurt his business?"

"I don't think so," offered Victoria. "In my experience, people like Peter seem to bask in the limelight of scandal. Also, nothing that he has done is, as far as I know, illegal, so what would be the point?"

"Perhaps, she could make another agreement for some sort of payment for using her skills to convince more governments to buy into Peter's product," suggested Sally.

"I think you all are being a bit naïve," said Alex. "You aren't going to convince Peter to give up anything. If Helen won't do what he wants, he'll just discard her and try to find someone else to do that work. Helen may be fantastic at what she does, but there are other people out there who can do a pretty good selling job.

"He obviously doesn't need her as a sex partner since he seems to get plenty elsewhere. So, it boils down to this: what does she have to bargain with? Unfortunately, I think the answer to that *is absolutely nothing!*"

There was an abrupt silence in the entire room. Each of the women looked at the others. No one wanted to be the first to speak.

"Okay," said Alex. "Since Helen can't persuade Peter to give her a reasonable settlement and also agree not try to block her from getting another job, what are her options? One possibility is that she can accept being unemployed, homeless, and indigent."

"No, that won't happen," stated Ruth. "I have already told her she can live with Hank and me as long as she needs to."

"But that doesn't really solve her problem, does it?" replied Alex.

"No, I guess not," said Ruth.

"She could always move somewhere else. Somewhere where Peter has no influence," interjected Sally.

"Given his world wide reach and his millions of dollars, cab you think of a place on the face of this earth where VYRO Solutions doesn't have influence?" asked Ruth

"I think there is only one viable solution," offer Alex. "We have to get rid of Peter."

"What! Are you out of your mind," shouted Sally.

"I don't think so," said a very solemn Victoria. "I think we have to recognize that legal and socially acceptable methods won't solve Helen's problem. We have to look elsewhere for solutions."

"Now, wait a minute. If you are proposing something illegal, I don't think I can go along with it," retorted Sally.

Ruth stood up and said, "Let's take a break for a few minutes and let everything cool down. There's coffee in the coffee pot and vodka martinis in the pitcher in the refrigerator. Everybody take a deep breath. Sally, can I talk to you?"

"Sure, Ruth."

"I think there are going to be some decisions made here which you won't be comfortable with. Would you feel better if you left now and didn't hear anything more?"

"Yes, I think I would." With that, Sally walked to the front door, opened it, and left.

Returning to the sunroom, Ruth said, "Sally felt uncomfortable with where the conversation might be going and she left. If anyone later asks her what she heard, the only thing she can say is that no specific plans were discussed, just a lot of statements of concern about our friend, Helen."

"Okay, then let's get down to brass tacks. If we are talking about 'removing' Peter, the only thing we can be talking about is his death," said Victoria.

"Well, I am not sure that's the only other option," said Lee Ann. "I don't even like the idea of considering murder. There must be other alternatives."

"Okay," said Alex, "offer another option."

"I don't have one at this moment, but that doesn't mean that there aren't other options. Before we jump on this bandwagon, I think we ought to consider if there are any other possible ways of dealing with Peter," requested Lee Ann.

The room became so quiet; one could almost hear the gears turning in four female brains. No one said anything, but Alex got up, went to the refrigerator and got out the pitcher of martinis. She poured herself a glass and silently offered it to each of the other women. Everyone accepted.

"Lee Ann, I understand your reticence, but I can't come up with anything more reasonable. Kidnapping would be much more difficult than murder and would leave Peter alive to take his revenge later. Trying to disable him would be even trickier. What degree of disability would allow Helen to escape the marriage with some sort of reasonable settlement? I have no idea and I don't think any of you have any idea how difficult it would be to produce exactly that sort of disability, even if we could agree on what it was. Given our mutual agreement that Peter would undoubtedly seek revenge for anything done to him, leaving him alive would simply be counterproductive," said Victoria.

Lee Ann crossed her arms across her chest. What about some form of blackmail to have him cancel the prenuptial agreement?

"What are we going to blackmail him with?" asked Alex. "he's always stayed just inside the gray area of legal."

"I know, I was just trying to think of alternatives," replied Lee Ann.

"Are we all agreed that killing Peter is the most likely answer to Helen's problems?" asked Ruth. She looked around the table and saw three suddenly pale faces. The direct use of the word *killing* seemed to bring all conversation to a halt. *Murder* was something than happened elsewhere, but *Killing* suggested they were personally involved. No one spoke for what seemed like an eternity. They were all stunned that they were seriously considering taking the life of another human being. That just wasn't something that was done in their social circles.

Finally Victoria spoke, "I think we are all uncomfortable with the idea of killing another human being, even one as loathsome a toad as Peter, but I can't offer any other course of action."

"I will go this far," said Lee Ann. "I'll work with you to come up with a plan to kill Peter only if you will agree to allow me to consider alternatives and bring them back to this group anytime prior to his murder."

"I am sure we can all agree to that, "said Alex.

Ruth and Victoria nodded their assent.

"Then how do you want to proceed from here? We have no idea how much time Helen might have to accomplish this. It certainly won't be this month, but Helen's told me that Peter has meetings set up with the last three major potential buyers for his HIV drug in the next few months. If they agree to buy his drug, she feels he'll have no more need of her. We don't know that's true and even if it is we have no idea how rapidly he'll act. Still, we need to get our ideas together while Helen still has choices," insisted Ruth.

"Fine. What do we want to consider when coming up with a plan?" Asked Alex.

"I think we need to look at what is possible for Helen to do herself. She obviously can't physically overpower him, although she might be able to hit him hard enough with a heavy object. I don't think she knows much about knives, guns or explosives. I know there are lots of ways to make a murder seem like an accident, but most of those require technical expertise that I'm not sure Helen has. So what are we left with?" asked Victoria.

"Poison," said the other three almost in unison.

"What do any of you know about poison?" asked Victoria.

"That's easy," said Ruth. "Any of the weed killers, rodent killers or antifreezes are poisons. I learned that watching CSI."

"True enough, but how would you administer any of them so that Helen didn't become a suspect?" asked Victoria.

"Come on Victoria, stop criticizing and offer some suggestions," demanded Lee Ann.

"Fair enough! If you are going to use a poison, it has to fall into one of two categories: nearly undetectable after death or so common it could be an accident."

Alex interjected, "I think there could be a third category. What if the poison was detectable, but it was impossible to tell exactly when and how it was administered. In other words, no one could place Helen at the scene of the crime, as it were."

"I think that's a good addition," offered Victoria. "Now what poisons do we know about and what characteristics do we want to look for in our poisons?"

"I think we want something that's fast acting," said Lee Ann.

"I disagree," said Ruth. "If it acts too fast it will still be present near the body when the police investigate. We want something that is very lethal, but takes at least several minutes to be fatal."

"We need consider how to administer the poison. Using a gas, for example, is too risky. We can't be sure that Peter would inhale enough or that Helen might accidentally inhale some. Putting it in a drink or food is also sort of iffy, as it would point very directly to the location in which he was poisoned. How would we explain Peter dying at home with arsenic, for example, in his wine? That would point rather directly to Helen, even if she were out of the house when it happened. We need something that can be administered and then somehow vanish," said Victoria.

"Come on, Victoria. How do you plan to have a poison vanish," asked Lee Ann.

"I think that's an excellent question, but I may have sort of an answer," said Alex. "What if the poison is applied to something which is normally thrown away? If the poison doesn't act too quickly, Peter will die away from where he was poisoned and whatever was used to poison him can be discarded or somehow disposed of. For example, if Peter reads his newspaper at home and leaves it there, it could be disposed of after he leaves. Ideally, he would die on the way to work and it might even look like a single car accident. Helen could even bring the newspaper over to one of our houses and we could burn it or bury it in our trash, or if that seems to risky, we could take it to a place like McDonald's and add it to their trash. We'd just have to find something that could be put on a newspaper that would kill him."

There was momentary silence in the room. Each woman looked at the others. Recognizing that a previously inviolate barrier had been breached, each woman slowly nodded in agreement.

"Okay, ladies," said Ruth, it is time for some research. We have to find a very lethal poison that acts within, let's say, an hour or so and can be put on or in something that is discarded. I, for one, am not sure exactly where to start, so I would welcome any suggestions."

"That's easy," said Lee Ann, wanting to make some sort of contribution, "Just go to the Public Library. Some of us could look at medical texts, others at murder mysteries using poison, and I am sure, there are books on poisons, themselves. How does that sound?"

"Let's divide it up. Who wants medical texts?" asked Ruth.

"I guess I am the best one to handle that, although all my very limited medical training was a long time ago," volunteered Victoria.

"I can start with books on poisons, but I hope they use small words, because I don't really know anything about them," said Lee Ann.

"I guess that leaves Ruth and I reading lots of mystery stories," said Alex. "I also think we need to keep in mind that whatever we find has to be something we can get a hold of, not some sort of exotic South Seas snake poison."

"I agree, Alex, but we also need to remember that it has to be something that can be applied to newspaper or something that can be thrown away, but it can't be obvious to Peter," offered Victoria.

"Let's meet back here in a week. Is that okay with everyone?" asked Ruth.

Nods of agreement from everyone were followed by a shriek from Lee Ann. "All the stuff we have written down on this paper. What do we do with it? "

"Relax, Lee Ann, Hank has a shredder in his office that will take care of everything. Just leave the papers here, but if you take notes later be sure to bring them here for shredding. Just don't leave them lying around.

After everyone left, Wu Lin and Ruth cleaned up. Ruth took all the paper to Hank's office and shredded it. Returning to the sunroom, she saw the Wu Lin had cleaned up everything, leaving her nothing to do.

"Gracious madam," Wu Lin said.

"Wu Lin, you are to call me Ruth, as I call you Wu Lin. In the United States there are no slaves." Ruth regretted that statement as soon as she made it because many of Wu Lin's relatives were virtual slaves in the United States. "Wu Lin, it would please me greatly if you called me Ruth. Would you do this for me."

"As my Mistress requires," was Wu Lin's response.

"God damn it, Wu Lin. You are an employee, not a servant. I am not your mistress and if you would allow it, I'd like to be your friend."

Wu Lin bowed her head and responded, "That would not be proper, Mistress.

Getting ready to produce a string of obscenities, Ruth hesitated and then said, "It is my wish that you call me Ruth. To do otherwise would not be respectful."

"Ruth, you are skilled in turning my words into cloths that will softly bind me to your will. I accede to your orders. However, such was not the reason I interrupted your gracious self. I would like to offer what poor assistance I might in your attempt to help your friend.

"Are you familiar with the fish called "fugu"? I assume it is called something else in this country, but unless prepared properly, it is very deadly."

Ruth thought a minute and remembered something she had seen on Animal Planet. What was that fish called? It was a puffer fish. "Why do you ask?"

Wu Lin replied, "When skilled cooks remove the liver from the fish, so it will be safe to prepare and eat, they sometimes save the liver. When the poison is extracted from the liver, it is more deadly than any other poison. A few drops will kill a grown man, although not immediately. I know of individuals in Portland who prepare this fish. They have access to this poison if you feel it will aid you in helping your friend."

"Wu Lin, thank you for your offer. It will be one of the things my friends and I will consider. If they think it will be the answer to our problem, I will be happy to request it of you. I am honored by your offer of assistance."

Wu Lin gave a small bow, turned and smiled to herself, pleased that she had been able to have helped her mistress.

Ruth wondered how many people would become involved in this plan to kill Peter. She knew that the more people involved, the more chance that someone would give something away and lead the police to Helen. What could she do about it. They were all amateurs, but they were also very bright people. She hoped nothing would go wrong, but perhaps she should talk to Hank. He was invariably good at coming up with answers to all sorts of questions. Perhaps this was an appropriate time to involve one more person.

Chapter 18

Helen sat in a lounge chair on the deck. She had a nearly untouched drink on the table next to her. She watched the rain come down and felt it clean the air. It had been dark and raining for several hours, but she was comfortable with it. Perhaps it would clean her as well as the air. She got up from her lounge chair and stepped out beyond the roof. The rain immediately plastered her hair to her head and her clothes to her body. She thought of the first time she and Peter had made love in the rain. It was such a delicious experience, but now she realized it had all been false.

Suddenly, she became cold. She needed to go inside, take a hot shower and have something to eat. She knew Peter would not be home for dinner or, possibly, for the entire night. She had no idea what she wanted for dinner. She could call Ruth and go over to her house or perhaps go out with Ruth and Hank. No, she had intruded on Ruth enough for one day. She knew she should eat, but she didn't feel like cooking. Should she go out somewhere by herself? That didn't seem like a very appealing idea.

She walked upstairs dripping on the carpet, but not giving a damn. She took off her wet clothes and flung them over her clothes hamper. She stood naked in the doorway feeling totally lost. Her life was going to change radically whether she did something or not. It was a very depressing idea. She turned and walked into the shower. She adjusted the temperature until it was a hot as she could stand it. Maybe this would wash away her problems. Naturally all it did was give her skin a beautiful rosy pink look, but there was no one there to appreciate it. She shut off the shower, dried and put on some old sweat pants and a sweat shirt that she had had for years. They felt warm and comfortable.

It was time to go down stairs and try to figure out what to do from this point on. She took some lettuce out of the refrigerator and made herself a simple salad. An oil and vinegar dressing and she had completed her preparations for dinner. She ate at the kitchen table. The table in the dining room was too often used when important guests were to be entertained and she didn't want to think about that.

When she finished, she put her dish and fork into the sink. She should really rinse them off and put them in the dishwasher, but she just didn't feel like doing the correct thing. She wandered from room to room. She turned on the television and then almost immediately turned it off. What was she supposed to do with herself?

She knew what she had to do, but she was actively avoiding dealing with the problem. She had to make some tough decisions about the rest of her life. She knew she didn't want to kill anyone. She also knew she didn't want to live with Peter or live with threats of his inevitable revenge hanging over her if she filed for divorce. On the other hand, if she let him file for divorce, he would have no reason to seek revenge. In that case, perhaps he wouldn't actively block her from getting a good job. Who was she kidding? The last time Peter fired a girl; he had bragged he had her beat up just to make his point.

Ruth said she would help her. Could she use her contacts to find her a job where Peter had less influence? Ruth and Hank were relatively insulated from anything Peter might do. Hank had a thriving business and refused to have anything more to do with Peter. Ruth had a very sizable trust fund left to her by her father.

Could she move to a new job far away from Peter and then file for divorce? That seemed like a reasonable solution. It avoided her having to do anything to Peter. It got her away from the possibility of his doing something to her and it gave her a new start in life. She would miss the finer things in life she had grown used to in her time with Peter, but *things* could always be replaced. She would miss the many friends she had made here. But if she could make friends in Portland, she should be able to make friends other places. She thought how glad she was that she and Peter had never had children.

Helen sat down on a couch in the small game room. She leaned over and opened the cabinet containing the bar. She had made a decision, now she could celebrate. She got up and took a tall glass from one of the shelves above the bar. Filling the glass with ice from the small refrigerator, she filled the rest of the glass with tequila. Back on the couch, she took a sip and relaxed as the alcohol warmed her all the way down. She'd call Ruth tomorrow. She'd also talk to Hank about investing what little money she had.

She sat quietly, finally at peace as she slowly sipped her drink. About halfway through her drink, her eyes closed, the glass slipped from her hand, and she was asleep.

A small noise awakened her. It was the maid cleaning up the mess she had made when she fell asleep and poured her drink over the carpet.

"Oh, I am sorry I made such a mess," she said.

"It is of no importance, Senora," the maid said, respectfully. She liked Helen and hated Peter, yet the job paid well enough to allow her to support herself and her three children comfortably. She would stay until her youngest was out of college and then perhaps, when money was not so important, she would find a job with a couple she could like and respect.

Helen had gotten off the couch and was looking at the carpet. The maid had cleaned up the glass and used paper towels to absorb most of the liquid. There was nothing for her to do.

"Later, Senora, when it is dried, I will come back and clean it with carpet cleaner. No one will ever know."

"Thank you, Mercedes. You are so kind."

'It is nothing, Senora."

Helen shook her head. Mercedes was more accommodating than any other housekeeper she had ever met. She had never refused a request Helen had made, although to listen to Peter, she was just another ignorant Mexican wetback and wasn't deserving of any consideration. Helen wondered what made Peter so hostile to those he considered his inferiors. Hopefully, before too long that would not concern her.

Reaching her bedroom, she took off her sweat pants and shirt and stepped into the shower. When she was done in the bathroom, she dressed in comfortable underwear. Jeans, a light sweat shirt, and sandals. It was really too cold for sandals and wearing them in winter was asking for wet feet, but she wasn't planning on going outside and she could always change shoes if that became necessary.

She decided to call Ruth this morning and ask her what her plans were. Hopefully, Ruth would have some ideas where she might find a job far away from Peter. In any case, she was sure that Ruth would help her move out of Peter's house and would most likely know who could sell her jewelry so she'd have money to live on while she searched for a new job.

She picked up the phone and hesitated. Was she asking too much of a friendship? Ruth had offered to help, but was it really fair to involve her in this? She couldn't do it on her own. She needed help and Ruth was her best friend. She dialed her number.

"Hello?"

"Hi, Ruth, its Helen.

"Hi honey. How are you holding up? If you've got some time I have some news for you."

"If its good news, go ahead. If not, I think I am full up."

"I think its good news. I called several of my girl friends over to my house after talking to you and I think we have a good start on coming up with a way to deal with Peter."

"No, Ruth, wait!" Helen howled. "I don't want *deal* with anyone. I want you to help me get a job somewhere far away from Peter. I just want to start over. I can sell my jewelry and start from scratch."

"Honey, I'd be happy to help and I am sure that Hank will help as well, but what sort of job would you be looking for?"

"I think something like what I am doing now—some sort of contract negotiator."

"When I am asked what sorts of experience you have, what do I say?" asked Ruth.

"Oh, I hadn't thought of that. What kind of a job do you think I could get without any references?"

"Honey, I am not sure it's the references that would pose a problem, but you'll be expected to list the places you've worked since graduating college. Have you worked anywhere except VYRO Solutions?"

"No, except for some part-time jobs while I was in college. Is there some way I could avoid listing VYRO Solutions?"

"I can't see how," said Ruth. "What would you say you'd been doing for the last ten years?"

"And anywhere I went, they would ask for the same information, right?"

"I'm afraid so, Honey. If you were 10 years younger, we could claim you'd been bumming around after college, but to have a ten-year blank in your employment history, that's asking for trouble. In any case, once you listed your social security number, a good detective could trace you back to VYRO Solutions. These days reference checks and drug tests are the norm."

"You're just telling me that my solution is no solution."

"I can't think of any way around it, Honey."

Helen began to cry. At first, only small sobs and then the dam burst and tears and sobs poured from her.

"Honey, honey," Ruth whispered, "don't worry. You have friends who will help you. Do you need me to come over there now?"

"Ruth, can I come over and stay with you and Hank tonight?"

"Certainly, the spare bedroom is already made up and we'd be more than happy to have you here."

"Thanks, Ruth. I'll gather up a few things and come over."

"We'll see you when you get here."

Helen tried to stop her tears, but they kept flowing down her face, blurring her vision. She went into her bedroom and grabbed an overnight bag. Stuffing it with a pair of jeans, some tops, some underwear, a long t-shirt for nighttime, and a pair of shoes, she put it on the landing at the top of the stairs. She went into the bathroom and somewhat randomly threw a variety of creams, lipsticks, powders, and other female paraphernalia into her cosmetic case.

On the way downstairs, she grabbed the overnight bag and took it and the cosmetic case to her car. She threw both cases into the back seat, got in the car and raced down the driveway. She got to Ruth's door in less than 15 minutes. She carried her cases to the front door and rang the bell. The door was opened almost immediately, as though Ruth had been waiting for her by the door.

"Come in honey," was Ruth's only response. She took the cases from Helen, placed them on the floor, and took Helen into her arms. "Everything will be okay, now. You just relax."

Helen folded herself into Ruth's arms as a child might do with its mother. Ruth patted her back as she had patted the back of her children when they had cried. She slowly rocked Helen back and forth until she felt Helen's muscles begin to relax. Then she walked Helen up to the spare bedroom, laid her in the bed and covered her with the sheet and blanket. She sat next to her on the bed, holding Helen's hand until her breathing became more regular and she slept.

Ruth walked downstairs and looked at Hank sitting in front of the TV. He eyed her questioningly.

"She's asleep. I think she's just totally exhausted trying to deal with all this. I wish there were an open season on hunting shits like Peter."

"I am afraid that wouldn't do you much good, my dear. There'd be so much competition; you'd be lucky to get a shot in. As a matter of fact, I would probably be one of the hunters."

"Hank, you always know what to say. How did I ever deserve to find a man like you?"

"Perhaps the same way I deserved to find a woman like you."

Ruth went over to the chair where Hank was sitting, bent over and kissed him. He grabbed her and pulled her into his lap and kissed her right back.

"This takes me back a few years ago," he said.

"Good, I'd like to go there now!" she answered.

When Helen opened her eyes, it was daylight outside her window, but she wasn't in her bed. Then she remembered she had come over to Ruth's home. She felt embarrassed that she had imposed, but she remembered that she had no other ideas of what to do. She was still in her light sweatshirt and jeans. She tried to remember if she had brought any other clothes. Pulling the covers off of her, she saw the over night bag and the cosmetics case near the end of the bed.

"I'd better get cleaned up and go downstairs," she thought. The guest bedroom had its own bathroom, so she showered, got dressed, ran a comb through her hair, applied some lipstick and even put on some mascara. She looked at herself in the mirror and was none too pleased at what she saw. It was quite clear that she wasn't handling her problem with Peter very well.

She walked downstairs to see Ruth and Hank sitting at the breakfast table. Hank was reading the Wall Street Journal while Ruth was jotting something down in a pink leather notebook.

"Good morning, sleepyhead," offered Ruth. "I hope you slept well."

"Yes, than you so very much. I guess I owe you an apology."

"Helen, the day you owe us an apology will be a very cold day in July," said Hank putting down his newspaper. "We want to do whatever we can to help you and if it means getting back at that son-of-a-bitch Peter, so much the better. Why don't you sit down and have a cup of coffee. I am moved to cook some waffles, if I can find where Ruth hid the waffle iron. You'll have some, of course."

"Look, I appreciate what you are both trying to do for me, but this isn't your problem."

"Bull crap," bellowed Hank in an unusual demonstration of anger. "That shit you are married to should be drawn and quartered and then hung out to dry. I'd be happy to do anything in my power to get his balls in a wringer."

Helen was more than a little surprised at both the profanity and the intensity of Hank's words. She couldn't remember any previous time when he'd been so verbally intemperate or so incensed. Obviously Hank was as much of an ally as Ruth.

Hank walked over to the counter where Ruth had just placed and plugged in the waffle iron. He picked up a bowl of batter from near the sink, stirred it a few times and then ladled several large spoonfuls onto the waffle iron. He turned on the oven and set it to low. He vanished into the pantry and came out with a large bottle of maple syrup. A plate appeared in his hands, the waffle iron was opened and the first waffle was placed on the plate and then into the oven.

"How many waffles would each of you like? Remember, I have removed all the calories from the batter."

"Sure you have, my darling, but I will have two anyway," said Ruth.

"Hank, I am nor sure I can eat any. I think I should just have a little coffee," Helen said quietly,

"Okay, two of my special waffles for Helen," shouted Hank as another waffle entered the oven. Soon the waffles were done and they all sat down at the breakfast table and started eating. The only noise was some soft smacking as the waffles were consumed. Surprisingly, Helen was able to eat both of her waffles.

"Helen," started Ruth, " I told you that several of my friends got together to come up with some ideas about how Peter might be successfully dealt with. I think at this juncture, you see that your options are very limited. While I don't mean to pressure you, I think you need to recognize the only effective options available to you."

"Ruth, I just don't think I can do that. I don't believe I can kill another living human being. Oh, I know all the reasons. I even know some that you don't. Remember I told you about the receptionist Peter fired and then had beaten up. Well, she has a boyfriend who actually developed the HIV drug that Peter is selling. Peter managed to get him accused of killing some of his experimental subjects. He lost everything and now works as some sort of clerk in a pharmacy. I know Peter is terrible. He has done incredibly cruel things to people, but I just can't . . . I can't kill someone."

"Helen, Ruth has told me all about your situation," Hank interjected. "I think you need to clearly consider what the rest of your life will be like as long as Peter is alive. You won't be able to get another job because as soon as you admit to working for VYRO Solutions, Peter will denounce you to whatever employer you want to work for. The way the pre-nuptial agreement is written, the house, the car, everything associated with VYRO Solutions and any other property that Peter has reverts to his sole possession as soon as either of you file for divorce.

"I could probably help you hide a small amount of money, but there is no way you could put together enough to live on. Yes, Ruth and I would be happy to have you come live with us as long as you wanted to do so, but how long would you be happy doing that. What I am trying to say is exactly what Ruth has been saying. If you want any sort of life after Peter, then Peter must die."

Helen hung her head. Her body slumped into a posture of abject defeat. She stumbled to a chair and fell into it. She started crying again. This time there was no sound, only tears running down her cheeks. Ruth rushed over to her and put her arms around her and held her. After several minutes, the crying stopped and gradually Helen's breathing returned to normal. Ruth slowly pulled her arms away.

"Honey, I know this whole mess seems terrible to you, but remember you have lots of friends and they will support you in anything you decide to do. While we all recommend killing Peter as the best solution. If you decide on another alternative, we will help you the best way we know how."

Through tear-streaked mascara, Helen looked into the faces of her closest friends. She still wasn't committed to killing Peter, but she was beginning to see all other options as dead ends. She started to ask the question, "Why me?"

and then realized that that was simply an exercise in self-pity. She wasn't one to wallow in self-pity. She believed in doing was had to be done and once she decided what that was, she tackled the problem head-on.

"Look, you two," she said, attempting a smile, "I know you want the best for me, but I am not sure I could ever physically murder someone."

Ruth broke in, "I understand, Honey. That's why the gals and I are looking at poison as the technique of choice. We have to do some research to find an acceptable poison and a very specific delivery system."

Ruth then described the meeting she had with Lee Ann, Victoria, and Alexandra. She brushed over Sally's leaving and tried to summarize all the suggestions and the basis for their conclusions. "So Lee Ann is looking at books on poisons, Victoria is going through medical texts, and Alex and I are reading murder mysteries where poison was used. We plan to meet again in a week to review our findings."

Helen was astounded that her friends had done this for her. She was quite surprised that four women could so systematically and dispassionately approach the killing of another human being. She didn't know what to say. Could she accept their help and actually poison Peter? The more she thought about it, the more plausible it became. She was actually considering killing another human being

"Can I meet with you when you get together again?" she asked.

"Of course. Since you are the one to make the final decision, it's critical that we have your input."

Helen turned to Hank. "What do you think, Hank?"

"Poison certainly has lots of advantages. You don't have to be in direct contact with the victim; you don't have to learn to use a knife or a gun; and you don't have to have overwhelming strength. I suspect that among the five of you, you'll develop a good idea that will be both effective and impossible to prove. If there is anything I can do to help, just let me know."

A few days later Helen called Ruth, "I think we may have a problem. This nursing student I know and her boyfriend are also planning on murdering Peter."

"Oh, oh. It sounds like we may be getting too many cooks in the kitchen. Do you know what they plan?"

"No, I only overheard part of a telephone conversation—just enough to let me know they were planning to murder him."

Ruth thought for a minute, "Since we are inviting Hank and John to our meeting, perhaps we should invite them as well."

"It sounds like we are getting a very large group. If we include everyone, we'll have nine people involved. I don't know if a group that large can make decisions," said Helen.

"Let's see what happens when we meet. If we can't come to any sort of consensus, then we can consider forming smaller groups," offered Hank.

"Ruth asked, "Who is going to ask your nursing student and how do you know they will accept?"

"I'll ask," said Helen. "I am getting to know Sheila fairly well and while she and her boyfriend Karol really hate Peter, I don't think they would mind hearing what we have in mind. I don't know if they will share their plans with us, but that's a bridge we'll cross when we come to it."

"Alright, I volunteer my house," said Ruth. "I have a huge table which will seat all of us with plenty of room left over." I'll ask if anyone wants to bring anything, but since we are discussing a murder rather than a party, I expect that coffee and tea will probably be plenty."

Hank looked at Helen then at Ruth. "I can't think of anything else, except to consider what I can contribute to the discussion when we meet. Helen, I think it would be a good idea if you stayed here with us. You can leave a voice mail message for Peter that you have taken a short vacation to Southern California to get away from all the rain and you'll call him when you are coming back."

"I think that will work. I'll just need to use my cell phone and I'll need to make a quick trip back to the house to pick up some more clothes and other stuff I'd normally take on a vacation."

"I'll come with you, Honey," said Ruth.

Chapter 19

"John, this is probably not the best time for it, but there is something very serious I have to tell you."

"Okay," he responded, "What is so important?"

"Helen is thinking of killing Peter. Well, that's not totally accurate. Ruth called several of us together to help come up with a way to help Helen kill Peter."

"What in the hell are you talking about?"

Vicki then proceeded to tell John the entire story: Helen's pre-nuptial agreement, the likelihood that Peter might institute divorce proceedings when Helen was no longer needed, the possibility of Peter's revenge if she instituted divorce proceedings, and the likelihood of Peter eliminating any reasonable job possibilities. John listened attentively, but kept shaking his head each time a murder scenario was discussed.

"Vicki, are you telling me that Helen is seriously considering murdering Peter? I don't deny he deserves it, but that seems a bit much, don't you think? You can't just plan to kill another human being."

"No I don't agree, John. Helen is in a situation in which if Peter is alive, he can essentially bankrupt her and make her homeless. Oh, yes, she has friends who will immediately take her in, but where does that leave her. You know how vindictive that bastard is. He would do anything to make sure that he remainder of her life was as close to a living hell as he could manage. Tell me, Honey, are you willing to let her live like that?"

John started to object and then realized that everything Vicki was saying was the truth. Peter would attempt to do everything in his power to eliminate every chance Helen might have to get a good job and enjoy life without him. Of course, he expected Peter would attempt to do the same thing to him, but he had plenty of money, Helen didn't. He had a career history apart from his time at VYRO Solutions; Helen didn't.

He struggled to come up with some reasonable alternative to murder. All he came up with was an affirmation that killing Peter was probably the best way of addressing the problems that Helen, Vicki, and he might face.

John said, "I think you are missing a very crucial point. How Peter is killed is a lot less important that making sure Helen isn't blamed for it. I would think that that is where was the only way to protect Helen and eliminate any the focus of our attention should be."

Chapter 20

Okay, here comes the pause that characterizes most rational human beings. I had to think of as many possibilities as I could and analyze the outcomes in terms of what I was looking for and the consequences of each of those actions. I had no intention of going to prison for this son-of-a-bitch, so if I were to commit murder, it would have to leave me free after its completion. Time to apply empirical methods to reach my goal. After just a few hours of library research, it seemed that almost murders were caught based on two things: motivation and evidence left at or observed at the scene. I was in trouble based on the fact that I clearly had a motive to want to kill Peter. So, I had to have an airtight alibi to make sure that I could not be suspected.

I started looking at the various techniques to murder an individual. They seemed to be grouped into five rough classes, although there were definite overlaps and what appeared to be almost infinite individual variations. I took out my notebook and started to make a list of my options, also noting the apparent pros and cons of each idea.

The first of these options were those techniques that use some sort of direct physical force to kill. These could be anything from manual strangulation, to stabbing, or shooting. It could include dousing them with gasoline and setting them on fire or running over them with a car. I dismissed this category of options almost immediately. I haven't the skills or the strength to strangle someone. I don't know how to use a knife to kill and the last time I tried to shoot a gun, I nearly injured a bystander. I was just as likely to set myself on fire if I attempted to use gasoline and I hadn't driven a car for over 3 years. I was clearly too unskilled and out of shape to kill using direct physical force. This would be a *last chance* category requiring I develop both the necessary physical skills as well as the practice to do whatever I planned efficiently.

A second category employed killing using physical force, but from a distance. These might include all sorts of explosive devices, long distance sniping, and the use of chemical or biological devices, activated from a distance. These options might seem to be more realistic than the first category, as it put me away from the actual scene of the murder, thereby reducing my chances of being observed. Again, I ran into problems with this category of possibilities. If I couldn't shoot close-up, the possibilities of killing from a distance were ridiculously low. I knew next to nothing about obtaining materials for a bomb or how to set it off so only Peter would be killed. However, every good library and the Internet should have numerous sources which could teach me to make and successfully set off a bomb. The use of chemical or biological agents would leave residues which might be traced back to me, as I assumed that these were items seldom purchased in the local hardware store, although there might be exceptions I could use. A simple straightforward bomb seemed to be a good place to start, but not before I had looked at the other possibilities.

A third category was those events which appeared to be accidental. These could include such things as tampering with the brakes of a car to cause a deadly 'accident.' Falling down stairs, being electrocuted in bathtubs, or drowning in bodies of water were commonly reported techniques. Additionally, fatal "accidents" could be caused by something the person is allergic to, such as bee stings. Again, I had some concerns that my skills would not easily lend it self to this methodology. I had no idea how to tamper with brakes, to arrange a fall down stairs or to drown anyone, especially as I am a weak swimmer, myself. I also knew nothing about bees, except they stung and produced honey. I didn't even know if Peter was allergic to bee stings. I decided to put these possibilities aside for the moment, but I would come back to tampering with a vehicle or a home's electricity if nothing else seemed more likely to work. After all, it shouldn't be that hard to learn how to tamper with an automobile or alter electrical connections. The difficulty would be disguising that tampering to appear accidental.

A fourth category could be to hire someone to do the actual deed. This allowed for a very wide variety of techniques and allowed the use of someone who already had the technical expertise, access to the materials/weapons needed, and no apparent motivation. Unfortunately, it had the disadvantage of being able to be directly linked to me if the hireling was caught. It also opened the possibly of blackmail, not to mention the original cost of hiring someone to perform the act. One additional thought was that I had absolutely no idea where someone went to hire such a person.

A fifth and most promising category was poisons. They could be delivered directly in someone's coffee or his food, or under some conditions absorbed through a person's clothes. They required no great physical skill and only a knowledge of the means by which a poison worked. The biggest drawbacks were that the poison almost invariably left traces, which a good pathologist could find. I also had no immediate idea about how to deliver these poisons other than directly in person or, for that matter, where they might be obtained. I also liked the idea of poisons, since most of my reading suggested poison was a woman's weapon. Again, I assumed that my best bet would be to start with the information in the library.

Okay, it looked like options two, three, and five were the most logical choices. It was time to begin my new research. I hadn't felt this exhilarated in years. On the way back to the hospital I stopped and bought some Lapsang Souchong and some Splenda. My mind was filled with the questions I had to answer. I needed to systematically record my research, but at the same time, I could leave no permanent trace of such records.

I returned to Sheila's room, trying to dispel all these thoughts and concentrate on her. I was astounded to see the improvement she displayed. She seemed wide awake and was sitting up reading. Her hair had been combed and she appeared to have put on a little lipstick.

"Well, hi there! You seemed to have improved a lot."

"I think it's because they finally reduced all the pain medications they were giving me which were making me so sleepy I couldn't do much more than sleep. The pain is slowly going away and they tell me I can probably leave the hospital in a couple of days."

"That's great," I said, but at the same time, wondered what sort of care she would need at home. I could spend some time with her, but still had to work 40 hours a week.

Then I thought about the $100,000. Perhaps, I could use some of that to take some time off without losing my job.

"Here, I brought you some Lapsang Souchong and some Splenda so you won't have to drink whatever the hospital is calling tea."

She smiled, "Thank you. That was very sweet. I hope that you'll stay long enough to have tea with me."

"I'd love that," I responded and stuck my head out the door to see if I could find a nurse to obtain some hot water. Naturally, no one was in sight, so I suggested Sheila press the nurse's call button next to the bed. We sat and talked about what she had planned for the future and I told her that I had no definite plans at the moment, but I didn't plan on being a pharmacy technician the rest of my life. She was getting ready to tell me more about the things she wanted to do after she graduated nursing school and was making some money, but the nurse chose that moment to walk in.

"Hi. You two look very intense. Is there something I can do for you?" she asked.

"We'd like to know how we can get some boiling water so we can brew some tea. I bought tea bags so we don't need a teapot," I told her.

"Let me see what I can do. We have a small kitchenette on this floor. I should be able to boil some water for you and maybe even find you a couple of cups." She turned and left.

We both thanked her and resumed our conversation. In a few minutes she was back with two unmatched mugs and a pot full of steaming water.

"Wow, that was fast," Sheila told her. "We really appreciate it. Would you like to have some tea with us?"

She looked from Sheila to me and then back again and with a funny little grin on her face and said that she was too busy now, but maybe later.

We poured the hot water into the mugs, added teabags and Splenda, waited a few minutes for the tea to brew and then clinked our mugs together and drank. I sat back and relaxed a bit. Oh, I still had research to do and plans to make, but right now, this very second, the only thing I had to do was be with Sheila. We sipped tea and talked about *what ifs* and *eventuallys*. It was a bit surprising that we liked so many of the same things, but luckily there were enough things we differed on to make it interesting.

She thought that we all should be our brother's keeper, while I felt that individuals needed to take responsibility for their own actions. I assumed that her feelings about taking care of others was what was leading her into nursing. I had never really analyzed why I felt the way I did. Perhaps that was something I should spend time thinking about.

I watched Sheila's eyelids slowly lower, her responses become more delayed, and I said I was tired and had to go home to get some sleep. I gathered up the cups, tea bags, pot of now cold water and put them on the counter near the window. By the time I was done, Sheila was asleep again. This time, I noticed, she had a smile on her face as she slept.

Chapter 21

I went home, cleaned up, and finally got into bed to go to sleep. It must have taken 5 or maybe 6 seconds after crawling into bed that I was asleep. The only dream I could remember from that night was me killing Peter by knifing him, shooting him, blowing him up with some sort of bomb, shoving him in front of a moving bus, electrocuting him with his own doorbell, and doing something to his car that made it run off the road. A very satisfying night!

I opened my eyes to find I had slept almost 8 hours and was feeling quite rested. It was Sunday, so the Library wouldn't open until noon. I decided that a little domesticity was in order. I took my dirty clothes downstairs to the coin operated washers and dryers and started three loads. I returned to my apartment and cleaned up the kitchen. Luckily, the way I had been eating that did take much more than making sure the trays I used under the micro waved meals were rinsed off, the silverware was clean, and the various drops, spills and drizzles had been wiped up. I made the bed with my second pair of sheets. It seemed wonderful to have two pair of sheets. Returning to the laundry room, I transferred the clothes from the washers to the driers—I was on a roll.

I sat down and tried to organize my activities. I needed to do my research, but also needed a way to make sure whatever data I collected wasn't available to anyone else to provide evidence against me. I needed to collect my $100,000. I needed to make some provisions for taking care of Sheila and I needed to do all this while maintaining my job, at least for now.

I thought that he best way to protect the results of the research was to put it in some sort of electronic media that could be smashed or deleted or thrown away when it was no longer needed. While I was no electronics whiz, I had worked with computers and was somewhat familiar with flash drives. Those little tiny things could hold huge amounts of data and were no more than 2 inches in length, half an inch in width and maybe a quarter of an inch thick. Such a small thing could be smashed underfoot rendering any information it held totally secure. Of course the flash drive was of no use without a computer, so that was one of the things I needed to put near the top of my list of needs.

I was making progress, but I now recognized that the first thing I needed to do tomorrow was to collect the $100,000. I needed the money to obtain any of the things I might need for research or for the commission of the execution. I had stopped thinking of it as a murder, but more of an extra-legal execution for crimes committed. I would call F. Downing Robertson and make arrangements to collect the money after work. I needed to find out what sort of things or help Sheila might need while she finished recovering, but that could wait a day or so.

By 10:30, I had collected the dried clothes and hung them up or folded them and put them away. The kitchen was reasonably clean and most of the litter in the bedroom and living room and been placed in the trash. I decided to visit Sheila in the hospital before going to the library.

I arrived to find Sheila out of bed and walking in the hall with the nurse by her side. This time she was walking independently, without any support. When she saw me, she stopped, smiled, and asked if I wanted to join her on her walk.

"Certainly," I said." Are we going anywhere in particular or just enjoying the morning air?"

"We are making a complete circle of this floor in preparation for being released tomorrow!" she exclaimed.

When we returned to her room, I could see that a walk of a few hundred feet had taken a lot out of Sheila and she readily returned to her bed. "Lunch in a few minutes," said the orderly as he passed by. This was the same clown who had said they were out of caviar a few days ago and made Sheila smile. I hoped he would offer something equally amusing as it was clear that even a short walk had tired Sheila more than I would have expected.

"I have to pee, but you don't have to leave. I can get to the bathroom by myself," Sheila said.

Thank goodness I didn't have to invoke the help of any of the gods or heroes given their ineffectiveness at the previous "pee" occasion. Sheila wasn't as steady as I might wish, but she made her way confidently to the bathroom and returned after a short while.

"Will you stay for lunch?" she asked. They'll bring you a separate tray."

I said I'd enjoy eating with her and suggested that we let the orderly know that we would like some hot water to make tea. I got another one of those wonderful smiles with that suggestion.

"Do you know when they will let you out of the hospital tomorrow?" I asked.

"No, they don't seem to decide that until the last minute so you can't really plan, but its just a short cab ride to my apartment."

"I'd like to be around to help if I could," I said.

"There's not too much to help with. The clothes I was wearing were mostly torn and while my purse was recovered, that's about all I have to take with me. The nurse told me that they'll lend me some 'scrubs' to wear home, but that's about it."

"Just let me know when. I'd feel more comfortable if you had someone to see you home."

"Just someone?" she asked with a pixy-like grin.

I could feel the flush beginning to rise from my neck to my face and I think I muttered something like, "I just want to make sure you get home safe and sound." I suspected it sounded just as fishy to anyone else who heard it as it did to me.

"Thank you." Again that pixie-like grin, "but I have a girl friend who lives nearby and she said if I called her, she'd help me into my apartment and make sure I was okay."

I was clearly outmatched here and decided that it was time to beat an orderly retreat. "I have a few things to do this afternoon, but I will come back and see you this evening, if that's okay with you."

"Certainly," she smiled

I decided to get out of there before I melted into the chair. This woman was certainly doing strange things to me. It was exciting, but not altogether comfortable. I walked out of the hospital a bit dazed, but took the bus to the library and began to refine my research.

Chapter 22

I learned that anything that put me in close proximity to the target (or victim, if you prefer) greatly increased the chances of being observed performing the act or, at least nearby, when it was accomplished. Since I had no way of isolating Peter from observation, I decided that this would be one of the criteria for eliminating a specific class of murder (although I was beginning to think of these as experimental procedures rather than acts of murder). Thus, anything which required I be in his presence when the *procedure* was employed was to be ruled out.

This meant I should focus on things which could be done either from a distance or which didn't require my presence to occur. I was now beginning to narrow down the focus of my research. Clearly, option one, the use of direct physical force was ruled out. Option two, physical force from a distance, still has possibilities, but that depended on my ability to learn how to apply what to me was a foreign technology, obtain the materials, and apply them in such a way that I would not be suspected. Explosive devices seemed to be a reasonable place to start.

As I read, I became more and more dismayed. Most explosives had chemical markers which could be detected and would lead detectives to the source of the product. This would greatly limit the materials I might use. On the other hand, a basic bomb seemed to be a very simple device. It required a container, explosive material, and some sort of trigger. There were hundreds of examples of bomb devices, but all of them relied on some sort of remote detonator, a timer, or some sort of switch to trigger the device. If I was to kill Peter, and Peter alone, a timer was not a reasonable option. There was no way they could discriminate who was or was not present. If I was to set off the explosive to kill Peter and only Peter, I would have to be in visual sight of him and that greatly increased the risk of being observed. On the other hand, if I could place the device somewhere where Peter would be alone, like his car, I might be able to use some sort of a switch which he could trigger, himself. This had some possibilities and category 2 became a much higher possibility for further research.

I had already decided that category 3 would require substantial research and, perhaps, training. I had no idea how to rewire electrical equipment to electrocute someone, much less do it without leaving evidence behind or how to alter something in a car which would cause it to fail leading to death. Yes, this category had some possibilities, but even the simplest of them would take some substantial training to perform without leaving evidence. Category three was to be considered possible, but only if no other category seemed practical.

I had already decided that category 4 was just too risky. While it offered the benefits of skilled and experienced personnel, I was not comfortable with having someone else know I wanted Peter dead. I also had no idea how I would obtain or pay for those kinds of services.

Category 5 intrigued me. Poisons seemed like such an appropriate way to deal with someone like Peter. I envisioned him in the same category as poisoning garden and household pests. Given my limited knowledge of poisons, this category would also require a lot of research to determine what was feasible. I knew that most poisons could be detected *post mortem*. I really liked that term and decided that paying attention to more of the crime series on television might give me some workable ideas and some hints of things to avoid.

I walked out of the library and noticed that it was actually a bright, sunny day, with only thin whips of clouds racing across the sky. This was a sufficient novelty in a late Oregon Fall that I decided to walk and enjoy the day. A walk would also give me a chance to think about all the things going on in my life. I'd like to say the clean, crisp air and bright sunlight led to some well-thought out decisions, but the truth of it was that I had been so preoccupied with Peter and Sheila, revenge and lawyers, and what I needed to do next that I just shut all of that out of my mind and enjoyed the walk.

It was almost evening when I arrived at the hospital. My walk had taken a good deal longer than I had planned. I went up to Sheila's room and found her sitting in a chair reading the newspaper.

"Hi," I said, "What's going on in the world?"

"Hi, yourself. I decided that I should probably start looking for another job since I'll need the money to pay for school."

"Don't you think it's a bit soon for that?" I countered.

"Since I was fired, I don't know how much of my medical bills will be paid by my insurance with VYRO Solutions. I think it covers me until the end of the month, but I have no idea how much is not covered by insurance. I also need to be prepared to pay next semester's fees and buy the required books in addition to the rent, car payment, utilities and all then other stuff."

She looked determined and I decided that this was not the time to assert my manliness and suggest I would take care of those things. Indeed, I had little to assert since I was just barely taking care of myself. I wasn't sure what I could actually do, but I thought that somehow I'd find a way to help.

"Can we forget about all that for now? I thought we'd have a quiet dinner together and talk before I have to leave to go home."

"Sure. That would be nice. You'd better tell the orderly that you want dinner."

I don't know exactly what we had for dinner. It certainly wasn't memorable, but I was paying much more attention to Sheila than I was to the food. We talked more about our plans for the future. I told her about my one trip to the Caribbean and snorkeling with hundreds of brightly colored fish. I told her how nice it was to walk into warm water and just relax while the fish swam by. I said I'd really like to go back and do it again. Sheila said that she'd never been snorkeling, but she thought that it would be fun to try. She told me about a trip she and her parents had taken to Utah and her visit to Bryce Canyon National park. Her descriptions of the varied colors of the rock formations and the various wonderful shapes that rain and wind had sculpted made me eager to visit.

A small, half hidden yawn from Sheila told me it was time to leave. I got up, told her 'good night,' and said I'd be back tomorrow after work.

"I may be at home by the time you get off work. Remember, they are releasing me tomorrow. You have my phone number. Let me give you my address. You can call before you leave work and see where I'll be."

"Okay, I'll try to call just before I leave. I don't have a telephone yet, but there's a payphone in the store." I was a bit ashamed to admit to having no telephone. Everyone had a phone, some people had two or three, but I didn't think that right now was the ideal time to explain my economic situation.

"You told me you work at an Albertson's pharmacy, but you never told me where the store was."

"Its at 18th and Glisan."

She furrowed her brow for a moment, then said, "but that's not all that far from my apartment."

"That will be easy then. If you are home, I can walk over and see how you are doing. Perhaps, I can even bring you some take out for dinner."

"That would really be nice, but you've already done so much for me, I don't want to impose."

"Sheila, the idea of having dinner with a beautiful woman is never an imposition."

She blushed and her faced turned a fabulous crimson. "I just meant, you don't have to do anything like that."

"It's okay. We'll talk about it when I call you tomorrow."

I squeezed her hand and left. I don't remember how I got home. I got there and that was enough. I laid out the uniform for tomorrow and went to bed.

Chapter 23

Morning came much too early. I was having a wonderful dream in which I had obtained the rights to my drug and was wealthy beyond all belief. Sheila and I were touring the world on my ocean-going yacht, seeing places I had only read about. We saw all the great sights, ate wonderful food, and were deliciously happy with each other. The anchor dropped with a loud heavy metal rock sound and I was back in the real world. I turned over, trying to re-capture the dream, but I knew it was useless. I pressed the cancel button on my alarm clock.

I struggled out of bed, listening, once again, to my joints and the music of old age. I rushed through my preparations to go to work. I needed to be on time and very alert to thank Sid for giving me the weekend off. I also needed to call F. Downing Robertson to arrange to sign over my life's work for a $100,000 check. I put his number in my jacket pocket and then decided to put it in my wallet. I noticed that there were only a few dollars in the wallet. I counted $6.00. Damn, I thought, I am really going to able to buy an impressive takeout dinner for Sheila with $6.00. I checked my pocket for loose change—31 cents. This wasn't looking too promising. I walked over to my dresser where I kept my penny jar, just to see if there was anything significant there.

There were a lot of pennies, but it all probably added up to less than a dollar.

I threw all the change in my jacket pocket, zipped it up, put on the jacket and left for work. I arrived a few minutes early and again had to wait for a licensed technician to open up for me. I was hard at work with the overnight faxed prescriptions when Sid came in.

"How's your friend?" he asked.

"She hopes to be released from the hospital today. She's still pretty banged up, but nothing that won't heal. I am going to call her after work and see if she needs anything."

Sid smiled at me, nodded, put on his white coat and went to work. I wasn't quite sure what that meant, but a smile from Sid was usually a good thing. I returned to my work.

On break, I asked Peggy, one of the cashiers, to total up all of my change. Hopefully, there was at least another dollar there. I went back to work, telling her that I'd be back during my lunch time.

At lunch time I returned. I had plenty of time as I couldn't afford to eat.

"Wow, Karol, you have just over $2.00 in change. What are you going to do with all that loot? Are you going to invest in a lottery ticket?"

"Peggy, thanks for counting everything out. May I please have bills instead of the change."

"Absolutely, Karol! But I still want to know what you are going to do with all this money."

"Come on, Peggy. Give me a break. I just want the money in bills."

Peggy smiled at me. That, in and of itself, was a bit unusual, but she nodded her peroxide blond hair and said, "Okay, lover boy."

I looked at her and asked, "What do you mean?"

"Come on, Karol. Are you that unaware of all the signals you are giving off? You look like a love struck idiot."

I started to bristle at this charge, until I realized that my behavior had changed and, apparently, others recognized it. Peggy, who has been a cashier since the store opened, obviously was more aware of changes in my behavior than I was. She smiled as if to say it was okay, her second and third chins bobbing in agreement.

"Thanks," I muttered, feeling like a fool and wanting to get back to the safety of my pharmacy bench.

Peggy handed me two dollar bills and 17 cents. "Good luck," she whispered.

I took the money and almost ran back to the pharmacy. How did anyone know what was happening? Maybe Sid had talked, but that didn't seem likely. I was very upset that people knew so much about what I was feeling. It was uncomfortable. Even more troubling, I wondered what sorts of signals I might be giving off as I planned Peter's execution. I couldn't afford to give any indications of those plans. I had never realized that my behavior was so easy to read. I'd have to think about how to hide my feelings or, perhaps, let people know about my feelings for Sheila as a cover for my plans to kill Peter. This involved more dissembling than I was used to and suggested a need for a different type of planning.

"Thank you, Peggy," I whispered back. I now had $8.00 and still couldn't afford a decent take-out dinner, but that was something to face later.

During the last part of my lunch break, I called F. Downing Robertson on the payphone in the store entrance to inform him that I was accepting the VYRO Solutions offer. While I waited for him to come to the phone, I began to wonder what the *F* stood for: Frederick, Frances, or perhaps Fortesque. His assistant came on the line and offered to handle any issues I had. I found it difficult to believe that anyone really talked like that, but I wasn't here to deal with his word choice. I said that F. Downing Robertson had sent me a letter offering me $100,000 to renounce any claims I had against VYRO Solutions. I said I wanted to take him up on that offer and wanted to know when he would like to finalize the agreement.

"I can fit you in at 4:00 pm this afternoon," he offered.

"I am sorry, I'll likely still be in a meeting at that time," I boasted, trying to sound like I still had important things going on in my life. "Perhaps, about 4:45, if that is convenient for you?"

He didn't sound too happy with the fact I was making him change his plans, but he did agree to meet me in the VYRO Solutions building at 4:45. 45 minutes was enough time for me to get from Albertson's to the VYRO Solutions building. I confirmed our meeting and hung up. As I did so, I remembered my promise to call Detective Williamson and arrange a time to come in to give him my statement. I had a little lunch time left, so I called him, reducing my funds another 50 cents. I said I could come in late Tuesday or Wednesday afternoon. He suggested Tuesday afternoon.

I pondered whether to spend another 50 cents to call Sheila since I was now down to just over $7.00. I decided to wait until after work to make sure she was home. As soon as I got off work, I called Sheila. She was home, but said that she had only arrived a few minutes earlier and was exhausted. Would it be okay, she asked, if I waited until tomorrow to come over. I told her that was fine and that I would call her tomorrow. I hustled over to the MAX light rail on my way to collect $100,000.

When I arrived at VYRO Solutions, I went to the 21st floor and asked for F. Downing Robertson. Naturally, I was told to wait. After 20 minutes, an emaciated skeleton came into the waiting room. He told me he was Daniel Salter, assistant to F. Downing Robertson. I looked at this creature who must have weighed 90 pounds dripping wet, while he stood close to 5' 9" tall. His clothes hung on him as though he had been the most successful contestant in a weight loss contest. His wispy hair was a very light brown, as were his eyes which appeared to bulge from their sockets.

"Good Afternoon," I said.

"Good afternoon. I don't really have time to waste on pleasantries so let's proceed to the business at hand." His voice was that of a tape recording played too fast, sounding very much like the high pitched shrieks of teen-aged girls.

I followed him to the elevator and we went down to the 19th floor to his office. I was not invited to sit nor offered a cup of coffee. I was handed the same document which had been attached to the letter from F. Downing Robertson. Basically, I gave up all rights to the drug, any interest in VYRO Solutions, and promised to do or say nothing which might suggest I was associated with VYRO Solutions. I asked for the check before signing. I was handed a cashier's check for $100,000. I signed and it was done.

Mr. Salter escorted me to the elevator. He didn't offer to shake my hand. He only gave me a copy of the agreement I had signed and told me that VYRO Solutions expected me to strictly adhere to the contents. I traveled the 18 floors downward in somewhat of a daze. I had just signed away everything I had worked on for over a decade. Then I smiled. At least now I had more than $7.00 with which to buy dinner for Sheila

The elevator doors opened on the ground floor and I faced Peter Stanford. I didn't know what to say or do. I needed to tell him I knew how he had cheated me, but no words came. His only comment was, "Get out of my way."

As he entered the elevator, I walked past him, smiled, and told him, "It's not over yet." The doors closed without any response, but I felt good. It was a start.

I knew that I had better cash the check before he decided to do something to stop me from obtaining the money. I found a Chase Bank few blocks away. I opened a checking and a savings account. They insisted on giving me a debit card, which would arrive in four to six weeks, a booklet of eight checks and an order form for more checks. I listened to the advantages of all sorts of overdraft protections, scheduled movements of monies from checking to savings, special loans, and other wonderful services. I thanked the young man handling the account and asked if I could have $100.00 in cash.

"Of course, Sir. We're here to meet your every need." He filled out a couple of forms, had me sign one, and I had $100.00 in twenties in my hand.

I now had $107 and change burning a hole in my pocket and I wondered what I should do first. I started thinking of all the things I could buy that I had been unable to obtain since my fall from grace. I had not had a good steak in over 4 years. My mouth started watering and I wondered where I could go when I stopped short and thought that if I started spending the money like this, I'd soon end up back where I was before—broke.

Chapter 24

I knew that one of the first purchases I needed to make was an inexpensive computer. That and a flash drive would allow me to keep my researches secure. I didn't need anything very powerful as I was primarily going to use a word processing program, perhaps a spread sheet, and some sort of internet connection device. Oregon is known for its recycling efforts and if I could find a Next Step outlet, I could probably find a computer that would meet my needs for less than $200.00.

A quick glance in the phone book came up with multiple stores offering used computers. There was one less than 15 blocks from the bank. I decided to walk over there just to get an idea of what was available. To be kind, the shop was unprepossessing; to be honest, it looked more like a refuse bin, with piles of electronic equipment scattered on the tops of table after table. A young, if somewhat greasy, long haired male approached me and asked if he could be of some help. I told him that I was looking for an inexpensive computer that could handle word processing, a simple spreadsheet, and the internet. He started asking all sorts of technical questions, most of which simply confused me. What type of processor? How much memory? How big of an internal drive? How many USB ports did I want? Did I need a fire wire port? Did I need a DVD player, a recorder, a printer? Did I want a Macintosh or a PC?

I told him that I didn't need a super fast processor as I wasn't going to work with large graphic files or complicated or big spread sheets. I didn't think I needed a DVD reader, but I needed a way to plug in my flash drive. I wasn't sure how much memory I needed and wanted his suggestions. I thought I could see his partially hidden smirk, but he took me directly over to one side of the store and pointed out several machines.

"I decided that you should probably look at PCs as they are less expensive and have more software options. You didn't say whether you needed a desktop or a laptop, so I'll show you several of each." I hadn't even thought of the type of machine I'd need. He went down one side of a long table naming each machine and indicting what sorts of features it had.

"Look, I obviously don't know that much about computers. I suspect that most of what I'll be doing is word processing and searching the Internet. I think that a laptop would offer the most versatility and, I guess, I'd like your suggestions."

He smiled, "You know it was pretty obvious that you really didn't know a great deal about computers, but at least you had the courage to admit it. Lots of you older folks just pretend you know everything, so it's nice to hear someone admit he doesn't. We got an HP laptop in day before yesterday that should fit your needs fairly well. It can only use Windows XP, but that shouldn't pose any problem for you. It has a DVD drive, which certainly isn't the fastest on the market, but it has over 200 Gig of memory and two USB ports. No fire wire, no SD media reader, no mouse—it's a pretty basic unit. I have just finished cleaning its memory and checking everything on it. You'll have Windows XP, Word, Internet explorer, and one game I haven't bothered to delete. If you need other programs you'll have to get them yourself. I need to tell you that it can't be upgraded to Windows 7. How does all that sound? Oh, I almost forgot, you have a built in wireless card, but you'll need to get a internet provider unless you only plan to use it at public WiFi locations."

"It sounds pretty good, I mumbled, not understanding most of what he had said. How much would all that cost?" I asked.

He smiled again. "I could let you have it for $125.00, but that wouldn't be fair. The battery is on its last legs. I scrounged one from another machine which still has some good life left in it, but it's still not the best battery in the world. You'd probably have to replace it after less than 500 hours of use. Tell you what, give me $100 cash and its yours."

I couldn't believe this offer. I wondered if it was too good to be true. I looked at the youngster and asked him if this was an up and up deal. "I don't blame you for being suspicious, especially since you don't know enough to know if I was cheating you. For what it's worth, you seem like a nice old guy, so I am giving it to you straight," he said.

'*Nice old guy?*' '*Nice old guy?*' 'That seemed insulting, but it was obviously that the kid meant it amicably. I swallowed hard and said that I'd take it. I started to pull the $100 from my wallet to hand it to him, asked if he knew where I could get a flash drive.

"What size?" he asked. I moved my fingers apart to indicate about an inch and a half long drive. I could see he was about to explode with laughter and asked what was wrong. He told me that the physical size of the drive had little to do with its storage capacity and it was the capacity he was talking about.

"What do you recommend?" I asked, finally getting used to the idea that this kid knew more about this electronic stuff than I'd ever know.

"Well," he said, rubbing his chin, "If all you are going to do is word processing, a 2 gig drive would be enough unless you were going to write a large number of Russian Novels, but if you may use a spread sheet and download data and perhaps a graphic or two from the internet, I'd go all the way to an 8 gig drive just to be safe."

"And how much would that cost?"

"I've got one here that I'll sell you for $5.00."

"Okay," I said, "one computer, a better battery, and an 8 gig flash drive for $105,00." I thought I might be getting taken on the flash drive, but later, when I looked at prices for new 8 gig flash drives in the stores, I realized what a bargain the kid had given me. I took all my cash out of my wallet and counted it out for him. When he saw what was left in my wallet, he said, "Look, let's just make it an even $100.00. I'll even throw in this laptop case," he said pointing to a battered piece of luggage which had clearly seen better days.

"Thank you," seemed like such an inadequate response, but it was all I could come up with.

He opened the laptop case, put in the computer, the newer battery, the tiny flash drive, and then proceeded to put in an electrical cord. I was about to ask him what the cords were for, but he anticipated my question. "This is a power cord which will run the computer and charge the battery. I recommend that you leave the laptop plugged in whenever you aren't taking it some place. That way the battery will always be charged. My guess is that you'll have close 90 minutes of battery life, with the older battery when it's fully charged, but don't count on it. If you are going to be working for more than 60 minutes, I'd make sure that I took the power cord with you.

If I were you, I'd get myself an inexpensive mouse. Its lots easier to use than this touch screen, but we don't have a good one right now. You have two USB ports so you can plug your flash drive into one and your mouse into the other. I would also think about how I was going to get data out of the computer. You can put it on a flash drive, but if you ever want a hard copy you'll have to have a printer. You can always come back here for something like that. At some point, if you are going to use the internet, I'd make sure to get some sort of firewall and a virus protection program. You can download a number of good ones from the internet for free. I don't think at this point that you'll have any other immediate needs, but here's my card, just in case." He smiled as he handed it to me.

I was struggling between two conflicting emotions. This youngster had probably saved me a lot of money, found me a machine which would do the job I wanted, and thrown in some extras for nothing. On the other hand, for someone who knew as little as I did about computers, he seemed to be a jack-ass, know-it-all who just took sympathy on a poor, ignorant old man. I didn't like that last characterization. I was a Ph.D. I had developed a world famous drug, even if I hadn't gotten credit for it, and here he was calling me a *nice old guy*.

"I don't know exactly what you plan to do or how much skill you have, but I do provide one-on-one training if you ever need it." Damn, this was a 20 something year old kid telling me he could teach me. Yet, if I looked at it rationally, that was exactly the truth. He was much more of an expert

171

in the use of personal computers than I would ever be. I had been spoiled by being able to use a massive computer which already had all the components installed, could work at tremendous speeds and had unbelievable memories. I had never had to program anything. Everything had already been set up for me with only verbal instructions needed to use it.

I still remember Edgar asking me what I needed Persephone (his name for the massive computer owned by SynthGen) to do. As I described the sampling procedures and data analysis and the graphic outputs I wanted, he kept nodding. "What other information do you need?" I asked him.

He wanted details on the types of sampling procedures used, the degree of error acceptable, and if any particular sampling sequences were required. On and on the questions went. He wanted to know things I hadn't even thought about, like output formats for reports, type face and size. Every time I said it didn't matter, he gave me some weird possible outcome and forced me to place some limits of what was acceptable. After two solid days of this, he stopped and asked if he could put together a small mockup for a trial. I was so grateful to have all these questions come to an end for a while, I would have agreed to almost anything.

I had a pile of paperwork on my desk to go through so I spent the day signing for equipment, going through all the little steps that grants demand, and checking off that people who had been hired had passed their security and drug tests. A thousand details and probably none truly relevant to the success or failure of the project. I was down to my last pile of urgent requests to approve or deny when I decided it was time to go home. I was just going out the front door when

Edgar stopped me. "If its okay with you, I'd like to try our little demonstration tomorrow morning."

"What demonstration?"

"Your verbally controlled computer applications."

Then I remembered the two days of quizzing was supposed to yield some result. "Fine, see you tomorrow."

The next morning I started in on the unfinished urgent requests. I had barely started when Edgar walked in carrying this tiny little box.

"This is your personal interface. It will allow you to 'talk' to the computer using normal English. It's an outgrowth of the word recognition programs such as *Dragon Naturally Speaking.*

"And what will that do for me?" I asked.

"Turn it on and try it."

There was just one switch on the little box, so I pressed it and one wall of my office lit up. Nothing else happened, so I looked at Edgar and said, "Now, what?"

"First of all, we have to train it to understand you. I have written a small program which will present some paragraphs for you to read. The computer has to learn how to relate the sounds you make to words in its vocabulary. I'll start the program since Persephone understands my voice.

"Computer, run training program one."

All of a sudden instructions came on the screen. I was to say the words on the screen. I complied and more words came on the screen. This went one and on until I was ready to tell Edgar what he could do with his machine. Finally, the computer stopped and **analyzing** came on the screen.

"Well, what do I do now," I asked.

"Nothing. Wait for Persephone to finish."

Completed came on the screen.

"Now, Tell her what you want. You must start by saying 'computer' and then making your request."

"Okay, Computer, compare the ages at which males versus females in our sample became HIV positive and specify the mean difference."

The mean difference is 1.87 years with females becoming positive earlier.

"Is that difference statistically significant?"

Based on a t-test with unequal groups, no. The probability of such a result occurring by chance is greater than .10%

"Computer, get me a cup of coffee."

While such a request is not within my design parameters, my connections to the equipment in the break room, have allowed me to switch on the coffee machine. It is estimated that the coffee will be ready in approximately 21 minutes.

"My God, Edgar, this is great. Don't I need to type in a password? What happens if I ask it to do something it can't? How will it know when I am talking to it and not another researcher?"

"Whoa, lets keep it to one question at a time. As soon as you touch the interface, she will recognize your thumb print, either hand as a matter of fact, and will be ready to respond to your commands. If Persephone doesn't understand or cannot complete your command, she will tell you so. At this point you can either stop and contact me or tell her to contact me and solve the problem. I have built in a few problem solving heuristics which may allow her to solve some simple problems without having to refer to me. When she does so, she will tell you the basis on which she solved the problem.

Your main concern will be to be specific. You asked Persephone to compare males and females. No problem, since she recognizes those terms. but if you had asked her to compare old versus young, she would have stopped and required a definition. Remember Persephone isn't smart. It's just that she can do so many things so much faster you and I that she appears that way. She also told you that she turned on the coffee pot. You, know of course, that no sensors have been connected to allow her to know if there is coffee, water, or even a filter in the coffee pot. You could end up with a burnt pot instead of coffee unless you have a human make sure that the pot is ready to go."

It went on like this for a couple of hours. I'd ask the computer, Persephone, to do something and I'd learn the computer's limits or my lack of specificity in the command given. I gradually became more aware of Persephone's capacities and my need for increased verbal precision, but from the time I walked into my office from that point on, I never had to make another keystroke. When I was too vague for the computer, she told me so. When I used Jargon, she demanded a definition. When I mumbled, she told me to repeat my question. Edgar had to come back a few times and make some modifications, but I had a machine I could just talk to.

Returning to the present, the youngster was saying, "There is a starter pamphlet with the laptop. It covers things like setting up your password, making and saving files, changing programs, and other pretty basic stuff. If you plan to do any more sophisticated stuff, you may want to buy a book which deals with whatever program you are planning to use."

"Thank you," I uttered with some difficulty. "It's hard to admit that someone half your age knows more about a subject than you'll ever know. I appreciate your help and apologize if I was rude in anyway. I'll probably be contacting you within the next few days for some basic lessons."

He gave me a half-smile, but all he said was "you're okay." I guessed from him that was high praise indeed.

Now I had to get all this equipment home and see what I could do with it. It turns out that a lightweight laptop, extra battery, power cord, flash drive, and case weighed a lot more than I had planned. I knew I'd better take the bus home.

I arrived home, lugged everything up to my apartment, plugged in the computer, inserted the flash drive and waited for something to happen. It didn't. Okay, time for a systematic check. I couldn't assume that the kid had cheated me, perhaps there was something I had forgotten to do: power cord plugged into the wall, other end plugged into the computer, computer screen raised, what was missing? I looked over the computer and noticed that there was a light which would indicate that the computer was getting power. What was I missing? Damn, the thing should be on. Whoops, where was the **on** switch? I found it looking a little bit like a miniature unlit lamp. When I pressed it turned white and the screen began to come alive. I let out the breath I had been holding and made sure that I had kept the card the kid had given me.

I decided that I didn't need to do anything more with the computer tonight other than let it charge the battery. I left it plugged in, pulled the top down, and left it alone. It was late enough that I should go to bed, but I was excited. I had the $100,000 minus $100 spent on computer equipment. I had the computer I needed as well as the flash drive and already had some ideas regarding what information I needed. I started making some notes on paper and realized that that was a bad idea and that was why I had bought the computer. I tore the paper into little pieces and flushed them down the toilet.

Chapter 25

Tomorrow. Yes, I'd start tomorrow. Right now I needed to get some sleep so I could do my work and see Sheila tomorrow evening. I got into bed, but I was wide awake. Clearly, I'd have to do something more to get to sleep tonight. I got up and went to the kitchen to fix some instant hot chocolate. It took less than two minutes in the microwave and I sat in front of my little TV sipping the hot chocolate. I am not quite sure what I was watching on TV—it had something to do with smuggling and the FBI, but when I awoke at 5:30 am, I realized that I had slept the entire night stretched out on my living room pillows. The TV was on some sort of morning show and the weather lady was telling us to expect showers—what else was new?

I got up, stretched, and realized that I actually felt rested. Off to the shower, dress, and a cup of Lapsing Souchong and I was ready for the day. Feeling strangely buoyant, I again arrived at work early and again had to sit and wait for the licensed tech to open the pharmacy. It was somewhat ridiculous, but I felt energized and ready to tackle whatever tasks came my way this day. I took the faxes and immediately started recording the orders which had come in overnight. I set up the trays so that the pharmacist could check and certify everything I had done. Somehow the work seemed to flow today. We must have had 50% more overnight orders than usual, but when Sid arrived everyone of them was in front of him, ready to be approved.

"What's happened, Karol? You seem to be moving at lighting speed."

Was this a criticism of my work? I looked up at Sid. He was smiling and said that I needed to slow down or I'd put a technician out of a job. His smile was so broad that I knew he was kidding. "I just want to make up for the slack you gave me last week," I explained.

"That's okay. By the way, when does the licensing exam come up for you?" Sid was referring to the exam which would make me a licensed pharmacy technician.

"I am not sure. I think its next month, but I don't know the dates."

Sid looked at me sternly and said, "I think you'd better find out and be prepared to pass the test."

He looked serious and I thought I'd better add this to the list of important things I needed to accomplish. This list was getting a bit long with research to identify effective *procedures* for Peter and with whatever I had to do to help Sheila. I thought carefully and said, "Sid, it would hurt me to disappoint you. I'll find out when the test is and make sure that I make it and pass it."

"Okay, Karol. Just do your best. I know that you have a number of things on your plate at this time, but relax and take things one at a time."

This was almost fatherly advice coming from Sid and I began to wonder what exactly was going on. I thought about everything he had said and then began to realize that he was simply telling me to do the things that would make a difference in my life. I began to wonder what I had done to make Sid treat me this way. I wanted to ask, but thought that would be a truly bad idea.

"Sid, thanks. I'll do my very best."

"I know you will, Karol."

I hadn't wanted to become a pharmacy technician as my career goal, but it was important to jump this hurdle as it would increase my pay and benefits and would provide a base for helping Sheila and developing procedures to deal with Peter. I dug out the Oregon Pharmacy Digest and looked through the issues trying to find out the next date for the licensing exam. I found it, but it was only two weeks away!

"Sid, the test is a week from next Wednesday, but it's in Salem. I'll need to use a personal day to take the test. Is that okay?"

"No. Any trainee is allowed time off to take any test which makes him more expert as a pharmacy assistant. You will not be charged with time off while you take the test. Can you get to Salem for the test?"

"I am sure I can. There are lots of buses between Portland and Salem on weekdays."

"And how will you make it there at 8:00 am for the start of the test?"

"If I have to, I will go down the night before and just wait."

"Dr. Rogers, I think that since I have business in Salem on that day, I'll be happy to give you a lift to the testing site."

I think my heart stopped. Perhaps it was only my brain. I am sure that my gut did a double-flip. Sid knew who I was and was offering to help me. I am sure I mumbled something, but I have absolutely no idea what it was. I was dumbfounded and didn't even have the presence of mind to say thank you. I think I just stood there with a dopey look on my face.

"I'll stop by your apartment at 6:30. Don't make me wait." He walked over to his station and began to work without another word to me.

To say I was astonished would be hugely understating my feelings. Here was a man I only knew from 8:00 to 4:30 who was offering me substantial help without batting an eye. I wanted to say something to thank him. I wanted to ask him how he knew, but nothing came out of my mouth except some soft grunts. I returned to my station feeling like an idiot, but determined not to let either Sid or Sheila down.

I am told I made no mistakes in filling any of the prescriptions, but to be quite honest, I don't remember much of that day. My mind was filled with alternating images of Sheila, Peter, and then Sid. I wasn't even aware when 4:30 rolled around, but Sid was.

"Have you called to register your name for the test," he asked.

""Well, no, but I don't have a phone, so I was going to do it after work, " I muttered.

"Not acceptable," he said. "Use the phone there and tell me when you have been registered."

I used the telephone to call long distance which I knew was a violation of company policy. I managed to get the office in charge of registration for the test. I gave them all the information required and was told to report no later than 8:00 am a week from Wednesday. I was to bring my paperwork and a signed letter from my pharmacist. I let Sid know I was registered and what I needed and he handed me an already prepared letter.

"Sid, how did you know?"

"I watched the 'Great Inquisition' on TV. I was astounded that someone who had developed such an important treatment would be subjected to such petty persecution. It seemed inconceivable to me that people would try to make political hay out of a few missing signatures and I was sure something about the whole thing stunk. I knew that there was nothing I could do to change things, but I hoped that I could give you at least some small chance to recover part of your life."

"Sid, I don't know how to say thank you."

Sid was about as good as I was about getting thanked, "Okay," he said and immediately turned away to resume his work. Sid was as good as I was about dealing with praise.

Chapter 26

I rushed over to Sheila's apartment after work and told her the news. I must admit I had a little trouble explaining how I had gotten in so much trouble if I had invented such a marvelous drug. It was difficult trying to explain the difference between inventing an effective drug and having it go through the various tests and then the approval phase before one could claim to have invented anything worthwhile. I tried to summarize my troubles with Peter, but she kept interrupting with questions.

"Sheila, my dear. I'll never finish this explanation if you keep asking for every little detail. Let me just hit the high points. I invented a drug which had a high cure rate for HIV. During the first human tests, two individuals died, When Peter wrote up the results of the first test, he emphasized those death over everything else, making it sound like my drug had been the direct cause of their deaths."

I tried to quickly summarize the witch hunt that followed, but Sheila was having none of that, "What did he do for you?'

"Sheila, let me just say that he said just enough to make everyone believe that it was my fault that the informed consents were not obtained in all cases and that at least some of the data may have been fictitious. That was enough to bring the congress and the press down on my head. At that point I could do little more that to try to defend myself—not very successfully, as you can see. If you checked everything he said, I doubt there was one statement that could be demonstrated to be untrue.

You see, I thought he had gone into hiding just as I had or had switched to some unrelated field. I had heard nothing from him nor read anything in the papers until I came across the article on VYRO Solutions. I was so thrilled to hear that my drug was successful and had already been approved for distribution, the only other thing I could think of was the money that would be coming to me and how it would let me live as I had before."

Needless to say, it took hours to explain everything Sheila wanted to know. Her final question was, "Why did you let him get away with it?"

I wasn't quite sure how I wanted to answer her. How should I describe my lack of viable options? I decided that truth was the best way since I wouldn't have to remember what lies I had told. I described my frustrations dealing with the committee, the press and the various lawsuits. I described my decent into poverty. I tried to express how I finally came to realize that Peter was the cause of my problems. I told her about seeing the two lawyers and what options they offered. Then I went through the process I had used to decide was sorts of actions were possible.

It was clear that Sheila had not taken the time I had to consider the various options to deal with Peter, but when I told her my conclusion that my only option was to kill him, she laughed.

"You aren't serious? she asked.

"Very," I responded and began to describe my preliminary research into the general types of procedures used to murder. I started to discuss some of the pros and cons of each class of procedures, but she interrupted me.

"What makes you think that you can kill another human being regardless of how vile that human might be? Do you think you could actually press a button to set off a bomb that would rip another person to pieces? Could you take a knife and actually cut into his body and watch the blood pour out?"

I started to tell her that of course I could do so, but deep down inside, she'd planted a seed of doubt. I had never considered the actual act of killing another human. I was just a scientist gathering data on effective procedures. After I selected an effective procedure, I would implement it. This sounded a lot more clean and abstract than pressing a button and watching a human being blown to pieces or placing a gun up to someone's head, pulling the trigger and watching the brains and blood blow out the back of their skull. I may have let my apparent scientific detachment keep me from seeing the visceral reality of killing someone.

"Well," I muttered, "that's an issue I really hadn't considered. I suspect that I'll have to factor that into my plans for choosing a procedure."

"Would you stop using words like procedure, research, and implementation. Talk about the method you plan to use to kill another human being." Sheila was bright pink with excitement. She was forcing me to look at the personal side of what I was planning.

"Okay, then you tell me what I can do to Peter after what he has done to both you and me!"

Sheila hesitated and the said, "I am not sure. I'd need to think about it. You've had years to consider what you'd like to do and now you are just trying to figure out how. I'll need some time to consider the alternatives. This is not just repayment for what he did to you, its also repayment for what he had his man do to me. I will likely bear some of those scars for the rest of my life, so I too want some sort of revenge."

"You're right. I've had a lot of time to think about Peter and to identify and discard possible actions. I told you some of them, but in the end, the only thing I could think of to exact my revenge was to kill him."

"Must you 'exact your revenge'?"

"Peter basically destroyed my life. He took away my career. He cost me almost everything I owned. I lost my friends because of the accusations made based on things he said. I cannot get credit or money for the drug I invented. I work as a menial pharmacy trainee. I have even had to sign away my rights to make any public statements about his actions. What would you have me do?"

"Karol, you need to calm down and think this whole thing over rationally. I need time to do the same thing. Let's skip dinner tonight and tomorrow night we can go out for dinner. How does that sound?"

"I'd love to go out to dinner with you. I guess another day to think about Peter won't kill me. What time would you like me to pick you up?

"If you don't mind driving my car, how about 6:30? I can't stay out too late as I still have nursing studies and I have to be prepared to pound the pavement to find another job."

"I'll be here at 6:30 tomorrow." With that, I bent down and kissed her lightly on the cheek. "Good night," I said.

She waved at me as I walked out her front door, but there was an expression on her face that I wasn't sure I understood. I guessed that she was thinking about what had been done to her and, perhaps, what she might want to do in return.

Chapter 27

The library was still open so I went there to use their computers to get on the internet. I plugged my flash drive into the computer so I could download information from the internet and take it home with me. I started my search with techniques for bomb making. There were literally hundreds of sites. As I opened sites and scanned them, I found that many of the sites were simply arguments against allowing bomb-making information to be placed on the internet. There were also a number of sites which referred me to other sites, books, and/or organizations from which to obtain information on bomb-making. I was a bit concerned that the FBI or Homeland security might be watching for persons who downloaded bomb-making instructions, classifying them as potential terrorists.

The simplest bomb seemed to be a pipe bomb, with all of the necessary materials easily commercially available. That would be important to avoid allowing the police to trace the materials back to me. I must admit I was a bit concerned about the warnings on most of the sites that great care was needed as even the simplest bomb posed a threat to the bomb-builder's safety. I decided that I would need to pay very close attention to all safety instructions.

I downloaded information from about 25 different sites, most of which were anarchist sites, before the library closed. I pulled out my flash drive and went home to review the material in greater depth. I read until my eyes started closing on their own. There was a lot of material and simply reading it over was not going to be sufficient. I shut down the computer, took off my clothes and crawled into bed.

The next morning came early as I had only gotten about 5 hours of sleep, but I got up, got ready for work, and made it to the pharmacy just as it was being opened. I went back to my usual activities trying to be both fast and accurate. Sid had said that if I finished my work, I could use my remaining work time to study for the test. The day passed surprisingly quickly, leaving me only thirty minutes of my work day to study the pharmacy trainee handbook. I stayed a few minutes after my shift to finish the chapter I was working on, then signed out to get ready to take Sheila to dinner.

Just as I was about to leave, I received a call from Detective Williamson. "Mr. Rogers, I must apologize. I am unable to see you this afternoon. I am involved in a rather urgent murder case. May I call you later in the week to arrange another time?"

This worked out well for me since I wouldn't have to rush to see Sheila at 6:30. "Sure, I understand. That's fine."

At home, I showered and shaved again and looked over my options to wear to dinner. The only suit I owned was in desperate need of cleaning and pressing. I had a bright blue sports jacket, but no slacks that really went with it. I decided that neat, casual, and matching was more important than formality, so I skipped the sports coat, pulled out my nicest pair of slacks, a crisp white shirt, and my favorite tie. I found a pair of dark socks and some black shoes which needed only a bit of polish to be acceptable. When I put everything on, I studied my image in the mirror and smoothed down my hair again. I wasn't very happy with how I looked, but I couldn't change anything that mattered, so I left my apartment and walked to Sheila's.

Naturally, I was early. So, for 25 minutes, I walked up and down her street until it was 6:30. I knocked on her door and she opened it almost immediately. She stood there in the doorway in a simple long-sleeved green cotton dress. Her hair hung down to her shoulders, framing her face and contrasting magnificently with the green dress. She looked beautiful. No bruises showed to detract from her loveliness.

"You look fantastic," I said.

"Thank you, kind sir, for the complement. After the way you saw me in the hospital, I truly appreciate the sentiment."

I longed to say something witty, but nothing came to mind.

Thankfully, Sheila seemed to understand and simply invited me in. Her apartment was small, but very pretty. Her living room was painted an off-white with photographs on each wall. On one wall, all the pictures were of people. I assumed these were her family. The other three walls featured colored pictures of beautiful scenes: a snow-capped mountain, an isolated island somewhere in the ocean, and a panorama of the American badlands. A couch, an overstuffed chair, and a low table completed the furnishings of the living room. Everything seemed to fit so well together, unlike my apartment which looked like a collection of items purchased at thrift stores. I made a mental note to look at my apartment with an eye toward re-decorating.

"How have you been?" I asked. "Have you had any trouble getting around?"

"I have been okay. I can't do as much as I'd like to because I get tired too fast, but I can take care of most everything around the apartment, including ZippyII. I haven't been able to go to class or look for a job yet. Thankfully, my girl friend went shopping for me, so I'd have food to eat."

"What's happening with the nursing studies?"

"Well, that's one of the things that isn't so good. I talked to my advisor and she said that if I could get the class notes and could pass the tests, I could get credit for one class, but all the others require I complete the on-ward hours and it seemed unlikely that I could do that, so each of those classes would have to be repeated. I talked to one of the volunteers, named Helen who said she'd do whatever she could to help me."

"Oh, Sheila, I am so sorry. It seems that Peter has managed to throw a monkey wrench into your plans too."

"It isn't something I want to think about now. Let's go out to dinner. Here are the keys to the car."

I was a bit anxious about driving her car as I hadn't driven anything for quite a while. Luckily, she had an automatic transmission and we only had to travel a couple of miles to the restaurant. Unfortunately, there were a number of things which had changed radically in cars since I had last driven one. When she handed me the keys, Sheila told me I didn't need them to open the doors. I walked up to the car and the doors unlocked. I didn't know how that was done, but not wanting to appear too naive, I said nothing and just opened the car door for Sheila. I looked around for a place to insert the keys to start the car. Sheila smiled and pointed to a button which said **start**. I pressed the button and the car started. I wasn't sure at first, but there was a low humming that sounded like something had turned on. I looked for the shift lever to move the transmission into drive and didn't see anything I was used to.

""Just move the lever there on the dash to the second position," Sheila said, pointing to a small lever.

I moved the lever to the specified position and the car started to move. I quickly pressed the brake pedal and the car stopped. "Okay, I think I have the idea now. I am not familiar with this type of car."

"It's a hybrid that uses a small gas motor and an electric motor to increase efficiency and reduce emissions."

I nodded as though I really understood and started to move the car out of the parking lot. I stopped to adjust the mirrors and found that my rearview mirror was partially obscured. It seemed like the top two-thirds of the back window was clear and the bottom had been covered with some sort of gray film. I could see through it, but it was disconcerting to have a clear view on top and a less distinct view on the bottom. I also noticed some sort of visual monitor on the dashboard. I didn't even want to ask about it as I might be thought a total idiot.

I probably went a lot slower than I needed to, occasionally looking at Sheila, but I suspect she thought that I was being extra careful not to do anything which might cause her any discomfort. The restaurant wasn't far and I avoided any large streets, so we made it without incident.

When we arrived, I opened my car door and moved around to open her door, but she had already opened it and was pulling her purse off the seat. I offered her my arm and we walked to the front door. I held it open for her and was rewarded with a smile. We walked up to the reception desk and I gave the maitre d' my name.

"Yes, sir. Reservations for two. If you will please follow me."

The restaurant was one of those Asian fusion things that had become very popular in the last several years. Sheila had mentioned it in one of our lengthy talks as a place she had heard of and wanted to try. It had been a long time since I had been to a restaurant—any restaurant. We were seated in a small room with only 4 other tables and only one of those occupied. There was a tiny pond with a bamboo pipe periodically pouring water into the pond. Huge menus were offered by the Maitre d'.

"What looks good to you?" Sheila asked.

"I haven't looked through half of this menu and quite frankly, there's a lot of dishes that I just don't understand. I guess I am not used to this fusion idea."

"What do you usually eat when you go out?"

"Sheila, I haven't been to a restaurant for over four years. I remember liking steaks and seafood, but I don't think I could name a specific dish that I was fond of. No, wait. There was a dish called Coquille St Jacques. It was scallops in a very rich sauce. I remember it because it was supposed to be so bad for you, with all the cream and cheese."

"There's a section on page 4 that seems to be mostly seafood. I am not too sure what I want either. Perhaps our waiter could offer some suggestions."

As though on cue, the waiter approached our table. "May I get you a before dinner beverage?" he asked.

"I don't care for anything right now, but if you want something, Sheila, please go ahead."

"I'd like some tea with my meal, but with all the medications I am taking I don't think I dare anything else."

I asked the waiter for some suggestions, telling him that we were unfamiliar with Asian fusion cuisine.

He smiled and said, "If you like spicy foods, I can recommend our Spicy Seafood Medley or our Asian Dream. If you prefer something with a little less zip, I can recommend any of our baked fish. If you are feeling adventurous and wanting to get a feel for Asian fusion cuisine, I would suggest you consider the Spice Trader's Platter or The Voyager as they offer a variety of dishes in smaller amounts. Let me get you some water while you consider those choices."

"I like the idea of sampling a bunch of different things," Sheila said. "If we find something we really like, we can write it down to have it next time we come. If we run into something we don't care for, it will only be a small part of the dinner.

"That makes sense to me. I wonder how big these sample platters are. I hate the idea of getting so much food that much of it goes to waste."

Sheila smiled and offered, "Why don't we ask our waiter about splitting one platter?"

"I like that idea. If it's not enough, we can always order more. Would you rather have the Spice Trader's Platter or The Voyager?"

"I think I'd rather try The Voyager. I am not too sure how well my stomach can handle spicy food. I think I'd prefer some milder options.

We ordered The Voyager and tea for both of us. The waiter seemed to approve of our choice and told us he would serve the soup portion in a few minutes, but the remainder of the platter would take at least 20 minutes to prepare.

Our tea came almost immediately, followed a minute or two later by the soup. It shared a characteristic with many other Asian restaurant's soups; it was loaded with corn starch as a thickener. It had some vegetables, most of which I couldn't identify, some chunks of tofu, some mushrooms, and some other small bits that I assumed were some form of animal protein. It was rather bland, but then the amount of corn starch would blunt the taste of most things. Sheila seemed to like it, but I guessed that after hospital food, almost anything would taste interesting.

I played with my soup, stirring and taking an occasional sip. Sheila finished her soup and looked over at me.

"Don't you like it?" she asked.

"It's got a bit too much corn starch for me."

"Hopefully, you'll like some of the other things better."

"I am sure I will." Then I asked how soon she thought she'd be able to return to school.

"I don't know. I expected to feel a lot stronger sooner than this. At least I have my books and can study for the class which doesn't require any lab or practicum time. I must admit that I am feeling rather angry about having to repeat an entire semester because of Peter Stanford.

"It's not just the money or having to repeat classes. It's the fact that he has delayed my career for a full semester. I'd like to spit in his face, but I am sure that isn't going to happen. I guess I'll just have to live with it. Helen, the volunteer, has said she'd help me with anything she could, and I like her so I am sure we'll get along."

"I admire your tolerance, but it doesn't dissuade me from my plans to deal with Peter."

"While I'd like to see him punished, I am just uncomfortable with the idea of killing another human being."

Our conversation was interrupted by the arrival of our food. I was happy we had ordered only one platter as it contained much more food that I was prepared to eat. The look in Sheila's eyes suggested she thought the same thing. The waiter named each different dish for us, but I forgot most of the names before he was even done.

"How do you want to approach this?" I asked.

"Let's start at one place on the plate and go around in a circle, each one of us getting a taste of everything. Then we can return to the things we liked best."

"Makes sense to me."

We started with some sort of vegetable dish, covered in what turned out to be a sweet and sour sauce. Whatever the vegetable was, I couldn't tell and the only thing I tasted was the sweet and sour sauce. Sheila shook her head and moved on to the next dish.

This dish was pieces of pork which had been cooked to the point it was falling off the bone. The sauce on this one was somewhat like a barbeque sauce and I liked it. Sheila was less impressed. We kept sampling until we had made a complete circle of the dish. I found a couple of dishes I really liked, while Sheila liked about one-third of the dishes. Each of us ate the remainder of the dishes they liked.

We both felt full and in no need of additional food. I called the waiter back and had him write down the name of the dishes each of us liked. I asked for the check, paid, and walked Sheila to her car. I drove her home.

"Karol, I'd like to invite you up since this has been such a nice evening, but I have to confess that I am so tired that I am about to fall asleep. Can you forgive me?"

"Of course," I said. "We can always do this again when you are a bit stronger."

Sheila opened her door and stepped out of the car. I handed her the keys and she leaned over and gave me a kiss. While it may not have been the most passionate kiss I had ever received, it was full on the lips and seemed to be filled with promise. I watched her walk up to her apartment. She opened the door, gave me a wave, and then stepped inside and closed the door.

Chapter 28

I felt wonderful as I walked home. I laid out my 'uniform' for work the next day then took off my clothes and climbed into bed. My dreams were, for once, filled with Sheila, walks on a sandy beach, and passionate kisses. Waking up the next morning was one of the hardest things I had ever done.

I was on time, rather than early, the next morning. I proceeded to my usual tasks and was well under way when Sid arrived.

"Tomorrow's the big day, right?" he asked.

"Yes and I think I am ready to ace that test. I'll be outside my apartment at 6:30 tomorrow, waiting for you. And, thanks again for the ride to Salem."

Sid smiled at me and then turned back to his work.

I could barely wait for my shift to end so I could call Sheila. I went to Radio Shack and purchased their cheapest cell phone and subscription service. For $15.00 a month I now had a phone. I used the store's phone to call Sheila and told her about my test the next day. I told her I now had a phone and gave her the number. She was excited about the test and said that she was sure I'd do well. I told her Sid was giving me a ride down to Salem, but I had to be ready to go at 6:30 in the morning.

"I am going to do some final review tonight, so I won't be able to see you. But, if I get back at a reasonable time, I'll give you a call and let you know how I think I did."

"Good luck, Karol, although I am sure you won't need luck. I have a check up tomorrow so I'll be able to tell you how the doctors think I am doing. Take care. Good night."

"Good night, Sheila."

I walked home and got the materials for the test out of their folder and spread them on the table. First, I put aside those papers I needed to take with me to the test. Then I opened the handbook and started my review. Everything seemed so familiar, I didn't spend more than a couple of hours reviewing. I heated up a can of soup for dinner and relaxed in front of the TV.

I was tuned into one of the early news shows. The anchor was wrapping up a story about a multi-car accident on Inter-state 5 which had resulted in the death of several people. He then asked the business reporter what the news stories of the day were. The first story was that Dr Stanford had received permission from the British to sell his drug in the United Kingdom. The expectation was that the European Common Market would soon approve the drug. The reporter then gave some estimates of the hundreds of millions of additional dollars this would bring in to VYRO Solutions. I turned the TV off. This was not the time to get upset. I needed to concentrate on passing the Pharmacy Technician test tomorrow.

I finished my soup, put my papers in a large envelope, and hung the clothes for tomorrow on the front of my closet. Then I went to bed, hoping to repeat the dreams of the previous night. Unfortunately, that was not to be. I relived the congressional investigation of my research and watched Peter laugh as I was hounded by newspaper reporters.

I awoke at 4:00 am, soaked in sweat. I decided that there was no point in trying to go back to sleep. I started the shower and turned it to as hot as I could stand it. As I stood under the spray, I felt my muscles finally relax. I turned the temperature down and completed my shower.

When I was dressed, I made some toast, cooked some oats, and made tea so I didn't start the test on an empty stomach. I ate, cleaned up the kitchen, and then gathered up the papers I needed to take. I collected my raincoat even though the weatherman has predicted no rain today. I'd lived in Oregon long enough to know how accurate that prediction was during the month of November.

It was a few minutes before 6:00 am and I was already to go. I decided that I might as well wait for Sid on the sidewalk rather than staying inside the apartment until 6:30. I gathered up everything I was planning on taking, going through it as I picked it up. I had everything so I walked outside. The temperature was quite brisk, but I only waited a few minutes. It was 6:25 and Sid pulled up to the curb. I got in and he took off for Salem.

"The test will be over at 4:30. I'll meet you outside, directly in front of the building. Even with traffic we should be back in the city by a little after 6:00. I assume that you plan to call your girlfriend and tell her how things went."

"Well, yes," I admitted. "I promised to call, although I doubt we'll get together tonight. When I get notification that I passed, then we'll probably do something to celebrate."

Sid nodded and smiled and said nothing for the remainder of the trip. I didn't have any inclination to talk as I was thinking of all the material I had reviewed last night.

The trip went smoothly and then 20 minutes before eight we pulled up in front of the testing site.

"Good luck, Sid said as I excited the car. "I know you'll do well. I'll be here at 4:30 so if you finish early, just wait."

I closed the car door and walked up to the entrance of the building, climbed the steps and went to the reception desk. It was an older lady sitting behind a desk who asked me if I was here to take the pharmacy technician test. I told her yes, gave her my name, and the letter from Sid. She asked me for my letter of admission and I pulled that out of the envelope and handed it to her as well. She gave me a small card marked with the date and the name of the test and told me to hand it to the proctor at the door.

"Which door?" I asked.

"Look down the hall and you'll see a sign."

I looked down the hall and there is a large, very obvious sign for pharmacy technician test. I felt a bit embarrassed but all I could do was nod and smile. I walked down the hall, handed in my card and was told to take a seat. The whole process reminded me of the Graduate Record Exam. Everything was filled out with number 2 pencils. I filled in each of the little ovals corresponding to the letters in my name and then my address. Each of us sat at a separate desk separated by at least a yard. A blue covered booklet sat facedown on the desk.

At 8:05 on the dot, we were told to open our booklets and answer each question. I knew there was a correction factor in scoring so I skipped any question I wasn't sure of. It turned out that there were very few questions I had any trouble with until I came to the ethics section.

In this section we were supposed to put ourselves in the place of someone who would actually hand out prescription drugs. I knew that we were supposed to check carefully anyone who came in for narcotics. I often wondered why we were so concerned about persons obtaining narcotics when I knew that huge number of people were under treated for pain. What difference did it make if someone got narcotics they were not supposed to have? I assumed that the Feds were worried about addiction, but if these people were trying to get narcotics, they were already addicted and the only thing we were doing was feeding their habit at low prices so they wouldn't turn to robbery or burglary to feed their habit. Obviously, I couldn't let my personal feelings affect my test answers, so I followed what I considered the party line and answered like a *responsible citizen.*

Just before 12:00 noon, we were told we had five more minutes. I was already checking my answers and looking at questions I had skipped to see if I could eliminate some of the possible answers to increase my score. At noon, we were told to close our booklets, hand them to a proctor and go to lunch. We had been given a list of nearby restaurants, with an attached map. All of the nearby restaurants seemed to require a car, so I went to the cafeteria and ate some sort of sandwich and a bowl of soup. To be honest, I can't really remember what I ate, but it was nothing that stood out in my culinary experience.

I returned to the testing site at 12:30 as the ambiance of the cafeteria simply did not lend itself to calming before an afternoon of testing. At 12:45, the doors were opened and we were allowed back in the testing room. I sniffed the air and thought that if there was a smell associated with frustration, this was it. I took my seat and waited for the proctors to pass out the afternoon exams.

On the dot of 1:00 pm, the proctors started handing out more blue booklets. We were told to fill out the front of the booklets. More ovals to be filled in with number 2 pencils. We were given 15 minutes to perform a 5 minute task and then told to open our booklets and start.

I was surprised to find that we were no longer filling out multiple choice questions, but instead were expected to answer open-ended questions such as "Why do you feel you would be a good pharmacy technician?" I paused, trying to remember the sorts of socially appropriate answers which would guarantee a high score. I finally opted for the socially responsible, caring persona that I thought the examiners wanted. I noticed the some people were starting to leave as early as 2:30, but I stayed until 3:30 trying to give the impression that I was really serious about these essay questions.

I gave my booklet to a proctor and walked out into the open air. It was cloudy, but, surprisingly, there was no rain. The air smelled a bit sweet and I wondered if the farmers were burning their mint fields. No, Oregon had outlawed that a few years back. I stretched to relieve the stiffness in muscles that had sat for too long. There was the usual music of advanced age.

I found a seat on a bench close to the street to wait for Sam to pick me up. I closed my eyes and thought of Sheila. I wondered if I was moving too fast in this relationship. "Hell". I thought, I wasn't sure I even knew what I was doing. I pictured scenario after scenario with Sheila and me. I wondered if I could be happy staying with a menial job such as pharmacy technician when Sheila would be earning much more as a nurse. I had a sudden pause. I was assuming that Sheila and I would be together on a permanent basis. Would she want to be with me? How would she feel about me after I had killed Peter? Was I assuming too much? How did I know that she thought of me as anything other than a friend?

I was immersed in these thoughts to the point that I was oblivious to the world around me until I heard a loud horn sound again and again. It was Sid, trying to arouse me from whatever state I was in. I waved and moved rapidly toward his car.

"How do you think you did?" he asked.

"It really didn't seem that hard. Many of the questions seemed to come right out of the manual. The only things I had any real qualms about were the ethics questions. I tried to answer them as I thought the board of examiners would want rather than I how I, personally, felt."

"What do you mean? Give me an example?"

"Well, there was a question about narcotics. It asked what sort of identification you would demand to issue a narcotics prescription. The book says that you need a minimum of an officially issued picture ID card, such as a passport or a driver's license. So, I put it down in pretty much those words."

"Good, that's the right answer. How would you have answered if it wasn't a test?"

"I'm not sure." I recounted my feelings about the under-treatment of pain and the fact that by providing drugs I was possibly reducing the need for an individual to commit a crime to obtain money to buy drugs on the street. "I think that providing narcotics free of charge would eliminate massive amounts of crime, but I guess that is a personal philosophy, rather than the expected response of a pharmacy technician."

"You're right there, Karol, but that doesn't stop you for campaigning for a change in the laws."

I was getting lots of surprises from this man who had struck me as a by-the-book, very conservative individual. I wondered what else I had mistakenly assumed about him. I was, obviously, not the best judge of another's character.

We didn't do much talking after that, but as we approached the Ross Island Bridge to connect to SE Powell Blvd, Sid turned to me and asked, "Well, what do you plan to do now?"

"Long term, I am not sure. In the immediate future, I plan to work in your pharmacy and save up some money. I want to work on my relationship with Sheila and I'm not quite sure how to do that. I guess I really haven't thought that far ahead."

"I don't really think you're going to be satisfied simply working in the pharmacy as a technician. I don't think there's enough challenge for you. And you certainly have the brains to make a whole lot more money doing something else. I can't advise you what to do because I don't really know. I just know you need to think about long-term planning. The technician job provides you with a starting basis. Get enough money to live on. You're building up a work history, since I assume you don't want to refer to your previous employment. You are bright, you have a substantial educational background and I think that perhaps you overlooked at potential jobs which will allow you to make use of that background."

"Sid, you're probably right, but like I said I just haven't thought that far ahead."

We sat there in the car as Sid approached my apartment. We didn't say anything else until we arrived. He wished me a good night and said he would see me tomorrow. I responded with a, "good night" and told him that I'd be in on time tomorrow.

Chapter 29

It wasn't quite six o'clock, so I thought it would be okay if I called Sheila, but I wanted a change into more comfortable clothes before I called. I opened the phone and tried to dial. Nothing happened. The phone didn't light up as the one had in the store. I quickly got out the instructions. To use the phone, you had to charge the battery. I am sure that every person half my age understood this, but somehow I was clearly out of step. I plugged the phone into an outlet using the included cord. As I read more of the instructions, it was clear that it would be several hours before I had enough charge to use the phone.

I decided to walk to the tea shop to use their phone. I walked over top the shop, getting there shortly after six, but the phone was busy. There was this young fellow who seemed to be making excuses for something he had done. I assume he was talking to a girlfriend since he kept saying, "forgive me forgive me." I ordered a cup of tea and sat down and waited for him to finish. A few hundred additional "forgive mes" and a single "I love you," finally finished his call.

I dialed Sheila's number and waited to hear her voice. She came on the line with a "Hello, Karol."

"How did you know it was me?" I asked.

"One of the things the detective suggested I do was to get caller ID. He thought this would be a good idea in case I got calls from anyone related to the assault. At the least I would be able to write down the number and give it to him so that he could track the caller down."

But this isn't my phone. I forgot to charge mine. How could you know it was me?"

Sheila laughed and asked me. "Who else would call me from a tea shop?"

I had to laugh at that. This one was no dumb bunny. "I just wanted to tell you that I think I did okay on the test, but I won't really know for another two weeks whether I got a passing grade. If I did, my pay goes up by almost 20% and I'm looking forward to having a bit more spending money."

"That's great, Karol. I'm sure you did very well and you passed. We'll have to do something special to celebrate once you get the official word."

"Sheila. that would be very nice. I'll look forward to it perhaps we can go back to that Asian fusion restaurant that we went to the other night."

"That sounds good to me. I know that when the next semester starts I'm going to be a little busier than I might want since I'm going to try to take an extra course to see if I can catch up. Helen, the volunteer that I told you about, laid out a plan that would allow me to graduate on time by taking one extra course each semester. It would mean a lot more work, but I wouldn't have to waste an extra semester waiting to graduate."

"That's great, Sheila. Will you be able to get a job that works around your additional school hours?"

"I'm not sure. I hope I can find something because my funds will stretch only so far, unless I can supplement them with some sort of a job. Helen has said that she will help me find something, but with unemployment the way it is today, I'm just not sure what will be available."

"I'll keep my fingers crossed for you." I wanted to say something more to keep her on the line, but my mind went blank. "I just wanted to call and say hi and ask you how you were doing."

"I'm okay. The doctor said I was improving and he saw no problems developing. I go back to the doctor next week for another follow-up and I am hoping he'll take me off all these medications. Its a little hard to concentrate with some of the stuff I am taking."

"Good luck, with the doctor. Are you up for another dinner this weekend?"

"That would be really nice," she said, "but I'll need to be home early to work on a paper I have to hand in for my class this semester. I also need to get the notes for the classes I missed so I can study for the upcoming tests."

"Maybe Helen can get you those notes. She sounds like a really great person."

"She is, but I don't want to impose. I mean, she's a volunteer and I don't want to add my personal stuff to her other obligations."

"What does she volunteer for? Does she have specific duties or does she just help out wherever she might be needed?"

"I'm not sure. I've never asked her. Perhaps it's not unreasonable to ask her. If it's too much trouble she can always say no. Thank you, Karol, I'll do that."

"Do you want to go back to our Asian fusion restaurant or you have something else in mind?"

"I chose last time, you choose this time. Pick something you really like. I'm pretty flexible about what I eat. I don't much care for raw fish or oysters, but other than that I like most anything."

"Okay. I'm not quite sure what I'll come up with but I will give you call and let you know. Would you prefer Friday night or Saturday night?"

"Let's do Saturday night. I will spend most of the day working on that paper and I am sure that I will want to break.

"I'll plan on coming by at six, if that's okay with you and we can have a nice leisurely dinner and still get you back at a reasonable hour. Is that okay with you?"

"That's fine."

"Okay, I'll let you go. Get back to all your studies.

As I made this offer, I wondered how the world I was going to find a good restaurant since I had no idea what restaurants were available in this area. I really needed some help, I didn't know who to ask. I guess I could try Sid. I would see him at work tomorrow and if he didn't have any ideas there was always the rest of the staff.

Chapter 30

I thought about working more at the library but I put it off for right now. There was plenty of time and I had downloaded a ton of stuff into my flash drive and it would probably be a good idea to go through some of that to see if I could start getting organized. I turned on my computer, waited for it to boot up, clicked on the start key and accessed my flash drive.

I had downloaded a huge amount of information. It was going to take me more than a single session to go through all of this so I thought I'd start with the information on bomb making. After reading a small part of the material I've downloaded, I found out that I could make a basic bomb using a metal tube with caps on both ends and black powder. That would eliminate any trace of my purchasing bomb making material. Unfortunately, that would not address the issue of black powder being left in my apartment, on my clothes, or my hands. I absolutely no idea of how long it would take to wash the black powder out of my clothes or off of my hands. I also realized that my apartment was certainly no place to test any bomb I made. I could rent someplace, but then there would be a record of my having done so and traces of whatever bomb making materials I had used at that place. Quite obviously, I have been naïve in my conception that I could use a bomb without leaving substantial traces of the bomb making materials. This was unacceptable.

Perhaps I could make a bomb using more common materials such as fertilizer but I'd have to do substantially more research to determine the practicality of such an approach. I began to realize that I had one hell of a headache and hadn't made much progress toward my goal. Well, perhaps that wasn't the case, eliminating ineffective procedures was progress.

It was late. It was time to turn off the computer and go to bed. I'd be fresher tomorrow and after work could begin again.

It was another night of weird dreams. I had bombs going off all sorts of places, but seldom where and when I wanted. I don't know how many times I blew up myself, Sheila, and for some strange reason even Sid. The dreams were a lot more vivid than most shows on TV and I awoke with a start just as Sheila was about to be blown up again with a pipe bomb in her purse.

I took a deep breath and started getting ready for work. My brain seemed to be working overtime, but I automatically showered, shaved, and dressed so that I got to Albertson's on time. There were only a few faxes to deal with so I got started on other things even before Sam walked in the door. It was soon obvious that this was going to be an unusually slow day. We were caught up with everything by 11:00 am and we were all standing around while trying to look busy. Sid told each of us to take a one hour lunch instead of our usual 30 minutes and then report back.

I had brought my lunch, so I went out behind the store to eat. I was done in less than 10 minutes and wondered what I should do for the remainder of the hour. I couldn't come up with anything that seemed interesting or useful, so I opted to return to the pharmacy.

"I thought I told you to take an hour lunch," said Sam.

"You did," I replied, "but I finished my lunch and couldn't think of anything else I wanted to do in the time remaining so I came back."

"Well, quite frankly, I am not a great believer in make-work so I am going to let a couple of the staff have the afternoon off. It will be you, me and Jason to finish the day. Is that okay with you?"

I told him it was fine with me. I felt that I had been given a lot more latitude that any of the other staff and working this would help balance that. I wanted to make sure that I wasn't being treated any differently than any other technician. I returned to my station and began to work. Within minutes, I found that even though there were only three of us instead of five, there simply wasn't enough work or customers to keep us busy.

I began looking for things to do so I wouldn't seem to be just sitting. I straightened things up, wiped down counters, and began an inventory of the shelves to see what drugs might need to be ordered for the following week. Soon Sid announced that Jason could take the remainder of the afternoon off. Sid and I worked the rest of the shift, although neither of us ever got really busy.

"Karol, I appreciate the fact that you were willing to work even when I let the others off. I guessed correctly when I thought you had character. I think its time we both left since Peterson and Soraire have come on."

I thanked him, grabbed my coat and prepared to leave.

"Have you heard anything from the Pharmacy Board?"

"No, I haven't. I thought it usually took a couple of weeks to get the results."

"That might be true," he said, "unless you have a cousin on the Board. I suspect that you won't hear for another week, but you not only passed the test, but you had the highest score of the group."

I wasn't quite sure what to do or say. I had just been given quite an emotional boost, but I wasn't quite sure how I should express my excitement to Sid. "I really appreciate you telling me," I finally said. "I'm just not quite sure how I should feel or what I should do at the moment."

"Perhaps you should call your girlfriend and tell her," he smiled.

"I think that's an excellent idea. I'll do that as soon as I get home." I said good night and walked out the door. I wanted to call Sheila, but was worried that she would feel obligated to stop what she was doing to celebrate. I decided to call her after dinner and tell her that Saturday we would have something special to celebrate. Keeping it a secret for a few days might make the celebration more special. In the meantime, it would give me more time to work on my plans for Peter.

The following day, after work, I went directly home and again started going through all the material I had downloaded. I was continually being amazed at what appeared to be the lack of logic surrounding the political statements these anarchists made. Some of these statements were so ludicrous, that I was surprised they weren't laughed into silence. On the other hand, these anarchist sites seemed to provide the most detailed instructions for making explosives.

Boiling down several days of reading, it appeared that I needed a container, gunpowder and a fuse. The container could be a pipe found in any hardware store, threaded at each end, with screw-on caps. I had seen all sorts of pipes in the plumbing departments of several hardware stores. I found recipes for gunpowder that looked fairly simple to make, but before I even thought of where to start buying the supplies, I remembered that I had access to gunpowder in a premixed form. It wasn't the right time of year, but in less than 6 months there would be enough fireworks available for me to purchase to make any number of bombs. Wait a minute; Portland had a reasonable-sized Chinese community. They had fireworks available for a variety of celebrations. There was nothing limiting me to the 4th of July time frame. As a matter of fact the Chinese New Year was less than two months away.

I really liked the idea of fireworks as a source, since they were legal. A huge number of people purchased them and those tests police ran for gunpowder residue would show the same results on me as they did for a few thousand other people who set off fireworks. The one sticking point I was having difficulty with was how to set off the bomb where it would hurt Peter and no one else. And I was adamant that I shouldn't be anywhere around when the bomb went off. This requirement eliminated all the simple, handmade fuses described in the papers I had downloaded. There were a number of recommendations for delayed explosions, for example using a clock as a timer, but those all left the possibility of the bomb going off when Peter was somewhere else. I had to find some sort of gizmo that Peter, himself, would activate to create the explosion.

One of the simplest methods appeared to be using a switch. A wire would go from one side of the switch to the explosive. A second wire from the switch to a battery or some other electrical device which could produce an electrical spark and the third from the battery to the explosive. What sort of switch? How big a battery? What sort of spark was required? I was becoming a bit frustrated at the lack of directions which specified all the relevant variables. I was also somewhat chastened by statements such as "If you forget the switch you can kiss your ass goodbye."

Clearly there were substantial risks in producing and setting off any sort of explosion, but I refused to be deterred. I thought I might need to change my approach. Rather than looking at all the variety of possible switches, triggers, etc., I should look at the conditions under which I wanted the bomb to go off. That would eliminate many possibilities and allow me to focus on whatever was left. So, what were the conditions under which I wanted the bomb to go off when Peter and no one else was present.

Just as I was ready to start entering possibilities into the computer, my phone rang. "Hello," I answered.

"Hello, Mr. Rogers," Detective Sergeant Williamson said. "I apologize for calling so late, but in addition to a heavier than usual workload these days, I didn't have your telephone number, except at the pharmacy, I got this number after I talked to Miss Cartwright. Is this an inconvenient time for you? "

"No, I was just reading some papers. You aren't interrupting anything important."

"Mr. Rogers, I realize that it has been quite a while since Miss Cartwright was attacked, but I still need to get some answers. If it more convenient for you, we could do it right now over the telephone."

"That's fine with me, although I am not sure what information I can provide."

"Don't worry about that. Just let me ask the questions and you answer the best you can."

"Okay," I said, still not sure what I could add to what the police already knew.

"Please tell me how you first met Miss Cartwright."

I described my visit to VYRO Solutions without going into great detail about my previous history with Peter. I told him about my meeting with Sheila after leaving VYRO Solutions. I gave him a summary of what she had told me about herself and her job at VYRO Solutions. "The next time I had any contact was when I tried to call her and got you, instead," I said.

"What sort of relationship do you have with Mr. Stanford?" Williamson asked.

"What do you mean? We used to work together. Now he owns his own company and I work at a pharmacy."

"Mr. Rogers, I detect more than a hint of anger in your tone."

"Perhaps, you do. The breakup of our former business was not done on the best of terms, but until last month I hadn't even seen or heard of Peter for over three years. He just gave me a $100,000 settlement for my previous work, so while I certainly can't count him as a friend, he certainly has been generous to me." I thought that statement was both sufficiently accurate and sufficiently misleading that Williamson wouldn't cast me in any sort of negative light. I considered what else I should tell him, but the only things I knew about the attack were things he had probably already heard directly from Sheila.

"Thank you, Mr. Rogers. You've been very helpful. May I ask what your relationship with Miss Cartwright is currently?"

What should I say? I think I am in love with this woman, but that's none of his business. "We have had a few dates. I find her a very remarkable woman."

"Good luck. If I need anything more, I will contact you. Good bye." Williamson hung up.

I thought about returning to my research, but since I had finally admitted to myself that I loved this woman, I thought I'd better do something about that. I sat there and kept trying to figure out just exactly what I should do. I was a bit new at this love stuff. Oh, I had slept with a few women and enjoyed my time with them, but this was something different and I felt woefully unprepared. I wondered if this was another area for research. No, this wasn't science, but what in the hell was it? I had a sinking feeling that this was going to be a harder issue to deal with than coming up with a way to kill Peter.

I backed up the material on my flash drive and cleared all my data off my hard disc. Closing my laptop, I decided it was time to call Sheila and plan Saturday night's celebration. I opened my phone, noting that it was fully charged this time, and dialed Sheila's number.

Chapter 31

John sat at his desk and thought about Peter. He felt sure that the son-of-a-bitch was going to fire him. Did that mean he was pushing too hard to come up with a way for Helen to kill Peter? That would certainly ease his problems at VYRO Solutions, at least in the near term, but was he doing it for Helen or because it would make his life easier? He needed to talk to Vicki.

He left the office at noon and drove home. He was beginning to feel very uncomfortable. His mood was as gray as the sky. He wondered if he really wanted to be in the group that was trying to find a way for Helen to kill Peter because he really wanted to help Helen or because he wanted other people around to share the blame, if anything went wrong

"Hi, Honey. What are you doing home so early? asked Vicki.

"Vicki, I am not sure why I am getting involved with Helen's plans to kill Peter. Is it that I want him dead, but don't have the guts to do it myself? I am starting to feel guilty that I am placing Helen in a situation where she does something that benefits me and at the same time may place her in danger."

"Relax, Honey. Ruth has talked to Helen and while the idea of murdering Peter came from Ruth, Helen now sees it as her only way out. I can see how you might feel that you were pushing your problem off on someone else, but that isn't the case. You are using your skills to help Helen come up with a way of solving her problems with Peter and not end up in legal trouble." Vicki put her arms around John and whispered, "It will be okay."

John hugged Vicki as though he were afraid of losing her. "Thank you, my darling. I needed to hear that."

Chapter 32

"Hello," she answered.

"Hi. Sheila. It's Karol. I just called to talk about our upcoming celebration."

"Oh, good. I am getting a little tired of all this school work and need a break."

"Would you like to go out for a drink or something else tonight?" I asked.

"No, I am too tired to be good company. Let's just talk for a while and plan Saturday Night."

"Okay, I asked around the pharmacy and got a number of suggestions for dinner. I looked up several on the Internet and they all seem fairly trendy. The Heathman is located in the Heathman hotel on Broadway and is supposed to be very classy. It's supposed to feature a French Northwest cuisine. The Metrovino Bistro Bar and Bottle is in the Pearl District on NW 11th. The chef there apparently combines his ingredients in truly novel ways. There is also the Nostrana on S.E. Morrison which specializes in wood fired dishes, from Pizza to steak. Do any of these sound interesting?

"Karol, I don't want to disappoint you, but I wondered if we could go to the same restaurant we went to the first time. It was our first date and now we know something about Asian fusion cooking. Perhaps we should make use of that knowledge."

"That's fine with me," I said, somewhat thankful that she had picked a restaurant that was unlikely to take most of a week's pay.

Sheila said, " This time we can order things that we like. Besides, I enjoyed the time we spent together there."

"What time would you like me to pick you up?"

"Karol, lets use my car again. If you agree, why don't you pick me up at 6:00 and we'll be able to spend a little more time together."

"Absolutely!" I responded, thrilled that she wanted to spend more time with me. "I'll let you go now so you can get a good night's sleep and work on your studies tomorrow. Good-night."

"Good night, Karol. Until tomorrow."

I hung up the phone and decided that I needed to go out and get some nicer clothes so that Sheila wouldn't be ashamed of me. I thought about starting to get the materials I needed for the bomb, but felt uncomfortable doing that while I prepared to meet Sheila for dinner. I went to bed and tried to sleep, but sleep didn't want to come. Then I woke up and it was morning.

The day at the pharmacy sped past so fast I was almost unaware of what happened. I left at 4:30 and went to the local men's shop. I didn't really know what I wanted. I talked to the lady who was helping the customers. She suggested a new pair of slacks, a new shirt and a very expensive sports coat. Even with my up coming raise, I thought this was just too much. I opted for the new pair of slacks and hoped I'd remember to send out my only suit for cleaning and pressing.

I was home by 5:30. I showered and shaved and put on my new slacks and one of my nicer shirts. I looked in the mirror and was, as usual, a bit disappointed with my appearance. It was obvious that clothes could only do so much. I grabbed my hooded coat, as it was raining again.

I walked to Sheila's apartment, this time arriving at one minute past 6:00. I rang the bell and the door opened at once. Sheila was wearing some sort of shimmery black skirt with a velvety-looking, bright, vivid blue sweater. I looked at her and wanted to say something nice, but somehow I just couldn't make my mouth work.

"Well, don't just stand there. Come in," she said.

I concentrated on making my legs move and cleared my throat. "You are absolutely beautiful."

"Why thank you, kind sir. Complements are always appreciated," she said as she walked into her living room.

"No, I mean it! You are one of the loveliest women I have ever seen."

Sheila blushed as though she had never been complimented in her life. She turned away, as though embarrassed.

"I'm just not used to such compliments. You'll have to forgive me."

"You are forgiven. You are very beautiful and I am very pleased to be taking you out to dinner tonight."

If anything, the blush became brighter. She turned away, went to the closet, and took out her coat. I helped her put it on and we went out to her car.

"Would you like me to drive? I noticed that you weren't familiar with my car last time we went out."

"That would be fine." I didn't think I needed to be Lancelot or Apollo behind the wheel of her car. I went around to open her door, but she had already done so and was sliding into the driver's seat I went around the back of the car and got into the passenger seat.

"Ready?" she asked.

"Sure," I said.

"Well, then put on your seatbelt. I don't want the police pulling us over for failing to have our seatbelts fastened."

I quickly pulled the seatbelt out and fastened it, somewhat chagrined that I had forgotten. "Anytime, you are ready," I said.

The drive was much quicker with Sheila behind the wheel than when I had driven. We pulled up, parked and were in the restaurant less than 10 minutes after leaving her apartment. The maitre d' greeted us as though we were frequent customers.

"If I remember correctly, you both prefer tea. Do you want to look at the menu or do you know what you'd like?" he asked.

"Tea would be fine," Sheila offered, "and yes, I think we'd like to look at a menu."

We sat down at the same table we had on our previous visit. I smiled at Sheila and she smiled back. I risked taking her hand and holding it. "I just want you to know how much I like being with you," I whispered.

"I feel the same way, Karol."

At that moment the tea and menus arrived. Hand holding stopped and we each opened the menu. It was just as gigantic as I had remembered from the first time we were here. This time, however, I remembered the chicken dish that I liked. I didn't want to risk anything by trying something new. Sheila said she wanted the pork filled pot stickers and the Satin chicken. I ordered the Sichuan Chicken.

"Very good. The pot stickers will be out in a few minutes," the maitre d' said.

"Karol, what's been happening with you since we last talked?"

I smiled broadly and announced, "I passed the test. I am now a Licensed Pharmacy Technician."

"Oh, Karol, I am so glad for you. What will you do now?"

"For the present," I said, "I will continue working at the Albertson's Pharmacy, with something like a 20% increase in pay. I haven't really thought about long term plans at this point. I guess I'd just like to adjust to the current state of affairs before I start considering longer-term goals. But, what about you? How are things going with your nursing studies?"

"Oh, that's not quite as good. I think I'll be able to manage to fulfill all the requirements for this one course where ward time is not required, but I don't know how I'll be able to take the courses in the order I have to in order to graduate when I had planned. There are some courses that are only offered once a year and they demand specific pre-requisites. My friend, Helen, is working to see if there is some way to bend some of the rules to allow me to take the courses I need even when I don't have the pre-requisites.

I don't know what will happen, but the worst is that I will graduate one year later than I planned on, because of the sequence of courses. I do think that I will be able to get the part time office job in the nursing office. Helen has been advocating on my behalf. It doesn't pay very much, but it does come with a reduction in tuition costs. With the pay and the lowered tuition cost, I should be able to make it without acquiring a huge amount of debt."

"That's great. I am sorry that it will take longer for you to get your degree, but at least you are on firm ground now. Hopefully, there will be enough time in your schedule for a few dinners or whatever with me."

"Karol, I'd really like that. You are one of the kindest men I have ever met. I truly enjoy being with you."

Luckily, the pot stickers arrived, as I had no idea how to answer Sheila. Did I want to spend a night with this woman or a few months or the rest of my life? I didn't know what I wanted and it was making me very uncomfortable. I knew I wanted to be with her and I thought that perhaps that was enough. Let the future take care of itself.

The pot stickers were delicious. I liked mine with just a touch of the hot mustard. Sheila dunked hers alternately in the fish sauce and the soy sauce. We were quiet for a while, except for some very pleasant lip smacking. Almost before I realized it, we had eaten all the pot stickers. Sheila was no slacker; she had certainly eaten her share. I enjoyed watching her eat. Hell, I seemed to enjoy everything about her!

"Karol, I don't mean to bring up something unpleasant when I am having such a good time with you, but I thought we might talk about your plans for Peter," she said, somewhat hesitantly.

"What specifically, did you have in mind?" I said, trying to avoid any sort of confrontation.

"Do you still believe that you only option is to kill him?"

"Quite frankly, Sheila, yes. It's not just your life and my life. I am sure that Peter has damaged many other innocent people. I think the world will be a better place without him."

Sheila reached across the table and took my hand. "I am not totally sure I agree with you, but if there is some way I can help you, I will."

I wasn't prepared for this response. I was prepared to argue my case for killing Peter, but I had just been presented with her offer to become an accomplice in a murder. If this wasn't love, I don't know what it could be.

"Sheila, I love you." Damn, where did that come from? When someone says they'll help you kill someone, does that mean they love you? Does that mean you love them? I was getting more than a little confused.

"Let's not talk about Peter or anything connected with him. Let's just talk about us," I said.

"Okay. I really like you, Karol. From the moment I first saw you in the hospital until you held my hand for hours and hours, I had never met anyone who cared that much. You asked nothing of me and you offered so much. I don't know yet if we would be happy together for the rest of our lives, but I can tell you, I'd like you to be with me now!"

I didn't know exactly what to say. I guess I was stunned. Here was this lovely woman offering herself to me. Did I want to take her to bed? You bet, but I wasn't totally sure that's all of what I wanted. I knew I didn't want a one-night stand with this woman, but what did we really know about one another. What should I say?

"Sheila, I am more uncertain that I ever remember being. I want you, but I don't want this to be a 'slam, bang, thank you ma'm.' The feelings I have for you run deeper than that. I want to get to know you lots better and have you know me much better before we decide exactly what we want from each other. I am thrilled to have you help me with my plans for Peter. I am thrilled to have you want to be with me. I am thrilled to be with you. Do I sound stupid being so thrilled?"

"Karol, I think I know where you are coming from and . . . ."

"Pardon me," said the Maitre d', placing our dishes in front of us, "here are your entrees. Please enjoy. I will bring more tea in just a moment."

We just looked at each other, smiled, and began to eat. My chicken was wonderful, with just the right veggies and spices. From the look on Sheila's face, she was equally entranced with her food. We were silent except for the noises associated with eating. We smiled at each other, but said nothing. In less than ten minutes we had each cleaned our plates.

"Mine was wonderful. How was yours?"

She looked at me and said, "It was fantastic. Now all I want is dessert."

"I didn't see any desserts on he menu," I said.

"What I want isn't on the menu. Let's pay the bill and go back to my apartment."

I signaled the maitre d' for the bill, paid in cash, with a healthy tip, and grabbed my coat to follow Sheila out the door. By the time I got to the car, she was in the driver's seat with the motor running. I got in the passenger side and we sped off. I mean we **sped** off. I wasn't sure, but I think we made it back to Sheila's apartment is less than 5 minutes. There was a rush to the door, some shedding of clothes, and we were in her bed.

The first time was frantic and hurried. The second time was much slower and much better. I slept better than I had slept in years. There were no bad dreams. When I finally awoke, I felt warm, rested, and ready to face the world. Sheila was already up. I could hear her in the kitchen.

"What would you like for breakfast?" she shouted from the kitchen.

"I am starved. What are you having?"

"Oh, I thought I'd impress you by having Eggs Benedict."

"Won't that take a long time?"

"Not when you get packaged Béarnaise sauce, add water and a little lemon juice and in the time it takes to poach the eggs and heat the ham, everything is ready."

"Do I have time to grab a quick shower?

"Sure, but make sure it is quick."

I literally ran into her bathroom and started the shower. I noted that she had set out an extra towel. This woman was a planner and knew her own mind. I washed as quickly as I could, dried off and practically jumped into my clothes. I tried to calm down a little and walked into the kitchen. There was the smell of Lapsang Souchong, Béarnaise sauce, and cooking ham. I went to Sheila and put my arms around her from behind and kissed her hair.

"That's very nice, but if you want Eggs Benedict rather than over cooked everything, you'd better let me get about my business."

I released her and asked if there was anything I could do. That was probably a waste of breath as she had the table set and was placing the English muffins on our plates. Less than 90 seconds later, we were seated at her table, with freshly made Eggs Benedict in front of us. I cut a small bite and tasted it.

"This is great!"

"Don't sound so surprised. I do know how to cook."

"That's more than I can say. Most of what I have eaten in the last several years has either been out of a can or something frozen and heated in the microwave."

"Well, enjoy. After this, I think I want to know what your plans for Peter are in more detail. If I am going to help, I need to know what you are planning."

I thought 'here we go again'. I'd have to take her though the entire process of selecting a bomb as the technique to use and the logic behind it as well as explain the need for some sort of switch that only Peter would operate. This time she just listened as I went through the entire rationale of selecting a technique which would put me well away from the scene, but would guarantee that only Peter would die.

When I finished, she looked at me and said she thought I had a good plan, but she could solve my switch problem. "You know that Peter drives a new Porsche, don't you? He is the only one allowed to drive it. I have heard that he won't even let valets park it for him when he goes out. Ms Carter, the woman you met before seeing Mr. Robertson, is quite a gossip inside the company. She said that even Mrs. Stanford wasn't allowed to drive it.

"You wanted a situation where Peter was certain to be alone. I think this is a perfect one. You don't even need to bring a battery. The Porsche supplies that. I don't know too much about car engines, but if you hook one end of your wire to the Porsche's battery and the other end to the explosive; then the second wire from the explosive to the accelerator pedal; and finally, the third wire close to the second wire under the accelerator pedal with the last connection to the battery, wouldn't you have the scenario you want?"

I thought about it. It made perfect sense. Peter was not the kind of individual to give a co-worker a ride. He would be alone. The only issue would be how to get access to the car where no one could see what he was doing. I broached this issue to Sheila.

"Oh, I thought of that. When he goes on business trips, he occasionally leaves the Porsche locked up in a garage underneath the building. There is a guard, but according to Ms Carter, the guy who works weekends is a drinker and is unlikely to be awake after 11:00 pm. What do you think?

I was a little shocked. This woman who had strenuously objected to my killing Peter in the first place, had, in a matter of minutes described the perfect solution to my problem. We might have some difficulty finding out when Peter would be off on a business trip. That could be a point in our favor since neither of us would be expected to know if the police decided to question us.

I wondered what changed Sheila's mind. I wasn't sure if I should ask her, but I thought it might be important, especially since our relationship had changed. "Sheila, I need to ask what changed your mind?"

"I guess I thought about what Peter did to me, what he did to you, and who know how many others and I decided he should be stopped. It took me a while to consider options for stopping him, but nothing I could come up seemed to be effective. I guess I was also influenced by Peter's attempt to eliminate my medical insurance retroactively."

"I didn't think anyone could do that."

"I know," Sheila said, "but the insurance man was so annoyed with Peter's attempt that he told me what he had done. I found out that most of my hospital bills will be paid as well as all of my doctor's bills."

"That must have made Peter really angry," I laughed.

"I bet it did, but that solidified my willingness to join you in dealing with him."

"Okay, then let's start planning. I can buy the pipes at any lumber store. I am not positive how big to make it, but the little information on effectiveness that's on the

Internet suggests that a 6 to 8 inch pipe bomb stuffed with gunpowder and placed close to the intended victim should do the job. I planned on getting a piece of 12 inch pipe and two caps, but there didn't seem to be any reason to do so right now."

"Let's make a list of what we need."

"No, I don't want any paper trail." I explained my purchase of the computer and flash drive. I also explained how I kept everything on the flash drive except for the programs on the computer.

"Fine, let's go to your apartment and get started."

I smiled and reminded myself never to get in this woman's way. Once she had made up her mind, she was a dynamo. Sheila put the dishes in the dishwasher and then disappeared into the bathroom for about two minutes. She came out, put on her coat, picked up her purse and car keys and looked at me.

"What are you waiting for? I'll drive. I'd like to see where you live."

I agreed. What was I waiting for? I hoped I'd remembered to clean up the kitchen. I wasn't much of a house-keeper. "Let's go!"

I gave Sheila the address and she drove to my apartment without a single wrong turn. Obviously, she knew Portland. She parked in front of may apartment and said simply, We are here."

As I unlocked the door, both Sheila and I perceived my lack of skills as a house-keeper. The floors needed some sort of sweeping and the living room pillows were simply scattered about the floor. The kitchen was a bit better, having only one empty glass sitting in the sink. Sheila opened the refrigerator door and sighed.

"You don't exactly keep a well-stocked refrigerator. Your bread is getting moldy and I hesitate to think what the contents of that dish are supposed to be," she said, with just a bit of humor in her tone.

"I did say that I don't cook and, yes, I admit I am not much of a housekeeper."

"Well, let's forget about that and get to the computer."

I powered up the computer, inserted the flash drive, and waited for it to boot up. When it did, I opened Microsoft Word.

"How would you like to do this?" I asked.

"Why don't you let me type. After all I did it for a living. Just start telling me the things you think you need. If I think of some additions, I'll mention them. After we have everything listed, we can go through the sequence of actions we'll need to take to accomplish killing Peter. If we can do that without coming up with any problems of the need for additional materials, we can discuss obtaining the materials. Okay with you?

"Sure," I said, somewhat surprised at her organizational skills. "We'll need one 12" steel pipe, with threads on both ends. Then we'll need to threaded caps to fit the pipe. I plan to drill a couple of holes in one cap to insert the wires. As far as the gunpowder is concerned, I plan to go to Chinatown and start buying the largest packages of fireworks that I can find. That's about it."

"Whoa, Karol. You've left out a number of things. Are you just going to tighten the caps or do you want to seal them so the explosion will be more intense?"

"How did you know about making the explosions more intense?"

"Look, I can make use of the library as well as you and I can do it from my home, on line. Secondly, do you own a drill that can go through steel? What sort of wire do you want? I assume it will be insulated except at the ends. And, finally, how do you plan to keep the wires inside the bomb?"

I couldn't believe how rapidly Sheila has found the holes in my plan. I hadn't thought of how to drill holes in steel. I had a small battery powered drill, but only had wood bits. I had no idea if the drill was powerful enough to go through steel even if I got metal bits. I had planned to use solid copper wire: 12 gauge should be large enough to carry a cars amperage, but I guessed I should check on that. Then how do I keep the wires inside the bomb? I had thought just shoving them through the holes should do the trick if the holes were small enough. I guess I had some more thinking to do.

"Look Karol, everything you want can still be purchased at any hardware store, except the gunpowder, of course. You should buy a good battery operated drill and a couple of small metal bits. I recommend we use Gorilla glue. I've used it under a variety of conditions. It often expands beyond where you put it and its expensive, but we don't care how it looks or the expense since we are only going to buy one small bottle. An instant glue can be used to hold the bomb in place while the gorilla glue dries and the same gorilla glue can be used to hold the wires in the bomb. When you determine the size of the wire you plan to use, you'll know what sizes of drill bits to buy. You won't need more than about 20 to 25 feet of wire, so the only big expense will be the drill. Do you have a wire stripper?"

"No, I don't."

"One last thing. We'll need to get into the car so we can release the hood. One of my two week practica was with a fire and rescue outfit. They showed us all the techniques they used to stabilize and transport patients. They also showed us all the tools they used. One of those tools is basically a very thin piece of steel with a little notch on the bottom. You insert it between the window and the outer part of the door. You slide it along until you feel it grab and then you yank up hard. The door is unlocked. They let me practice a couple of times and I am sure I can open the car door."

"We have to get a piece of steel."

"No, as it happens, I have one. I locked myself out of the car often enough that I got one to keep in the house with me."

"That's it then," I said.

"No, not quite. How many fireworks are you going to buy? Where do you plan to store them? I presume that ripping them apart to get the gunpowder and then pouring it into the pipe will be rather messy. Where do you plan to do that?"

I was stumped. I guess I had thought I'd just do everything in my apartment, but that didn't seem like a good idea anymore. Sheila was truly surprising me. This wasn't the same woman who wanted me to hold her hand in the hospital. This woman seemed a lot smarter than I was and if this killing was going to work, I'd be glad I had my female genius at my side.

"As part of my rent, I have a small lockable storage cabinet," Sheila offered. "It would probably hold most, if not all, of the fireworks you'd need, but its too small to be a work space."

"I think I know what to do. I can buy one of those cheap plastic tarps. They sell them everywhere. When I have enough fireworks, we can go down near the river and open the fireworks on the tarp, pack it into the metal tube, and then leave the tarp and any leftover material there. If we wear plastic gloves, we won't leave fingerprints on anything. In addition, any of the homeless people who hang out near the river will grab a free tarp within hours of us leaving it there. The paper from the fireworks will probably end up in one of their cooking fires. That will destroy almost all the evidence.

"I'll have to buy the drill and bits so we can make the holes for the wires. We can insert them and glue them in after we have packed the powder inside. We can use duct tape to cover the holes while we transport the tube."

I thought to myself, we have all the bases covered. We can get the materials without suspicion because they are so common and easily obtained. We can make the bomb without leaving traces in either of our apartments. The hood of Peter's car can be opened after Sheila opens the door. The wires can be fed through the openings already in the firewall. A little glue will hold them there and then, when Peter presses on the gas pedal, he will blow himself up.

"When do we start?" I asked. "How about today?"

"I have other plans for the rest of today. Let's just list the supplies, put everything on the flash drive, clear the computer's memory and go back to my apartment."

"I like that idea," I said trying hard not to grin.

The drill, the bits, the wire, the tarp, the gorilla and the instant glue, the plastic gloves, the wire strippers, the metal tube, and the caps were all purchased over the next week. We went to Home Depot and Lowe's since they were big National chains. Their products would be available to thousands of people and no one in either store would be likely to remember us.

Sheila went to Chinatown to look around. When she returned, she told me that they were getting ready for the

Chinese New Year and anytime we wanted, we could buy all the fireworks we could ever need. In the next two days, Sheila and I bought about $250.00 worth of fireworks. My raise had certainly helped our ability to carry out this plan.

The two holes were drilled in the top cap. The bottom cap was screwed and then glued on. We were almost ready.

"When do you want to load the powder into the tube?" I asked.

"We can do that anytime you want. Incidentally, I got one of those larger cloth grocery bags to carry the tube in. Even if anyone sees us, it will just look like some sort of groceries."

"That gives me an idea. Sheila, what do you think about taking a lunch along so it would look like we were have a picnic if anyone came along?"

"That's a great idea. I love it!" She leaned over and kissed me.

I thought I'd better come up with good ideas more often. "I am off this Sunday. Would that work for you?"

"Sure," Sheila said. "What do you want to have for our picnic?"

"Oh, I don't know. Maybe some sandwiches and chips."

"How dull. Here we are going out to prepare to murder someone and all you want to eat is sandwiches and chips," she smiled.

"I didn't know that there were appropriate foods you had to eat when you were picnicking and preparing for a murder"

"Let me take care of the picnic. I think I have some ideas about what might be appropriate and tasty. I'll load the picnic staff and the fireworks into my car and drive over to pick you up. What time do you want to leave?"

I thought about that for a moment. I didn't know how long it would take to cut open the fireworks and load the powder into the tube. At the same time, people didn't usually go on picnics at 8 o'clock in the morning. "What about 10:00 or 10:30?" I offered.

"That's fine with me. I'll pick you up a little after 10:00, depending on how long it takes me to load the car. Unfortunately, I need to go home now. There is still schoolwork that has to be completed and turned in and I want everyone at school to think I am a deadly serious student" The smile on her face as she said "deadly serious" was somewhere between a pixie and an evil witch.

Sunday rolled around and so did Sheila, at just after 10:00. "I have the perfect place picked out." We drove North of the airport until we could see the Columbia River. Turning East, we cruised along until we found a turn out that lead through some woods to a level spot.

There was absolutely no one around. We could hear the planes landing and taking off in the distance, but we could also hear the Columbia close by.

"Let's get everything out and get started," I said. In about 30 seconds, I changed my mind as it started to rain.

We got back in the car. I looked at Sheila and Sheila looked at me. We both started to laugh.

"What fantastic criminals we are. We didn't even check the weather," she said.

"What should be do now?" I asked.

"Well, I don't think we have much choice. We take everything back and have our picnic inside. We can always plan for another day, but this time we consult the weatherman first."

We drove back to Sheila's place, took everything out of the car and put it away, getting rather wet in the process. I was grateful that the fireworks were still wrapped in their plastic packages. When we were done, we went inside. Both of us were cold and wanted to get out of our wet clothes. We got warmed up in the shower and even warmer in bed afterwards.

I had the duty both days of the following weekend as two staff members had managed to get the flu and one was on vacation. Sheila and I were trying to see each other at least a couple of times a week, but with her schedule ands mine, it wasn't easy. I told her that I would be off at least one day the weekend after next and perhaps we could plan our 'picnic' for that time. She said that would work out if the weather co-operated.

Two weeks later with no rain in the forecast and new picnic food, we were off. We found the same place and unloaded the car. We placed the tarp on the ground, put on our gloves, and then placed everything else on top of it. The tube was taken out of the plastic bag along with a box cutter I had bought. I used the box cutter to open a package of fireworks and then removed each piece. With the pieces laid out before us, I had Sheila hold the tube while I cut open each piece and poured the gunpowder into the tube. I discarded anything that didn't look like gunpowder. It took two and one-half packages of fireworks and just over an hour to fill he tube.

We screwed the top cap on the tube, put duct tape over the two holes and returned it to the plastic bag. We gathered up all the empty fireworks and tossed them into the bushes near the river. They seemed to mix with all the other detritus that seems to pile up along rivers. We put the remaining fireworks and the filled tube into the trunk and took out the picnic basket.

"Wow, I didn't think it was going to take so long. My nerves are a bit on edge," I said.

"My hands are stiff from holding that damn tube for so long. I think I want a drink of that wine I brought and perhaps some of the humus and pita chips."

"I'll be happy to get that for you, my dear," I said. I took the wine out of the basket, pulled out the opener, and as I began to pull the cork, I felt the first raindrop

"Shit! It looks like the picnic is off again. Let's put everything in the car and go to your place and eat it there."

Sheila smiled, "That would be just fine with me."

The next day, I glued the two wires into the holes in the top cap. I had left plenty of wire attached so that I could easily reach anywhere within the hood of the Porsche. All we needed at this point was to find out when Peter would be out of town so we could attach the bomb.

Chapter 33

"Okay, everyone's here. Please go into the dining room," Ruth barked in her Sergeant Major voice. "There are plenty of seats. Just take one. There is coffee and tea on the sideboard. Help yourself. If you need anything else just ask."

There was a lot of seemingly random movement as individuals selected seats, changed their minds, got up to get coffee or tea, and then finally reseated themselves. Eight people stared at Ruth, assuming she would be the one to get the meeting started.

"Before we get started, I want to make sure everyone knows who everyone is. None of you, except Helen, have met Sheila or Karol before." With that Ruth began the introductions, giving both their name and some history of the individual's previous interactions with Peter. When she was through, handshakes were extended around the table.

"We are here to discuss what everyone has learned about possible poisons which can be used on Peter. Please feel free to speak your mind, but remember we want to hear all ideas, not just shoot them down. Does anyone want to start?"

Veronica raised her hand, "If I may."

"Of course," responded Ruth.

"My task was to look at medical texts. I tried to identify poisons which were hard to detect and or difficult to treat. I also talked at length to Lee Ann who was looking at all available poisons. We decided that just looking at every possible poison was too formidable of a task, so we tried to come up with some criteria which would help us eliminate poisons which would not be very useful for our purposes.

"We eliminated any poison which required a prescription or which was government controlled—such as radioactive materials. The reasoning behind this decision was that we wanted to leave no paper trail which could be followed back to Helen. We also eliminated plant and animal poisons. Plant based poisons usually have to be extracted from the plant which requires more sophistication than I think any of us has. Animal based poisons have two problems. It is often hard to determine when an animal will bite, so timing is not under our control. Secondly, the amount of toxin actually injected can vary substantially from incident to incident, so we'd like the ability to guarantee the delivery of a lethal dose."

"Just a second," Helen said. I understand your two objections, but what if you could obtain the poison separate from the animal. Like if you had the venom from a fugu fish. Ruth said she was able to obtain such a poison."

"That's a good point, Helen. I must admit that neither Lee Ann nor I had considered that possibility. The fugu, which is called a puffer fish in the United States, is found in relatively warm waters, so the poison is obviously imported. That means there is a chain linking you to the people involved in its importation. You'd have to trust whoever gave it to you with your freedom. On the other hand, fugu poisoning has got to be unbelievably rare in Oregon. I can't imagine that there are many coroners in Portland who would even know what to look for, much less be able to identify it. If I remember what I read, it causes numbness which spreads from the mouth to the face and throat, followed by respiratory problems and finally paralysis. The onset is usually fairly rapid. On an empty stomach, I read it can occur in 10 or 15 minutes. If it is diluted with liquids or other foods, the onset of symptoms can be delayed for hours. I suspect that this is one poison that can stay on our list for further research.

"We also wanted our criteria to exclude gases. In most cases they require more expertise than we have. An exception is carbon monoxide. We've all heard or read stories of people who were killed or who committed suicide by sitting in a car with a hose going from the tailpipe to the interior of the car. We would have to immobilize Peter in order to use carbon monoxide in a car. If he were asleep and we could figure out a way to deliver the carbon monoxide and a fairly tightly enclosed space, we could use it in that way, but quite frankly I have no idea where to get carbon monoxide other than the tailpipe of a car and I don't see us rigging up a hose from a tailpipe to his bedroom.

"We decided that any poison must have at least a short delay in reaction time. If it doesn't, then Peter falls dead at the feet of Helen or at least immediately adjacent to whatever we used to poison him. This delay does not need to be terribly long, but long enough so that Peter and the poison source are separated. We also need a poison which is very lethal in very small doses. Water is lethal if consumed in large enough doses, but that sort of thing is totally impractical for us."

"Does anyone else want to offer some input?" asked Ruth.

"Well, I . . . . . I think I should tell you about the plan that Sheila and I developed. We have made a bomb which we plan to plant in Peter's car."

The room immediately erupted with questions: What sort of bomb? Where did you get the parts? How big is it? How many did you make? Have you tested it?

"Let's settle down people," the Sergeant Major spoke again. "Let's let Karol finish."

"We made the bomb from materials available in any hardware store except for the black powder." Karol described the components of the bomb and how it had been assembled. There was some laughter when he mentioned the picnic lunch.

"How are you going to set off the bomb? If you wire it to the starter motor or the ignition, Peter will blow himself up in the driveway," asked John.

"One wire from the bomb will be connected to the battery. The other wire will be connected to a small metal plate under the accelerator. Another wire will be connected to the metal of the accelerator pedal. When the accelerator pedal contacts the small metal plate, the circuit will be closed and the bomb will explode.

"But what about the black powder? Where did you get that?" asked Hank.

With a slight smile on her face Shiela described their various trips to Chinatown to purchase fireworks. She discussed the problems with chemical markers sometime left in explosives. "That will be no problem as we purchased several different bands from several different dealers

"I don't know how our plans will fit in with what you have planned. The only time we can get to Peter's car is when he is out of town. He sometimes leaves it locked in a garage under the VYRO Solutions building. I don't see where that would fit in with your plans to poison him."

"Karol, Peter doesn't always leave his car in the underground garage when he goes on a trip. He often locks it up in our garage. You can always tell because he leaves my car outside. He does that because I don't have a key to the garage."

"That means that you could work on it in his own garage and he wouldn't use it until he was at home," said John.

"What's so valuable about that?" asked Karol.

"If a car blew up and bomb fragments were found, how hard do you think any coroner would look for poison? Using both poison and a car bomb, we increase our chances for success!" crowed John. "While it is quite possible that Helen might be suspected of poisoning Peter, it seems extremely unlikely that she would be thought capable of blowing him up."

There were slow nods all around the room. There was a consensus that combining the two approaches would better protect Helen and increase likelihood of Peter ending up dead.

Ruth interjected, "We still need to address the issue of what poison we are going to use and how we are going to administer it. As I read through mystery novels that used poison, the killer was often tripped up by some remnants of the poison on his person or in his house. The other main reason was some trail of evidence linking him to the poison. That could be a fingerprint on the glass holding the poison or a receipt or some other evidence showing he had bought the poison. We need to keep those issues in mind."

"I have a possible poison, I'd like you to consider," said Alex. "It's a rat poison called 1080. It has a real name, but I can never remember it. It is extremely deadly. According to the World Health Organization 0.5 to 2mg per kilogram of body weight is lethal. Peter weighs about 185, I think."

"One eighty," said Helen. "He's very vain about his weight."

"That's about 82 or 83 kilos. So using 2mg per kilo to make sure, we'd need about 165 mg. That's less than 1/100 of an ounce."

"But I understood that it was illegal in the US except for specially licensed exterminators," said Veronica.

"That's correct. But the same limitations are not in place in Canada or Mexico. It is extremely dangerous. You must not breath it or get it on your skin. If you take it internally, you start showing symptoms in 30 minutes to 3 hours and once you show symptoms, there is no medical cure. My only concern here is how dangerous it could be to Helen."

"Let's just add that to the list of possible poisons and look at its danger as a possible drawback," said Helen

"What about the standard poisons? If we are going to blow up Peter in his car, why look for esoteric poisons when the coroner is unlikely to suspect poisoning in the first place?" asked Ruth.

"What, pray tell, are 'the standard poisons, dearest?" asked Hank.

"You know the ones used in all the old murder mysteries: strychnine, arsenic, and cyanide."

"You can eliminate cyanide. It works too quickly," said Vicki.

"What about arsenic and strychnine?' asked Ruth.

"Arsenic doesn't break down in the body. It is fat-soluble and it remains in the victim's hair and fingernails. While it takes at least 30 minutes for symptoms to develop, death may be delayed for as much as 24 hours. I don't think we want Peter to hang on that long," said Vicki.

"If he's blown to bits, does it make a difference?" asked John.

"Okay, what's the problem with strychnine?" asked Ruth.

"There really isn't any. It has a bitter taste, but that's about its only drawback. It will start to show symptoms in 20 minutes, a bit longer if taken on a full stomach. It is also found in fruit which is grown in Hawaii and looks something like a Mandarin orange. If a few of those were found in his car, they could easily explain how he was poisoned, although we'd want to use rat poison as a much more concentrated form of the drug," answered Vicki.

"Which of these poisons is most likely to be fatal?" asked Sheila.

"Given the appropriate dosage, all are fatal," responded Vicki.

"Then it seems to me that we should choose the one that is easiest to obtain and to use," said Alex.

"I agree," said Helen. "I'd like to eliminate the 1080 poison since the other two seem to be less hazardous to me."

"That certainly makes sense," said Ruth.

Vicki offered that both of the remaining poisons had real advantages. "The fugu poison is so rare that even if a coroner suspected poison, he or she would be very unlikely to come up with fugu as the cause. Even if he did, how could he trace the fugu back to Helen? Fugu works reasonably fast, but not immediately, so giving it to him just before he left in his car should produce the result we want.

"On the other hand, with strychnine, we have the possibility of suggesting that the cause is a natural one by placing the fruits containing strychnine as a natural ingredient in his car. This would tend to eliminate any suspicion that the poisoning was anything but accidental. Strychnine also works reasonably fast, but not immediately."

"The only difficulty with strychnine as an accidental poison is that we'd have to get some of those fruits from Hawaii. That means we'd have to find out what they are called and have someone get them from Hawaii," said Lee Ann.

"I have a number of contacts in Hawaii and if someone could find out what those fruits are called, I am sure I could get some air shipped here in short order," offered John.

"Doesn't that leave a fairly clear trail? You are asking someone to ship a dangerous product into the Continental US. That implies some amount of paper work. If nothing else, a shipping manifest. One of the things we wanted with our poison was to avoid leaving tracks to the extent humanly possible," stated Vicki.

"Damn, you're right. I guess that leaves the fugu as the best choice," said John.

"Only if we can be sure that it can't be traced back to Helen." Said Vicki.

"I think I can guarantee that," said Ruth. "The person who offered it to me does not like Peter any more than the rest of us."

"If we are all agreed on the fugu, we need to consider how we are going to administer it," said Hank. "Are we all agreed that the fugu sounds like the best choice for poisoning Peter?"

There were nods of agreement and a number of quiet "yeses." from all around the table.

"Let me digress a minute or two," asked John. "Is Peter still the nit picker at home as he is in the office?"

Helen said, "I'm not exactly sure what you mean."

"Once Peter threw a fit when he received a set of stapled papers where the staple was not completely folded over on one side. He was more than a little annoyed when a letter he was sending out was not completely sealed. His secretary is always careful to bring him his Kona coffee. Any other brand and he lets his secretary know he's pissed. I once offered him for Starbuck's coffee and he literally spit it out on my office floor. He also told me I was never, never to offer him that sort of coffee again."

"Yes, he is pretty fussy at home, but generally the staff knows what upsets him and avoids those kinds of problems. We have only Kona coffee in the house. The stapler in his office is an industrial variety which is supposed to fasten up to 100 sheets of paper. I suppose there are lots of other things, but I can't think of them at the moment," answered Helen.

"Then perhaps we can arrange to have Peter give the poison to himself," smiled John.

"What do you mean?" asked Ruth.

"Well, I was just thinking that if Peter gets upset at things which are not done to his standards, if we give him something like that, he may be inclined to fix it."

"Oh, John," shouted Helen, "I know just what you mean and I also know just what will work. You already mentioned that he gets upset when a letter is incompletely sealed. I know as he has yelled at me when I have not licked the glue well enough to fasten the flap of the envelope.

"What would happen if I asked him to mail some letters at the office and one of those letters was unsealed? He'd be mad as hell, but he'd also be most likely to seal it himself."

"I don't understand. What good is that?" asked Sheila.

"I think I see," said Hank, "and I think that it is a fantastic idea."

"Okay, explain it to me," said Shiela.

Karol laid his hand over hers and said, "If the fugu poison is on the flap of the envelope and Peter licks it, he will essentially poison himself. Since it won't act immediately, it will give him time to get out to the car and start it before it takes effect."

"Oh, that's terrible. I love it!" said Sheila.

Ruth asked, "Are you sure that the fugu poison will stick to the glue on the envelope?"

"I think so. It's in the form of a liquid and since it needs so little to be fatal, I can just dab it on with a q-tip. The q-tip will go in the garbage at the local grocery store along with any wrappings it came with and the remaining fugu poison will go down the drain," offered Helen.

Alex said, I can't believe it. We amateurs have put together a perfect murder plan. No clues will lead back to any of us. While many of us have motive, the number of people who hate Peter is so large that it would take months just to interview them all."

Ruth decided to be officious again. "Alright people, we have two procedures designed to kill Peter. With any luck at all, they will both occur at the same time, but either should kill him. I want everyone to take a moment or two to consider any flaws in the plans or any additional considerations."

"I have a minor thought. While I think Karol and Sheila's plan is excellent, I can think of one improvement. If the bomb is placed next to the gas tank, an explosion and fire is guaranteed," said John.

"That's a great idea. I'll check to see if I have enough wire to reach back to the gas tank, but getting more if needed should be no problem," Karol said. "And fastening it to the gas tank should add no difficulty to the procedure."

"Okay," said John, "what else do we need to do before we can proceed?"

"For our part, we have the bomb ready as well as all the equipment needed to install it. We have gloves to avoid fingerprints. All we need at this point is know when Peter will be out of town so we can break into his garage and car and place the bomb," said Karol.

"I still have to get the fugu poison and I am not quite sure exactly how long that will take, but I assume it will be a matter of days. We have plastic gloves around the house. Oh, that means I have to dump them with the q-tip and fugu wrappings. I'll have to write some sort of letter to put into the envelope and have at least a couple of other envelopes to go along with it. I could do that today.

"In fact, I need to renew my license as a notary public. It's one of those things that Peter likes me to have so he can seal a deal on the spot. He'll certainly want that letter sent and I can put it together with some letters to girlfriends," offered Helen.

No one else spoke, so Ruth ended the meeting by telling everyone that they would meet in one more week. By that time, everything that can be prepared ahead of time should be prepared. She cautioned again not to speak to anyone outside the circle about their plans and continue to look for problems with any of the plans. "See all of you here next week, same time, same place."

Chapter 34

The week passed slowly for everyone. Karol and Sheila went over their plans and their equipment. Helen wrote a letter to each of two close friends. She wondered if they would ever receive her words. She decided that she would write them as soon as this was over. Ruth went to Hank and asked him if it would really work. He held her in his arms and said, "If God is just, it will work!"

John and Vicki went over both plans multiple times. Neither could find anything missing or anything wrong. Vicki said, "You know, I am really uncomfortable with all this. I wish we didn't have to kill Peter, but I don't see any other reasonable solution."

"I know," said John, "but remember the old saying: *The only thing that evil needs to succeed is that good men do nothing.* We can sit on the sidelines and do nothing or we can support those who would rid us of someone as evil as Peter. I am ready to do anything I can to help."

"I understand, darling, but I don't want you to do anything that would take you away from me."

"Relax, Vicki, no one seems to want to do anything which would actually get me physically involved in either of the two plans. Not that I wouldn't be willing to help, but no one has asked."

"John, honey. I understand your willingness to, participate, but I need you too much to have you sacrifice yourself for a nasty bastard like Peter."

"Don't worry. With the two plans we have in place., I don't think there is any possibility that Peter will survive."

"Okay, John. I want to believe that this whole thing will soon be over and that we all can return to a more normal life."

"Trust me. It will soon be over and we can return to our normal lives." With that said, John put his arms around her and hugged her to his chest. "You don't need to worry, Vicki. In a few days or at most a couple of weeks, Peter will no longer be around to create any more pain for another human being."

"Thank God," Vicki whispered.

Chapter 35

Helen was awakened by Peter going through his closet and muttering that several of his suits were missing. He wasn't happy with the shine on several pairs of shoes. He yelled downstairs to Mercedes.

"Where in the hell is my dark grey silk suit with the light grey lines? Damn it, I told you time and time again to put things back where you found them."

"Yes, sir, you did," responded Mercedes, "but that was one of the suits you had me send to the cleaner. It and three other suits should be back tomorrow."

"That does me a fat lot of good. I am leaving this afternoon for a meeting and I wanted to wear that grey silk suit. Shit, I can't trust a anyone in this house to do what I need.

"Okay, pack my midnight blue suit along with a couple of blue slacks. I thought I'd told you that I wanted my shoes polished to a high gloss at all times."

Mercedes gave a small sigh, "Yes, sir, you did, but Silvestro has been sick for several days now and has not been able to shine your shoes. I can try to shine them, but you always seem to feel my efforts are less adequate than Silvestro's."

"Oh, crap. I can't count on you for anything. Put two pair of black shoes in my hard sided bag, along with the suit and pants. I'll select my own ties since you people don't seem to have any taste."

Helen put on her robe and walked into Peter's bedroom. "Is there anything I can do for you?" she asked.

"No. Oh wait. Perhaps you could find some competent staff since Mercedes and Silvestro don't seem to be able to do their jobs."

Helen started to defend Mercedes and then realized it would do no good. Peter was in one of his 'no one does a good job except me' and 'why am I saddled with all these incompetents.'

"I'll help Mercedes pack your things. Where are you going?"

"Why do you care. You're not going. This is a one on one meeting with Mikhail Alexandrovitch. He wants to discuss payment options and I want to tie up any loose ends."

"Does that mean you'll have to go all the way to Russia. It is extremely cold in Russia this time of year and perhaps we should be looking at warmer clothing to pack for you."

"Relax Helen. I am not going to Russia. I don't even want to get close to that stinking place. I am meeting Mikhail Alexandrovitch in Morocco where the weather will be warm and sunny, even if the natives are worthless creatures."

"I guess that means I should move my car out of the garage. Do you want me to drive you to the airport?" asked Helen.

"No, I have a limo coming for me in just over half an hour so I need to get everything ready to go. Why don't you help Mercedes as I am not sure she has the ability to do it by herself."

Helen looked at Mercedes and lifted her shoulders in a 'what can I say' gesture. "How long will you be gone?"

"Its not really your business, is it?"

Helen kept her temper in check and simply replied, "I just thought that you'd want clean underwear each day and unless I know how long you'll be gone, I won't know how much underwear to pack."

"God dammit, a reasonable request at last. I will be gone for no more than three days, so pack accordingly."

Peter strode out of his bedroom and down to his office. While he gathered whatever papers he would need, Helen and Mercedes packed his bag. They looked at each other with understanding, but only Helen knew that this was possibly the last time they would have to do this.

"I apologize," whispered Helen.

"It does not matter," responded Mercedes. "His words are like the rain and simply run off my body."

Peter went out to the garage. He backed Helen's car out into the driveway and moved his car into the garage. He locked the garage and returned to the house.

The clothes, toilet articles, and paperwork packed, Peter walked to the front door, opened it, and smiled as the limo drove up the driveway. "Good bye," he said and walked out the door. The chauffeur quickly stopped the vehicle, got out, and opened the door for Peter, and then rushed to collect the luggage and put it in the trunk. In less than two minutes, the limo was heading out the driveway toward the airport.

Helen was still in her robe. She faced Mercedes and said," I am so sorry that Peter was so rude to you." She started to tell Mercedes that Peter's rudeness would soon end, but she thought better of it. "Perhaps things will improve with time."

Mercedes looked at her with sympathy. "I don't think Mr. Stanford will ever change, but I am happy to work for you."

Helen reached for and hugged Mercedes. Mercedes was very surprised, but hugged Helen to tell her she was on her side.

"I'd better get dressed," Helen said. "I still have a couple of things I need to do."

Back in her bedroom, she called Sheila and Ruth to tell them that Peter would be out of town for three days starting today.

Surprisingly, Ruth had already received the fugu poison and Sheila and Karol were ready to go. All the pieces of the plan were starting to come together.

Late that same night, Sheila and Karol came over to Helen's home. They carefully picked the lock to the garage. John joined them as they entered the garage. They had decided to use small flashlights as they didn't want the neighbors wondering why the lights were on in the garage when Peter was out of town. The three of them worked silently and carefully to plant the bomb next to the fuel tank and then connect the wires to the battery and to a couple of plates underneath the accelerator pedal In less than 45 minutes the three of them had rigged the bomb to go off when Peter pressed down hard on the accelerator.

The three of them left the garage after attempting to relock the garage door. They were unsuccessful relocking the garage door, but assumed that it would be a minor issue as Peter would undoubtedly unlock it when he arrived home.

While the three of them were working on attaching to bomb to the car, Helen and Ruth were placing the fugu poison on the envelope which contained the letter for the renewal of her notary public status. She had even included a check to make sure it seemed legitimate.

They all went into the living room and sat down. They looked at each other, waiting for someone to say something.

"It's all set," said John. "The only thing left is to wait."

"Peter won't be home for two days so we'll have that long to just wait," said Helen.

Chapter 36

Peter stormed into the house, yelling about what a stupid pig that Russian was. "He just played around. He never was interested in buying my drug. I had to sit there for almost two full days listening to that idiot talk about the past glories of the Soviet Union and how the future of Russia would be equally glorious. What an idiot!

"Have the maid unpack my stuff and send the suit and pants to the cleaners and wash and iron the rest. I am going into the office and see what can be done about dealing with that bastard."

"Peter, before you go, could you mail some letters for me. I have to get my renewal for my notary public certificate in the mail or I'll have to go through the re-application process and I know you like me to be able to notarize at the drop of a hat," Helen said, with some concern that she may have oversold the need for mailing the letters.

"Damn it. Why can't you be pro-active and get your shit together ahead of time. You know I hate this last minute stuff. Go get the stuff you want me to mail. I guess I have to take up the slack at home as well as at the office."

Helen rushed into her office and picked up the three envelopes. "As long as you are mailing the renewal application, I didn't think you'd mind mailing a couple of letters to friends of mine."

"Are you sure you don't want me to do something else? Perhaps you'd like me to go out and get some gifts for your friends. Perhaps I should wrap them up, as well. Alright, just give them to me."

Helen handed the letters to Peter and walked out of the room and upstairs to her bedroom. Peter glanced down at the envelopes and muttered, "You stupid bitch, why can't you even seal a letter."

Naturally, it was the important one—the one for the renewal of her notary public certificate, he thought.

Momentarily, he thought about calling Helen downstairs and taking her to task for her sloppy ways. Then he decided he didn't have time for that. He'd discuss it in detail when he got home. He licked the glue on the envelope and sealed it. He was further annoyed at the fishy taste of the glue. He'd have to talk to Helen about where she was buying her stationery. Damn it, did he have to do everything himself.

He walked to the garage and unlocked it. "Strange, he thought. It was like it was already unlocked." He knew that couldn't be the case since he was the only one with a key. He got in the car and started it. Slowly backing out of the garage, he closed the door with his remote and backed out into the street. He started toward his office as he noticed a numbness in his lips and tongue. "Probably nothing," he thought, "but better get to the office and have one of the physicians take a look."

He felt the numbness slowly spreading over his face and down to his neck. I'd better move it, he said as he pressed down hard on the accelerator.

Chapter 37

The telephone rang and Helen picked it up. "Hello."

"Hello. Mrs. Stanford?"

"Yes."

"My name is Detective Sergeant Williamson and I am sorry to inform you that your husband has been killed."

There was silence on the other end of the telephone as Helen tried to determine what she should say next. "I don't understand, he was on his way to his office. He just left here a couple of hours ago."

"We don't have all the details, Mrs. Stanford, but we know there was an explosion while he was driving his car. We have bits and pieces of paper bearing his name and that of VYRO Solutions, but will need to speak to his dentist to get his dental records to confirm his identity. I am afraid that the damage to his body is so great that no one could possibility recognize him."

"Oh, my God," gasped Helen. They had done it!

"Do you have a friend you could call who come stay with you? I will come by later to take your statement and ask a few questions," said Detective Sergeant Williamson.

"Oh, I don't know. I am going to call my best friend Ruth. What am I supposed to do?

"Go ahead and call Ruth. You probably need some time for this to sink in and then for you to deal with it. I'll call before I come over."

Yes, okay . . . I guess. I am going to call Ruth now.

Chapter 38

Ruth, Hank, and Helen sat in the enclosed sun room, with the fireplace blazing. Each had a tall drink in their hands and they looked very relaxed.

"I think the interview with the detective went off very well, don't you?" asked Ruth.

"Yes, I do," said Helen. "Now I have to think about what I want to do about VYRO Solutions. I think I know I know a man who has lots of experience with our drug who would be very good at leading the research efforts there. I also think I know another one who would be an excellent administrator.

Chapter 39

John picked up Victoria and carried her into the bedroom. "This is a wonderful occasion and we should celebrate"

"Oh, I agree," murmured Vicki, "and then lets go out to dinner."

Chapter 40

Karol was sitting on Sheila's couch drinking his second cup of Lapsang Souchong tea. Sheila cuddled next to him and asked, "Don't you think that one apartment would be enough for the two of us?"

Karol started to answer as ZippyII climbed up into his lap, "I am not sure. Perhaps we need to think about a house for the three of us."